CW00350948

# The
# Solstice

ALSO BY MATT BROLLY

Detective Louise Blackwell series:

*The Crossing*
*The Descent*
*The Gorge*
*The Mark*
*The Pier*
*The Bridge*

Lynch and Rose series:

*The Controller*
*The Railroad*

DCI Lambert series:

*Dead Eyed*
*Dead Lucky*
*Dead Embers*
*Dead Time*
*Dead Water*

Standalone novels:

*Zero*
*The Running Girls*
*The Alliance*

# The
# Solstice

## MATT
## BROLLY

THOMAS & MERCER

Text copyright © 2024 by Matt Brolly
All rights reserved.

Published by Thomas & Mercer, Seattle

www.apub.com

Amazon, the Amazon logo, and Thomas & Mercer are trademarks of Amazon.com, Inc., or its affiliates.

ISBN-13: 9781662520396
eISBN: 9781662520402

Cover design by Tom Sanderson
Image credits: © S.Borisov © encierro © EB Adventure Photography
© Jacek Lidwin © Matthew Storer / Shutterstock

Printed in the United States of America

*For my 'best men', Matthew Lower and Ryan Skeets.*

# Prologue

His hand was shaking as he took the mask. It was such a privilege and he was desperate not to ruin the moment. He savoured the smell of the dank, well-worn disguise, heady with history and the sweat and tears of those who'd worn it before. He felt the change as he placed it over his head and became something else, something better.

He noticed the change in the others, too. For a brief moment they were all transformed, and everything else in the world no longer mattered, as he felt his blood rush through his veins.

He was the Hare. They were the Fox, the Badger, the Boar and the Raven.

All humanity disappeared from their features, their faces becoming the death stare of their respective animals. It should have been scary – and no doubt to the boy it was – but he saw only beauty.

In what they'd become and what they were about to do.

One by one, they lit their torches, the Fox and the Badger dragging the boy through the cave opening. The Raven began the chanting and, again one by one, in a wondrous crescendo, they all joined in, their voices muffled but coming together to create a singular voice that reverberated against the cave walls.

He wanted it to go on forever. He was enthralled by the ceremony and his own transformation, but he was also desperate to see what happened next. In many ways this was his initiation. It was an honour to have been invited, and he was privileged to have this small role to play.

The Raven had been here before. She stopped by the entrance to the chamber. She stood tall, her glorious death mask seeming to grow in the dim glow of the fire torches. 'It is time,' she said, the Fox and the Badger dragging the boy through the squeeze passage into the chamber, where he cowered in the corner.

It was a shame he would never understand the beauty of what he was doing, the sacrifice he was making for the sake of others, but there were more important things than the boy, more important things than the five of them.

As the Raven read from the book, the time counting down to midnight, he watched the Fox, the Badger and the Boar seal the chamber, from behind the blur of his camera lens.

Until there was no space left for the boy to look out from.

Until he was entombed in the cave forever.

# Chapter One

Louise Blackwell had hated Sundays as a child, and now that sense of melancholy returned with a blunt force. The scene in front of her reminded her of the more idyllic days of her childhood. She was in the living room of her house in Weston-super-Mare, the sound of lapping waves in the distance catching her ear every now and then, as on the carpet her niece – and now adopted daughter – Emily played with Louise's fifteen-month-old son, Jack. Next to her on the sofa, Thomas was taking photographs on his phone, and in the two armchairs her parents looked on, unbidden smiles etched into their faces as they watched their grandchildren play. In the corner, Molly, Louise's Labrador, tried to get some sleep.

'Look,' said Thomas, showing her an image of Emily and Jack caught in a moment of pure joy, exchanging looks with such an evident sense of love that it tore Louise's heart to know she would be returning to work tomorrow.

Not that the last sixteen months hadn't been an adjustment. It had been hard enough moving in with Thomas – sharing her life with someone after living alone for so long, let alone being with two children for the better part of each and every day. But she wouldn't have exchanged that time for anything. She was closer with Emily than she'd ever been. And little Jack was a blessing who had changed her life in all the ways everyone had told her he would.

'It's not too late,' said Thomas later that evening, after her parents had gone home and the children were asleep upstairs, the sound of Jack's breathing like faint white static on the monitor.

'For what?' said Louise, distracted as she got her clothes ready for the next day.

'To quit. I'm earning enough money now. Just tell Robertson you've had a change of heart, and you don't want to go back.'

It was a conversation they'd had many times over the last six months, and with each repeat Louise grew more and more tempted. After leaving the police, Thomas had endured a few knockbacks as a civilian, but the last couple of years had seen his career flourish. He was now national head of security for a cyber software company based out of Bristol. It meant more money, but also more days, and nights, away, and he was currently working on a long-term project that was taking him to Surrey every day. With Louise as a stay-at-home mum during her extended maternity leave, it hadn't proved to be a problem, but that would all change now.

'I can't let him down like that,' she said, talking about her boss, DCI Iain Robertson. Her voice barely sounded like her own, as if she was trying to convince herself.

'He would understand.'

Louise had gone through so much with Robertson, and she agreed that he probably would understand, but she still felt she had to go back. Even if she only returned for six months, she had to try; had to see if she had the same hunger as before. 'Maybe so, but I wouldn't forgive myself.'

Thomas nodded. She was sure a part of him didn't want her to return to work, but he understood how much it meant to her. As they'd discussed, it wouldn't be so long before Jack was off to pre-school, and then what would she do with herself?

'Take Molly out before you come to bed,' she said, the dog's ears pricking in anticipation as Louise skipped upstairs before Thomas had time to object.

◆ ◆ ◆

The following morning, Louise left in time to take Emily on her customary journey along the seafront in Weston before dropping her at school. The sun had yet to burn through the cotton-wool clouds, and a fine mist had descended over the water, blanking out the view of Steep Holm and its compacted relative, Flat Holm.

Louise would usually have taken some joy in the sight, but her mind was preoccupied with her first day back at work and the impact this was going to have on her family. She'd loved her time on maternity leave, and her role as a police officer felt more distant than ever. She glanced a look in the back. Emily was glued to the view of the eerie mist over the seafront, and Jack was looking at his sister with something approaching awe.

Louise had known this day would be difficult, but after dropping Emily at school she felt her stomach lurch, and she almost didn't take the short journey to Clarence Park and the childminder's where Jack would be staying today.

They had already completed a couple of trial days with the childminder, but that had been different. The significance of returning to work couldn't be understated. As she stopped opposite the park, trying to ignore the memory of the murdered teenage girl they'd found in the same place a few years ago, Louise understood that today would change everything. There would be many different milestones over the years, as Jack grew from toddler to infant, from junior to teenager, but this felt like the most heart-wrenching.

She picked him up from the child seat, the first rays of sun bursting through the layers of cloud as she carried him to the front door. 'I'm going to miss you today,' she said, as she rang the doorbell. Jack giggled in response.

She wasn't the first parent to have gone through this, she thought to herself, as the childminder, Yvonne, answered the door, but it was a struggle to hand her son over.

'It'll be fine,' said Yvonne, in a tone that suggested she'd done this too many times before.

'I didn't know it would be this difficult,' said Louise, surprised by the visceral reaction the thought of leaving Jack had on her body, in particular the threat of tears behind her eyes.

Yvonne smiled, her expression sympathetic but firm, as if she was on the verge of telling Louise to pull herself together. 'I'll send you some pictures through the day. We have a full house and I'm sure Jack will be the centre of attention.'

Louise kissed her son goodbye. She could sense Yvonne trying to cajole her away from the house, and knew it made sense to make a clean break of it. 'I'll see you later,' she said, a look of bewilderment reaching Jack's face as she backed down the pathway, before Yvonne, with a little wave, shut the door.

Louise sat in silence for a few minutes before setting off for Portishead, via the bypass and M5. She knew it would get easier, and Jack would get older, but leaving him had drained all her energy, and now she had another challenge to face in returning to work after so many months away.

The last time she'd had more than two weeks off work had been during a suspension many years back, after her altercation with the now disgraced former DCI Tim Finch. It was much different now. She'd kept in contact with her colleagues during her maternity leave, but stepping into Avon and Somerset's headquarters again, she momentarily felt like an outsider. It wasn't as if she'd expected the world not to move on without her, but she'd reached CID before she saw anyone she recognised.

As she expected, the welcomes were pleasant but muted. 'Welcome back . . . Coffee?' said DS Greg Farrell, who'd made the move with her from Weston CID a few years back.

'Thanks, Greg,' said Louise, whose taste for coffee had returned following Jack's birth.

'Louise? Good,' came the voice of DCI Robertson from the other end of the office.

'Sir,' said Louise.

'Come on then,' said Robertson, beckoning her into his office. 'Welcome back and all that,' he added, in his Glaswegian accent, as Louise took a seat.

Louise laughed. 'I wasn't expecting bunting, but some enthusiasm wouldn't have gone amiss,' she said, sitting opposite him.

Robertson nodded, a slight grin appearing, then vanishing. 'You are irreplaceable, Louise. Both figuratively and literally. It seems that the powers that be thought you were so good at your job that it was pointless paying for someone to take your place during maternity leave, so they didn't bother.'

Louise knew that wasn't completely true, as her colleague and good friend Tracey Pugh had told her of the litany of relief workers who had come and gone in her absence. 'I'm back now, Iain, you can rest easy.'

'How are you with dark cavernous spaces?'

'Is this a set-up for some elaborate joke?' asked Louise.

'No,' said Robertson, deadpan. 'Banwell Caves. You heard of it? Close to your neck of the woods.'

'I know it,' said Louise, who had visited the tourist attraction with its collection of animal bones as a child.

'Couple of cavers, potholers, whatever you call them, were exploring the area and found something.'

'Some bones?' said Louise, thinking back to the eerie collection of animal bones, which had been arranged as if they were in a library.

Robertson frowned, clearly surprised by her response. 'Yes, but they were not where they should have been. One of the cavers is a surgeon by trade and he recognised what he'd found immediately.'

'Which was?' said Louise, understanding her first day back wasn't going to be an easy one.

'Human bones, he believes. CSI are on their way, but the surgeon believes they belong to a child between six and ten years old.'

Louise took in a big breath. These types of findings were usually hundreds of years old and would simply result in an archaeological search of some sort. It was the kind of thing she would usually pass on to a junior member of the team, and she had to wonder why she was being singled out. It was probably Robertson's way of easing her back into the role, but she would rather have got stuck into something else. 'I haven't even had a coffee yet.'

'Take it to go. And take the new DC with you. You haven't met yet. Miles Boothroyd. A bit wet behind the ears but I'm sure you'll get along.'

Louise stood up. 'You know I've just travelled in from Weston, don't you. Would have been a hell of a lot easier to call me in advance.'

'What can I say, I wanted to see your smiling face. How is the little fella, by the way?' asked Robertson, as she reached the door.

'Thomas or Jack?'

Robertson's lips formed into a half-smile.

'All fine. First day at the childminder today.'

'There you go then. You'll be that much nearer to pick him up.'

◆ ◆ ◆

DC Miles Boothroyd was waiting for her in CID. Six-four, with strawberry-blond hair, he had the body of a hardened rugby player with the smooth facial features of a baby. Wide-eyed, he hurriedly placed down his coffee cup as Louise approached, looking around him before saying, 'Ma'am.'

As Louise looked at him, he moved his hand as if he was unsure whether he should offer it to shake. 'You must be Miles. I presume you're old enough to drive?'

'Ma'am.'

'Let's go, then,' said Louise, as Miles fumbled around in his desk for some car keys.

Louise waited until they were approaching Banwell before telling Miles that he could call her Louise. She had to stifle a laugh when he let out an audible breath of relief. 'I was so pleased when I was told I would get to work with you. You're a bit of a legend in the station,' he said, heat reaching his cheeks.

'Where are you on the training programme?' asked Louise, as they pulled in next to two patrol cars in the driveway of a large house.

'A few checkpoints to pass yet,' said Miles, switching off the engine.

Louise nodded and left the car, not waiting as Miles locked up and jogged to catch up with her.

A man was waiting for them in the front garden. He was wearing what Louise considered to be typical country wear: green protective trousers, wellington boots, and a gilet over his shirt. Louise placed him in his seventies, and he appeared to be in great health. Behind him was a detached property, the brickwork painted white. 'DI Blackwell,' said Louise, displaying her warrant card. 'My colleague, DC Boothroyd.'

'Malcolm Landry,' said the man, offering his hand. 'This is my property.'

'You live here alone, Mr Landry?'

'With my wife. I've told this to your uniformed friends.'

'I understand, sir. If you don't mind repeating a few things for my benefit? It wasn't you who found the bones?'

'God, no. We occasionally allow people access to the caves. The two young men you need to speak to are in the house.'

Louise followed the man through the side entrance of the house to an extended garden area, where in the distance was a large stone tower.

'We have two caves here. The stalactite cave, and the bone cave. We know both the men very well. Very experienced cavers. We believe there might be an unexplored network of caves beyond the bone cave. Lots of dead ends, collapsed tunnels, that sort of thing. They had discovered a new tunnel a few hundred yards in, and that is where they found the bones. They will tell you more of course.'

'What's this?' asked Miles, as they passed under a stone archway, part of a set of arches.

'That is part of the Druid's Temple,' said Landry. 'It was on the land before the discovery of the caves.'

'This place is no longer open to the public?' asked Louise. 'I came here as a girl.'

'No, too much trouble. As I said before, we allow private visits subject to permission.'

'And that?' said Miles, pointing to the tower with the enthusiasm of a child.

'That is Banwell Tower. Grade II listed. Was used as a lookout in the war.'

'Still in operation?' asked Louise.

'It is now. You can take a look if you like?'

'Maybe later,' she said, stopping at the police tape at the entrance to the caves, where the CSIs had set up. Louise placed coverings on her hands and feet before stepping under the barrier. 'Hold the fort, Miles,' she said, as one of the CSIs in full overalls returned from within. Louise recognised her as Janice Sutton, head of CSI in the region.

'You're back,' said Janice, removing her mask.

'Miss me?'

'Sure did. How is the little baba?'

'He's fine. With the childminder this morning.'

Janice beamed, and not for the first time, Louise noticed how much more inquisitive people had become about her life now that she was a mother. 'What do you have for me?'

'The two cavers are inside the house, I believe?' said Janice to Mr Landry.

'They are,' said Landry. 'No point them waiting out here.'

Janice moved back towards the cave, nodding for Louise to follow. 'Unfortunately, they didn't leave all the bones in situ. There is a small opening inside I can show you. It's a marvel they could get through it. We'll need specialist teams in here, as I can't risk any of my lot going through yet. Here,' she said, pointing at a single bone in an evidence bag on the floor of the cave.

Louise looked at the bag, her mind already running in a number of different tangents. 'Definitely human?'

'It appears to be the femur from a human, yes.'

'How many other bones were found?'

'There was a whole skeleton. The caver decided to bring this in case something happened to the tunnel before we could take a look.'

'You're sure this is definitely human?' asked Louise, delaying as she collected her thoughts. She could see it was human, and she was thinking about a lost and lonely child trapped within the cave structure, and despite herself, her thoughts turned to Emily and Jack.

Janice grimaced an affirmative. 'I'm no expert but the femur appears to be quite smooth, less eroded than some I have seen in the past.'

'Meaning?' said Louise, thinking about the surgeon's summation that the bones belonged to a child aged six to ten.

'I can't even guess at how long they've been there. But the smoothness indicates that they haven't been there that long. Certainly not as long as the animal bones inside.'

'How long exactly?' said Louise, all thoughts about an easy first day back at work evaporating.

'If I was to guess, and it would only be a guess, I would say these bones are less than thirty years old, and maybe even younger.'

Louise accompanied the specialist team inside the bone cave when they arrived thirty minutes later. The coolness of the cave was a welcome respite from the cloying heat outside. Lights had been erected and the bright rays accentuated the oddness of the place. It wasn't called the bone cave for no reason. It was like a mausoleum for animals, thousands of animal bones arranged on every side in little cordoned-off sections. Like a bone library.

'Imagine stumbling across this,' said Louise, moving deeper inside.

'Someone did,' said Mr Landry, who had insisted on joining them. 'It was an accidental discovery, long after the stalactite cave had been discovered a few hundred years ago.'

Louise bent down to examine some of the bones, touching the rough exterior of the collection that was caught behind a wire mesh.

'You'll see what I mean about the smoothness of the femur bone when you get to touch it,' said Janice, as the specialist team began examining the opening in the side wall.

'It was once believed that the bones were remnants of Noah's Ark,' said Landry, sounding wistful as he glanced around the illuminated interior.

*Two of every animal,* thought Louise, leading Landry away as the specialist teams began setting up ropes and pulleys.

Sweat prickled Louise's body as she returned outside and shielded her eyes from the sun. 'I'd like to talk to the cavers,' she said to Miles. 'Go with Mr Landry, and I'll be there in five.'

Once Miles had walked away, Louise called her mother. Although her thoughts had turned to Emily and Jack on occasion in the last hour or so, her focus had been on work and she wasn't sure how that made her feel.

'Hi, Lou. How's the first day back?'

Louise realised that ever since Robertson had told her about the discovery of the bones, it had felt – to her – as though she'd never been away. 'It's going fine. I know it's day one, but it's already turning into a long one. Could you pick the kids up? Thomas is in Surrey today and won't be back until late.'

After Louise's brother died, Emily had moved in with her grandparents. It was only after Louise became pregnant that Emily had moved in with her and Thomas. Although her parents had welcomed the return of their freedom, they missed having Emily around and had readily agreed to look after the children on days like this when Louise had to stay late and Thomas was working out of the area.

'Of course, don't worry about it.'

Louise thanked her mum and hung up, trying her best to ignore the nagging guilt of not picking Jack up after his first proper day at the childminder's. She wouldn't have minded if Thomas had been able to do it, but it felt wrong that neither of them would be there for their son at the end of what would have been – for Jack, and maybe even them – an important and exciting day.

Mr Landry was making tea as Louise entered the kitchen area to the rear of the house. 'DI Louise Blackwell, this is Steven Webster and Patrick Morton.'

'Gentlemen,' said Louise. 'Please, stay seated,' she added, as both men got to their feet. 'I'm sure DC Boothroyd has already mentioned to you, but we need to ask you a few questions.' She took a seat at the large rectangular kitchen table. 'Which of you was the first to find the bones?'

'That would be me,' said Steven. 'We were on our way back. We'd climbed through the squeeze passage and had reached a dead end. I can't believe we didn't see them the first time around.'

'Can you tell me how they were arranged?'

'Freakiest thing ever. I could see it was a full skeleton, but the bones were all tumbled together, almost in a pile.'

'And you took what you believed to be the femur?'

'That was me,' said Patrick. 'As I've told your colleagues, I'm a surgeon. Not in orthopaedics, but that was hardly needed.'

'Why did you take the bone?'

Patrick frowned, as if slighted. 'We took some pictures, but I thought you would like proof before sending anyone in. I was also concerned about the solidity of the tunnel. The femur, and I recognised it as such, was the closest to hand. Did I do something wrong?'

Louise ignored the question. She would rather the bones had remained where they'd been found, but it wasn't as if the man had tampered with a recent crime scene.

'How long have you been caving in this area?' asked Miles.

'Years now,' said Steven. 'The only reason we came here was to look for potential openings to other cave structures.'

'As experts, how do you think the bones ended up there?' asked Louise.

Patrick fielded that question. 'My best guess is that the child – as I presume these remains do belong to a child – who found their way to that area had become stuck. It could have been via the bone cave, or another tunnel entrance that has since collapsed.'

Louise thanked the men, as Mr Landry placed a cup of tea in front of her. 'We would like to take some fingerprints and DNA samples from you both if you don't mind,' she said. 'Purely pre-cautionary, to rule you out if we get any prints on the bones or surrounding area.'

'You think this was foul play?' said Patrick.

'I don't know what to think, but procedure is procedure. DC Boothroyd will go through the details with you. Thank you for bringing this to light,' Louise said, taking her tea and returning outside.

◆ ◆ ◆

The days were getting longer, but night had fallen before the bones were recovered from the cave.

Thomas called and told Louise that her mother had dropped the children at home. Louise had been absorbed in the investigation all day, but it hadn't stopped her constantly checking her watch as the time for collecting Emily and Jack passed. 'Did he go down OK?'

Thomas hesitated before answering. 'He missed his mummy, but he settled in the end.'

Louise had spent the odd night at her parents' in anticipation of this moment. She'd needed to prepare Jack for her absence after she'd stopped breastfeeding. Though deep down she knew she'd needed it for herself too. Those nights aside, it was the first time she hadn't been there for Jack's bedtime, and it felt like a milestone; a milestone she wasn't ready to accept.

The CSIs and the specialist teams had recorded the scene as much as possible, videoing and photographing the skeleton as best they could before bringing it back through to the bone cave. Despite the decomposition of the body, and the removal of the femur, the bones were still formed in the shape of a small human, and the teams had done their best to keep the skeleton as intact as possible.

The small remains were laid out on a gurney in the bone cave, ready to be taken away for further analysis. It was a sombre sight, the floodlights illuminating the area and its collection of animal bones, and the brittle remains of what appeared to be a child taking centre stage.

Louise bent down to the remains, her mind ruminating on what had happened to the child. The jawline was a mixture of baby and permanent teeth. 'Some are still intact,' she said to Janice Sutton, who was standing next to her, eyes downcast.

'These have been looked after. Possibility of finding dental records?' said the CSI lead.

'Let's hope so,' said Louise, contemplating the long road ahead of them, which despite the tragic circumstances felt much more significant than she had originally thought.

It was another couple of hours before Louise returned home. Perhaps it was overkill, but she'd wanted to supervise everything on her first day back and had even sent Miles home earlier. Thomas was asleep on the sofa. She switched off the television and woke him. 'Get to bed, sleepyhead,' she said.

Thomas groaned and opened his eyes, his face a comical mask of bewilderment as he adjusted to his surroundings. 'What time is it?' he murmured.

'Bedtime. Go on up. I have a few things to do.'

Louise watched him drag himself upstairs before collapsing down on the sofa. She was too wired to sleep. She was sure it was the excitement of a new investigation, but already the case seemed to resonate with her. Sometimes it was difficult to separate the personal and professional, and it was impossible not to think of Emily and Jack when she considered the remains they'd uncovered. She wondered if, somewhere, a parent was lost and alone and hoping for news of their missing child. The intact dental structure of the skeleton suggested that the remains belonged to someone who had disappeared more recently than they'd anticipated. It reminded Louise of one of her last cases before going on maternity leave – the body of Aisha Hashim, who'd been found in a shipping container in the Avonmouth Docks. If Janice Sutton was correct, then the remains belonged to someone close in age to Emily, and the very thought of a child being stuck within the caves, slowly starving to death, sent shudders through Louise.

Fatigue washed over her and at some point she fell asleep. The next time she looked at her phone it was 4 a.m.

She tried to recount her uneasy dreams as she climbed the stairs, blinking out disturbing images of Emily and Jack lost underground as she fumbled in the darkness and lay down next to Thomas, hoping her next set of dreams wouldn't be as horrific.

# Chapter Two

It was the nights she hated the most. During the day, Fiona O'Sullivan had the others in the group to keep her company, but at night she was alone in the caravan they'd been assigned when they'd moved here.

Her boyfriend, Pete, had lasted nine months before leaving, and now it was just her and her ten-year-old son, Max, who was zonked out after a full day in camp.

She'd asked if they could be moved further into the camp, but had been told it was too soon, and they liked keeping families in the caravans.

*Families.*

That was a joke. Their family had been destroyed the day Pete upped and left, with only a few lines of goodbye on a letter to remember him by.

He'd been all for it; in fact it had mainly been his idea. They'd met a few people in the group already at the environmental rallies they'd attended, and Pete had pushed her into taking the online tests. No one had forced them to join. They'd slowly been inducted, introduced to the group's beliefs and practices. She'd been a little reticent, but Pete had been gung-ho and eventually she'd succumbed to his enthusiasm.

They hadn't had much, and they'd been happy to give it up for the security of the commune and the way of life, especially for Max. But Pete's enthusiasm had soon waned. In hindsight, she should have known then that things wouldn't last. Pete was a fervent environmentalist, but he'd been less keen on the spiritual activities. That side of things hadn't been made clear to them, and while Fi had loved the ceremonies, the songs and gifts for Gaia, Pete had remained on the periphery, too quick to dismiss everything as nonsense.

Fi had found something within the commune that Pete hadn't, and while she was still happy with the arrangement, she hated being here at night. The caravans were situated nearly a mile from base. Some people loved them. The area was secluded, the caravans woven into the scenery as if they'd always been part of the forest. Yet, although Fi appreciated the beauty of their surroundings, she was always wishing the night away.

She opened the front door of the caravan and lit a cigarette. Her nearest neighbours were less than a minute's walk away, but gazing into the darkness – with only the moon, a splattering of stars, and the embers from her cigarette for illumination – Fi felt as if she was all alone in the heart of the forest.

A forest that was perfectly still. No breeze rippling through the trees, only the same constant heat from the last few days. She hated herself for thinking it, but it was at times like this she missed Pete. She had loved sharing these moments with him. If he'd been here, she wouldn't have felt alone at all. With Pete here, the remoteness had been perfect. They'd had the best of both worlds – the community and their own space.

Fi returned inside, carefully disposing of the cigarette butt. She poured herself some of the group's homemade beer, wincing at the sour taste, and wondered to herself if it was really Pete she missed, or if it was simply company she longed for.

She switched on the radio and listened to a late-night chat show about modern architecture. She began to relax. *It won't always be this way*, she told herself, and anyway, Max was doing great. He'd made lots of friends and was living the kind of life she'd always dreamt of, growing up; away from the banal cruelties of modern living. She thought about her own childhood – the cramped flat in the Downley estate, her neglectful mother and absentee dad. The endless days of getting herself ready for school while her mother slept on the sofa, and returning to find her in the same position. It would have been too easy to succumb to that way of life, and those bitter memories only cemented her belief that she was doing the right thing by staying here.

She curled up on the sofa bed she'd once shared with Pete, plugging in a night light to ward off the envelope of darkness surrounding the little home. Eyes closed, she strained to listen. Usually there was an abundance of night sounds to keep her company – the scurrying and howls of nocturnal animals, the night breeze passing through the trees – but all she could hear was her own breathing.

Fi wrapped the sheet tighter around her body. She was attuned to nature, and the silence felt odd, as if it was a portent. She shivered, wondering what dangers were lurking beyond her door. The thought stuck with her, her mind making up more and more elaborate scenarios, from a wildfire swarming through the woodland to supernatural forces invading the forest. She shivered, despite the heat, and was so wrapped up in her perceived nightmares that she couldn't stifle a scream when she heard two gentle knocks on the caravan's front door.

'Shit,' she whispered, waiting a beat before moving, hoping Max hadn't been woken by her screaming.

She checked the old carriage clock she'd stolen from her parents before leaving them for good. It was 9.30 p.m. Perhaps not so late for visitors. She peered through the side window, but the glass was smeared and she only saw darkness. Moving to the door, she said, 'Who is it?'

'Hi, Fi, sorry to bother you. It's Teresa. Sorry if it's too late.'

Fi stood still, the sound of her heart beating in her chest audible as she breathed a sigh of relief. She undid the lock, the door creaking as it eased open. Teresa was one of the elders. She'd been one of the first people Fi had met at the camp. Fi wasn't sure if she lived on camp but Teresa had worked through all the paperwork with them, and had been there for her when Pete had upped and left. 'I'm really sorry to call on you so late,' said Teresa again.

'That's OK,' said Fi, hoping the darkness hid her tiredness. 'Would you like to come in?' she added, noting a second person standing behind Teresa.

'No, that's OK. We don't want to disturb you. I wanted to introduce you to Silas. He's a long-term member and is taking over the Pattersons' caravan for a few months. Thought it best we introduce you now in case you bump into one another.'

'Pleased to meet you,' said Fi.

'And I you,' said Silas.

Fi smiled as an awkward silence passed between the three of them. She wanted to know why the Pattersons were being moved, and if they were going to the main camp then why she couldn't join them, but she held her tongue.

'Well, we'll leave you to it,' said Silas, finally.

'Lovely to meet you,' said Fi, feeling awkward as she watched the pair shuffle off down the hill into the darkness, and wondering if the stranger's arrival was another portent she should be concerned by.

# Chapter Three

By Friday, Louise was finding it a little easier to drop Jack at Yvonne's. The childminder was still reluctant to allow Louise through the front door in the morning, insisting it was easier for Jack if Louise didn't linger too long, but saying goodbye was becoming less of a drama. That morning, Jack went to Yvonne without complaint. Although Louise was pleased he'd settled in so quickly, she couldn't deny a stab of jealousy that he'd acclimatised to the days without her so easily.

More of a concern to her now that she was back to work was the overwhelming fatigue. Here she was starting day five, and she felt as exhausted as she usually did at the end of a major investigation. She'd spent the week working on new cases, and waiting for results to come in on the skeletal remains found at Banwell Caves. She knew better than to focus all her energies on one particular case, but she'd been desperate to know more about the remains, so much so that she'd called in some favours to push through the analysis and had arranged to meet the forensic anthropologist who'd been assigned the case.

DC Miles Boothroyd was waiting for Louise outside the building in Bristol when she arrived forty minutes after dropping Jack off. He was wearing a tight-fitting suit that showcased his broad shoulders, and his pale face was lined with a film of sweat from the early summer sunshine.

'You could have waited inside,' said Louise, walking past him to the entrance. It was early days, but she'd been quietly impressed with Miles so far. He was deferential, but not scared to speak up and ask pertinent questions. It seemed that Robertson had put her in some sort of mentor role, and for now she was enjoying having the young officer's help.

They signed in at reception and made their way to the basement, where they were met by the forensic pathologist, Dr Chloe Baker, who was leading the analysis on the bones. Louise thought she was feeling her age, but all the same, Chloe appeared impossibly young for such a senior role. She looked like she was fresh out of university, and even dressed down in her white overalls she seemed to shine with youth and beauty, something that Miles had obviously picked up on if his blushed cheeks were anything to go by.

Chloe led them through to a room that had all the appeal of a surgery, with an amalgamation of modern technology and age-old scientific instruments. 'I was working late on this,' she said, moving towards an aluminium table where the skeletal remains were laid out.

Chloe gestured for Louise to come closer as she picked up the small skull. With a gentle touch, she pointed to the dental arch. 'The presence of a mixed dentition, with both primary and permanent teeth, suggests a pre-adolescent age group, likely between eight and twelve years.' The speed of her words took Louise by surprise.

'I imagine you already know that,' she added, placing the skull back and guiding them to the long bones, then hurriedly explaining the science of bone growth and the indicators that helped pinpoint the age of the young individual. 'The state of the

22

epiphyseal plates, the growth regions of the bones, aligns with the age estimation derived from the dental analysis,' she continued, her fingers tracing the lines of growth on a femur, the same one Patrick Morton had chosen to rescue initially.

Chloe turned her attention to a set of radiographs displayed on a light-box, explaining the subtle signs of bone maturation and the early stages of development in the wisdom teeth, still nestled within the jaw, unseen to the naked eye but revealed through the X-ray.

'So we're definitely looking at a boy aged eight to twelve?' asked Miles, as if desperate for something to say. He beamed again as Chloe looked away. Louise had to suppress a laugh, thinking that the young officer would make a terrible poker player.

'That's correct,' said Chloe, Louise noting a hint of a smile forming on the pathologist's lips.

'Do we have an idea of when he died?' asked Louise.

Chloe frowned, faint lines appearing at the sides of her eyes. 'The isotopic signatures and the state of preservation suggest he passed away approximately a decade ago,' she said. 'If you can trace the dental records, we should be able to narrow that down.'

'And where are we on that?' said Miles, his flushed face returning to its normal colour.

'Here,' said Chloe, picking up a file and handing it to him. 'A full dental chart.'

Louise took the file from Miles, scanning the document, which contained detailed X-rays of the teeth. 'Anything to help us?'

'Quite possibly,' said Chloe, leaning in close to Louise, a light aroma of vanilla on her skin. 'From what we can see, the upper-left second premolars are absent. It's possible he was born without these, which is the kind of detail that could well appear on a dental record. Not unique at all, but something of a distinction. If dental records exist, I would suggest this would have been noted. In the meantime, I need to run some more tests and will get back to you when I have more for you. Unfortunately, I am backed up at the moment as I'm covering Cornwall and Devon, so it could be a couple of weeks before I have something more in-depth for you.'

Louise wasn't surprised by the delay but it still rankled. There were things they could get on with in the meantime, but it was still an unwelcome pause.

◆ ◆ ◆

Back at the station, Louise created a small incident room for the investigation. She was joined by Miles, Greg Farrell, and Tracey. Tracey had been a regular visitor at Louise's these last sixteen months, and was known as Aunty Tracey to Emily, and to Jack in a more abbreviated form. Tracey headed up another section of CID out of headquarters in Portishead, but had worked with Louise on numerous investigations and Louise wanted her input.

On the whiteboard in the room were pictures of the skeletal remains found in the cave. Louise discussed what Chloe had told her with the group. 'I know it's very early days, but we're looking for a boy who would have been eight to twelve years old about ten years ago. We can start locally and increase the scope of the search once we have exhausted that. Obviously, our priority will be on missing persons with official dental records,' she said.

Louise noted the subtle shift in atmosphere. They were all professionals, but things were always a little more on edge when children were involved. Louise caught Tracey and Greg exchange a look of doubt. She understood how they felt. There was no central dental database, and the search would be painstaking. They would first have to find a missing person fitting the particular criteria, and then hope for a potential dental match. It wasn't needle-in-a-haystack territory, but it wasn't far off.

'I can lend you a couple of bodies. Can even lend you myself for a couple of days if you like,' said Tracey, brushing a swathe of unruly dark hair dotted with small patches of grey behind her ears.

They spent the next twenty minutes determining roles for each member of the team. The investigation would be a huge undertaking. The number of missing persons registered was much higher than the majority of the public understood. Louise knew the chances of an instant hit on the databases was unrealistic, and sooner or later Robertson would ask her to pass it over to the cold-case team, but for now she needed to give it her full attention.

She stayed an hour later than intended – having to call on her mother to collect Jack again with Thomas still working on his project in Surrey – trawling through one missing persons case after another, marking some for further analysis of dental records. It made for depressing reading. So many boys to have gone missing over a four-year period in Avon and Somerset without ever resurfacing. Thinking of Emily and Jack, she had to wonder how many of those boys were still alive and living off-grid, and what they would have endured during that period and might still be enduring now. She shuddered at the thought of either of her children going missing, and had to fight the urge to go to be with them.

Yet, despite those concerns, she was the last to leave the incident room, having all but forced Miles out of the office. Although it was 7 p.m. on a Friday night, it felt too early to return home with the bones still unidentified, but she was exhausted and there was nothing more that would be achieved at that late hour.

She turned off the whiteboard, the flash of lights leaving the residual image of the boy's skeleton in her vision, and left for home.

# Chapter Four

Morning changed everything. All her doubts and fears had vanished with the light, although Fi could have done without Max being such an early riser. Max was playing inside as Fi drank coffee and smoked outside, before getting ready for the day ahead.

She didn't miss Pete at times like this. The place was too free and liberating, and she found it easier to dismiss those doubts that surfaced in the darkness. 'Shall we go?' she said to Max, who was full of energy and skipped through the woods towards camp, Fi upping her pace to keep up.

'Hi there,' came a voice from behind her, and Fi turned to see the man from last night running after her. 'Hope we didn't give you a fright,' said Silas, as he caught up with her. 'I told Teresa we should have waited until the morning but she insisted.'

Last night, Fi hadn't really been able to make out his features in the darkness. He looked a bit older than he'd sounded – late forties to fifties – with a full head of silver hair. 'No, not at all. It's so quiet out here that sometimes the smallest sound can spook you,' she said, wondering as she did if she'd said too much.

'I imagine it must take some getting used to. How old is your boy?' asked Silas, joining her as she continued walking.

'Ten.'

'Does he like it here?'

'Loves it. He loves the freedom, but also Miss Carlisle who teaches him. He learns so much more here than he would on the outside,' said Fi, surprised at how easy she found it, talking to the man.

Silas smiled. 'He's a great addition. You must be very proud.'

'I am. He's adjusted so well. Couldn't be happier,' said Fi, as they entered the path towards the main camp area. 'Right, must drop him off now. I'll see you around.'

'I hope so,' said Silas, holding her gaze for a few seconds before heading back into the woods.

◆ ◆ ◆

Fi found herself thinking about Silas through the day. She hadn't entertained the thought of another man in her life since Pete had left, but couldn't deny her attraction to him. His eyes had promised something mysterious, and her pulse had quickened when he'd held her gaze.

'Who was that you were with?' asked Denise, when she arrived in the kitchen where she was working on lunch. Denise had been her friend since she'd first joined the group. Like Fi, her partner had left her, though that had been prior to Fi signing up.

'Who?'

'Don't be like that,' said Denise, with a teasing grin. 'That piece of hunk I saw you walking with earlier.'

Fi felt herself blushing. 'My new neighbour. Silas. Don't know his second name.'

The look on Denise's face changed, her eyes narrowing as if she knew something about the man.

'What is it?' asked Fi.

'Oh, it's nothing,' said Denise, as one of the supervisors arrived in the kitchen. 'I'll talk about it later, now pass me that pot before we get shouted at.'

◆  ◆  ◆

The day moved slowly. Fi was preoccupied with Denise's earlier reaction to her mentioning Silas's name. With lunch prepared, she joined the rest of the team to help serve it. Some of the camp were protesting against a proposed new-build close to the green belt in Hampshire, so there were fewer people than usual, but it was still an age before she was able to sit with the kitchen team and enjoy the fruits of her labour. She kept glancing at Denise as she ate, her friend doing her best to ignore her, until finally she got her alone, following her to an open space next to a copse of sycamore trees where Denise was rolling up a cigarette.

'Here,' said Fi, handing her one of hers, pre-rolled.

'Thanks.'

They lit their roll-ups, each taking an exaggerated drag as if preparing themselves.

'That was hard work today,' said Denise.

'Come on, Denise,' said Fi, wanting to get straight to the point.

'OK. Sorry, I didn't want to say any more with people listening. I didn't realise that man was Silas Oakley.'

'Neither did I. Sounds like a Harry Potter character,' said Fi, with a nervous laugh. 'So, who the hell is he?'

The stoic expression on Denise's face hadn't changed. 'He's one of the higher-ups. Cosy with Teresa.'

'That I do know, she introduced us, but so what?'

'Sorry, Fi, I am terrible at hiding my emotions. I overreacted, that's all.'

'You're scaring me, Denise. What is it?'

'That's not my intention. Listen, there are rumours about him. I shouldn't have got all het up by it and I don't want to freak you out. You've probably heard some of the rumours yourself. About the more . . . salacious side to our group?'

'Salacious?'

'The sex stuff, the ancient rituals.'

Fi felt a sharp pain in her stomach. It was the same pain she'd felt when Pete had said he was leaving. It was another portent, as if her world was about to unravel. She'd heard the rumours before but hadn't paid them much heed. She'd been told about them when she'd joined – about how the outside world was scared of them and created these wild stories to discredit their work. 'I thought that was all nonsense.'

Denise took another drag on her roll-up. 'Of course it's nonsense,' she said.

The group didn't have a name, not officially. It had once been known as the Verdant Circle but that moniker was frowned upon now. Fi had read the articles online before joining, had discussed them with Pete, who'd dismissed them out of hand.

Since its foundation, the group had been focused on saving the planet from the humans who were ruining it. At least, that was the image it portrayed to the outside world. Some of the articles suggested a sinister underbelly to the group, hinting at occult practices and the mistreatment of its members. Although Fi had initially dismissed these rumours, the longer she was with the group, the harder she found them to ignore.

The hierarchical structure to the group was undeniable. There were elders, such as Teresa Willow, the de facto head of Fi's particular commune, and all resources were managed without members' input. To join, they'd had to give up everything, and the money had gone into the group. Fi had accepted it as a necessity; everything was provided for them and she didn't really want for anything, but she understood why people outside would treat the organisation with suspicion.

'Then why do you look so scared?' she said, about to ask Denise more when Max appeared and wrapped his arms around her.

'Sorry, I shouldn't have said anything,' said Denise, ruffling Max's hair as she walked away before Fi could interrogate her any further.

# Chapter Five

The Marine Lake Causeway was flooded, the tidal Bristol Channel spilling into the lake itself as a diagonal streak of sunlight danced off the smooth water. Louise sat in the sand, watching her parents hand in hand with Emily and Jack as they moved to the water's edge. Louise couldn't remember seeing the lake so busy with rowing boats and people enjoying the sunshine. She'd left work early, having promised Emily an hour at the beach after school. It felt like she was bunking off work, not something she would have considered before Jack and Emily had become her everyday life. She called Thomas but his phone was off. She would be glad when his Surrey project was over, and he could get back from work at a normal hour.

Days were passing faster than she had imagined, and already she was settling into a routine. It was different from the past, when she would work all hours and end up crashing at home late at night in front of the television. Now she had to take into account pickup and drop-off times, feeding and sleep routines. Not that she was any less exhausted. Coming home earlier and looking after the children was a blessing, but at times she found it harder than being at work. Even now, as the children skipped to and from the water, she couldn't drag herself away from her phone.

It was a week since Louise and Miles had met with Dr Chloe Baker, the forensic pathologist. Since then, a forensic odontologist had also been appointed to the team, and for the last few days had been checking dental records for boys who had gone missing during the period of their search. It was a laborious process. Once the missing person had been identified, then there was the painstaking work of finding the dental records and gaining permissions before the odontologist could get to work. Each new set of X-rays brought fresh optimism, but so far there had been nothing approaching a match.

No messages.

Louise sighed, looking up to find that Emily was now almost waist-high in the lake. She'd pulled up her school dress but Louise knew it would only be a matter of time before she was soaked head to toe. Not that she cared. It was a pleasure seeing her niece enjoying herself, and the new lease of life in her parents with their latest grandchild. Jack was taking a much more cautious approach to the water. He'd started walking three months earlier, but still clung on to his grandparents' hands as if his life depended on it, forcing them to swing him in the air every time water came near.

Louise was about to join them when her phone vibrated. A message from Tracey:

I know you're at the beach but we think we have a hit

Louise got to her feet, wondering at the strange noise she made at the effort of getting up, and called over to her mother. 'Need to make a call,' she mouthed.

Her mother turned, smiling as she nodded.

Louise walked on to the promenade, searching for a quiet spot. The beer gardens in the bars opposite were full of people making the most of the sunshine, and she walked on until she found a quiet nook in the sea wall.

'I thought you were at the beach,' said Tracey, answering her call.

'You think I would be able to get on with my day with a message like that?'

'No, I didn't, but I thought I'd give you the option. We have a name. Hugo Latchford. Went missing twelve years ago from a foster home in Shepton Mallet. Biological parents had done a runner when he was aged seven.'

'Lovely. Do we know why?'

'Looking into that. It seems they sold their house not long after. Debt, drugs?'

'And the foster parents?'

'We've made contact. I've arranged for you to see them tomorrow morning. Ten thirty a.m. OK? I'll send details over now so you can read later.'

'That's fine.'

'We've hardly had a chance to catch up since you've been back. How are the kiddiewinks?'

'All good,' said Louise, catching sight of Emily – now soaked head to foot – and Jack, returning from the water. 'Listen, get Miles to meet me there tomorrow.'

'OK. I'll keep you updated if we hear any more about the biological parents.'

'Sure, thanks,' said Louise, distracted by the sight of Emily doing her best to dry herself, and the news that they finally had a name for the set of bones they'd found in the caves and what that might mean.

◆　◆　◆

The good weather continued into the next day. It was another high tide as Louise drove along the seafront, the distant sights of Steep Holm and Flat Holm coated in the sheen of sunlight. After speaking to Tracey yesterday, she'd spent a restless night reading up on Hugo Latchford and his family. The seven-year-old had gone missing after playing football in a local park in Shepton Mallet. As would be expected, there had been extensive searches but the body had never been found.

Hugo had been given up for adoption by Jeremy and Valerie Latchford the previous year. Undertakings were already underway to track down the two parents. It was rare for children to go into care at that age by choice of the parents. Usually, children were moved into care by the authorities. Sometimes because of abuse or addiction problems. Sometimes because the parents could no longer cope. In this instance, both parents had been working and had money. The only possible reason Louise could see for the parents giving up Hugo was that Valerie had been on heavy medication at the time. Still, it was a lengthy process, and the fact that it had happened was a red flag she needed to investigate.

Miles was waiting for her outside the house of Hugo's foster parents. Louise wondered if his impeccable punctuality would last forever or if he was still trying to impress. He left his car as Louise parked up, his large frame moving a little more sluggishly than usual as he approached.

'Late night?' she asked, causing him to blush.

'How did you know?'

'When you reach DI, you get these superpowers.'

The colour remained in his cheeks. 'So, tell me who I was out with then?'

Louise knew little about the young man and nothing about his friends and acquaintances. She made a quick mental note of everything Miles had been involved in since she'd met him, and only one possible name came to mind. 'Dr Chloe Baker,' she said, recalling the way Miles had blushed during their meeting last week with the forensic pathologist. Louise remained expressionless on the off-chance that she was correct.

Miles's mouth hung open, and his eyes went wide. 'How?'

'Superpowers,' said Louise, turning away so Miles couldn't see her smile. She thought about how relatively young the pair were, recalling the mistakes she had made as a young officer – in particular her affair with the now disgraced officer Tim Finch that had almost ruined everything. Miles didn't need mothering, and she'd ended up marrying a colleague so was hardly in a position to give out warnings about professional relationships, but there were risks in getting emotionally involved with a colleague in this environment that Miles could do with hearing about. She decided to leave it for now, and she walked up the pathway to the house, pushing past overgrown vines in the front garden blocking her way. 'Remind me of their names again,' she said, testing the young officer's recall.

'Deborah and Leslie Jenkins.'

'Leslie is male?'

Miles pursed his lips. 'I presume so.'

Louise shook her head and sighed, aware of Miles blushing for not checking as she rang the doorbell. The detached house was a small plot close to woodland. The exterior, painted a garish shade of red, had seen better days. The wooden window frames were crumbling, the side guttering hanging from the wall.

The door opened, answered by a frail man with long, black, greasy hair, with a matching peppered beard that stretched to his chest. 'Mr Leslie Jenkins?' asked Louise, glancing quickly at Miles.

The man looked at Miles as if for explanation.

'You are?'

'DI Blackwell and DC Boothroyd. May we come in?' said Louise, displaying her warrant card.

'What's this all about?'

'Please can we come in?'

Mr Jenkins hesitated for a few seconds, his brow furrowed in thought. 'Come through,' he said, finally, turning his back on them.

The sound of crying filtered through from the back of the house, Miles closing the door behind them as Louise moved through the dimly lit hallway to an open-plan kitchen area. Concertina doors spanned the width of the room, leading to a field-like garden, the grass burnt back to a yellow-brown colour. 'This is my wife,' said Mr Jenkins. 'Deborah. Deborah, the police.'

Deborah Jenkins was holding a toddler on her lap, a frowning boy who clung to her tightly. 'How old?' asked Louise.

'Twenty-two months. We've had him a year, haven't we, Nathan?' she said to the boy.

Louise was surprised the boy was that much older than Jack, as they looked to be a similar size. She wondered what had happened to the boy's parents, and was briefly thankful for the life Jack had at home. 'I have some very sad news, I'm afraid. Last week we recovered the remains of a young boy in Banwell Caves. We believe the remains are of Hugo Latchford.'

Colour drained from Mrs Jenkins, as Mr Jenkins slumped down on a kitchen chair. 'You're sure?' said Mrs Jenkins.

Louise nodded. As foster parents at the time of Hugo's disappearance, the Jenkinses would have naturally been treated as possible suspects, but nothing had been uncovered to suggest they'd had anything to do with the boy going missing.

'Such a terrible thing,' said Mr Jenkins. 'Can I get either of you something to drink?' he added, his initial brusqueness having faded.

'I'll take a tea,' said Louise, keen to keep the pair talking. 'He wasn't with you that long?'

'Hugo? No,' said Mrs Jenkins, bouncing the toddler on her knee. 'He was such a sweetheart. I felt so sorry for him. When we take on older kids . . . if it's not because of abuse or neglect, it's usually because of death in a family or illness. With Hugo it felt a little different. From what I understand, the mother was having mental health issues, but why they would give up their little one like that I'll never know.'

'Did you ever meet them?' asked Miles, squeezing into one of the kitchen chairs as Mr Jenkins prepared cups of tea.

'No. Not usually a good idea. Even when Hugo went missing, we never saw them,' said Mr Jenkins.

The file on Hugo Latchford stated that Valerie and Jeremy Latchford had been living in a commune in the Mendip Hills at the time of Hugo's disappearance. It had taken the authorities over a week to track them down, the commune being off-grid, close to the village of Priddy.

'What happened to him?' asked Mrs Jenkins, the toddler on her lap falling silent as if he too wanted to know the answer.

'We're still trying to find that out. Tell me about the day he went missing,' said Louise.

Mr Jenkins, who was now the only one still standing, glanced at his wife before looking away. Louise wasn't sure if his reaction was from distaste at having to live through those events again, or because of the inconvenience that her and Miles being there presented.

'Here, take him,' said Mrs Jenkins, to her husband.

Louise studied the exchange as the child was passed from one foster parent to the other, Mr Jenkins' large hands holding the child and lifting him away effortlessly.

Mrs Jenkins took a big breath and began to speak. 'We had three boys then and one girl. Hugo was the youngest of the boys. The other two – Steven who was twelve, and Ash who was fifteen – had taken Hugo over to the fields to play whatever it is boys play. Steven came home first in tears. He'd gotten into a fight with some local lad and had a bruised eye to prove it. Ash didn't come home until much later. It was still light, so we weren't worried. Ash was responsible and we knew he'd look after Hugo for us. It was only when he returned that he told us he'd spent the last three hours looking for Hugo.'

'When was the last time Ash saw him?' asked Miles.

'Hugo had gone to play by the river with some of the younger boys. None of them had come back so Ash went looking for them. When he came back, we called around. We knew all the boys, and the parents said they'd all returned safely. All except Hugo.'

'Is there any need for this?' asked Mr Jenkins, who had placed the toddler in a playpen, the child playing with his toys in his makeshift prison. 'You must have a record of all this. We nearly lost all the children after Hugo disappeared.'

They had, and Louise had spent all night studying the details. After calling around, the Jenkinses had gone straight to the police. Within hours, search times had been allocated, helicopters posted, and divers had been sent into the river. Time did strange things to recall, and she was interested to hear how the Jenkinses remembered that period. 'I need to clarify, I'm sure you understand. Do you ever hear from Ash and Steven?'

'Steven, yes. Ash, no,' said Mrs Jenkins.

'It hit Ash hard. It hit all of us hard. But Ash blamed himself. I imagine he still does,' said Mr Jenkins.

Like all the boys there that day, Ash had been questioned. They had an address for him on file and would speak to him soon. 'In all these years, have you ever heard from Mr and Mrs Latchford?'

'No. They didn't even turn up to the memorial. Imagine that,' said Mrs Jenkins, shaking her head.

That was information not in the file, and it piqued Louise's interest. It was believed both parents were still with the commune. They'd been off-grid since giving Hugo up for adoption, and at present the police didn't have a known location for either of them.

'Thank you both. I realise this must have been very hard for you,' said Louise. 'Before we go, is there anything you may have remembered since that time that might help us find those responsible?'

'We must have had forty more children come to stay with us since Hugo disappeared. Despite everyone trying to get us banned. We do our best every day to help these kids and get nothing in return. I treated that boy as my own,' said Mrs Jenkins, her eyes watering.

'Right, that's enough,' said her husband, trying to usher them out of the room.

Mrs Jenkins rubbed her eyes, composing herself before saying, 'All I can tell you is that he cried for his mother every night. Every single night. As I've cried for him every night since he disappeared.'

# Chapter Six

No sooner had Louise sat down at her desk in headquarters than a call came through from the duty sergeant informing her that a DI Gerrard Pepperstone had arrived to speak to her. Louise had spent the journey back from Shepton Mallet ruminating on Mrs Jenkins' final words, and the haunting vision of Hugo Latchford crying himself to sleep every night for a mother who had abandoned him; a mother he would never see again.

'Who?' asked Louise, thinking that the name sounded made-up and she was somehow being pranked.

'He's from the Met,' said the duty sergeant.

'Hang on, I'll be down now,' said Louise, wondering why someone would travel all the way from London without calling ahead.

DI Pepperstone stood as she entered the reception area. He was smaller in height than Louise, five-six at a push, and was wearing a creased, cheap-looking linen suit. His patchy hair was overgrown, as was the hair on his face, which was almost a parody of a beard. 'DI Blackwell, Gerard Pepperstone,' he said, his voice a nasal wheeze.

'Louise. How can I help you, Gerrard?'

'It's about the bones you found,' said the DI, surprising Louise by speaking in a mock-spooky voice. Louise was used to gallows humour in the force but didn't take kindly to anyone mocking the death of a child. Pepperstone had already put her on the back foot.

'They don't have phones where you come from?'

'I was in the area, thought I'd come to see you face to face,' said Pepperstone, his voice returning to his monotone wheeze. 'Any chance I can buy you a coffee?' he asked.

'I think we can stretch that far, come on,' said Louise, getting them buzzed through and taking Pepperstone to the canteen, where she got them both one.

Pepperstone took a sip, closing his eyes as he drank, like it was nectar. 'Sorry, I know I should have called ahead. I head up, sort of, a unit in the Met looking into a group that goes by the name of the Verdant Circle, amongst others. I'm sure you've heard of them?'

Louise had heard of the group before. They'd made national news on occasion, and she understood there were still a number of current investigations being made into their community. 'The Verdant Circle' was not a term they actively used any more, but to many they were considered a cult due to the hierarchical nature of their organisation and the accusations from former members who claimed the group had taken their life savings. 'I've come across them, yes. What has this to do with me?'

Pepperstone took another sip of coffee. 'When Hugo Latchford went missing twelve years ago, we tracked down his parents, Valerie and Jeremy, to a subset of this organisation,' he said, using air quotes on the last word.

'You still think they're with them?' said Louise.

'That's the thing. We didn't know for sure then, and we don't know now. The Verdant Circle have been around since the seventies under various guises. They started off as an environmental lobby group, but it wasn't long before the nutters took over. By the eighties they were dabbling in religious and, we believe, occult practices. They work in your classical cell structure, often going by different names, under the guises of environmental campaigners or spiritual groups.'

'I may have encountered them before,' said Louise, thinking back to an old investigation at Cheddar Gorge. 'Not sure if it was definitely the Verdant Circle, but I investigated a commune in the Mendip Hills during a missing persons case. From what I remember, they were more an environmental outfit than anything else. Do you have people on the inside?'

Pepperstone's eyebrows shot up his forehead. It seemed that even if they did have people on the inside, he wouldn't be sharing the information. 'They are well funded, often by their followers, and well protected. You'd be surprised how hard it is to take legal action against them. At least successfully,' he said, with a sneer. 'Furthermore, everyone takes a new name when they join the fraternity, as it were. Classic move, ridding the poor saps of their identity. If the parents are still involved, they would have long since stopped using the monikers of Valerie and Jeremy. Probably Moonshine Child and Flower Warrior by now.'

Louise frowned. She didn't know that much about the group, but found the DI's flippancy unnecessary. She'd encountered different environmental groups in her time. It was an emotive subject, but the majority of the people she'd met had their hearts in the right place.

'Look, don't get me wrong, I feel sorry for these people. I've been tracking this group for years. They sucker them in with promises of eternity, and this idea of the divinity of nature, and before you know it, they've sold all their worldly possessions to be part of this hive mind.'

'And that is what happened to the Latchfords?'

'Most definitely,' said Pepperstone, wiping his nose with a handkerchief. 'Sorry, allergies. The thing is, Louise, we haven't heard hide nor tail from those two in the last twelve years beyond the occasional sighting. And to be honest, we'd long lost interest in them. But now you've found the bones of their son, they are obviously back on our radar.'

'You're actively looking for them?' said Louise, wondering what Pepperstone was getting at.

'Not quite. We have our feelers out but our interest is the top of this organisation. We're close to bringing a case against them. Fraud, embezzlement, money laundering, tax evasion, you name it. Our investigation suggests there are a minimum of forty-six subgroups working nationwide, so finding them won't be easy. To put it delicately, I need you to tread carefully on this investigation. I was hoping we could work together on this discovery. As the bones were found here, it would make sense to start working locally. I have people in the area I can put you in contact with.'

'Have you ever come across something like this before?'

Pepperstone shrugged his shoulders. 'Human remains? Not that I'm aware of, but I'm happy to share our work with you. You'd be staggered at some of the things we've come across.'

'You think the environmental campaigning is a front?'

Pepperstone pursed his lips as if he'd eaten something distasteful. 'I know we're not supposed to say it, but they are a cult, simple as that. They may not have started out that way, and their environmental campaigning is real, but the money only flows upwards in their organisation. And when that happens, the power balance shifts.'

'Meaning?'

'When they initially started, as the name would suggest, their environmental credentials were mixed firmly with their pagan beliefs. Some of the groups have taken this to its limits.'

'What are we talking about?'

Pepperstone took another sip of coffee. 'Most of it is harmless enough. Praying and dancing to Gaia, that sort of thing. But there are reports that things get weird out there. Suggestions of occult practices, that sort of thing. We've encountered animal sacrifice in the past, as an example,' he said, wiping his mouth with the back of his hand.

Louise sat up straight. She'd encountered the sacrifice of slaughtered sheep when investigating the disappearance of a teenager in Cheddar, though that had been down to the work of one person. 'What are you saying?'

Pepperstone nodded to himself for a few seconds, as if he was listening to a beat. 'As I said, my investigation centres around the financial. However, people go missing in the Verdant Circle. The thing is, they're already off-grid by the time they are indoctrinated, so measuring how many go missing is all but impossible.'

Louise closed her eyes, thinking of the arrangement of the bones in the cave, and the little boy they had belonged to. 'You mean . . .'

Pepperstone shrugged again. 'I don't mean anything. All I'm saying is that I wouldn't put anything past them, and I certainly wouldn't rule out the possibility that Hugo Latchford's death was not accidental.'

# Chapter Seven

Everyone in the camp was assigned a role, although today being Monday Fi had a day off from working in the kitchens. After dropping Max at the camp's schooling area, she decided to take a walk. The atmosphere in the camp was muted following the news that the bones discovered in Banwell Caves had belonged to Hugo Latchford, the son of former camp members. It brought fresh, unwanted attention to the commune, and there had been several meetings at the camp, though Fi hadn't been involved.

She left the main camp, taking the steep incline back towards her caravan. She didn't stop there, deciding to walk further into the woods. She paused as Silas's temporary home came into view. She still didn't know what to think about the man. Despite what Denise had told her, she still felt a stab of attraction. Silas had been nothing but pleasant since arriving, though she hadn't seen much of him lately.

She'd heard about the boy before joining. It was one of the rumours circling on the internet that she and Pete had contended with before joining. The group made no secret about the controversy that had come their way when Hugo Latchford disappeared, his parents having given him up for adoption before joining the group. Although she'd never understood why the parents had done such a thing, she'd accepted that both they and the group had nothing to do with Hugo's disappearance. The fact that everyone had been so open about the accusations had only cemented her desire to remain. Where Pete had grown suspicious, she had appreciated the openness with which the group faced their detractors. She felt sure she had the same resolve now, but the news of Hugo's remains being found in the cave, and the underlying suggestion from the reports that his death hadn't been accidental, had unnerved her.

She walked further into the woods, enjoying the earthy smells and the jagged lines of sunshine punctuating the covering of trees. It was such a heavenly place, and now that she'd recovered from Pete's departure, she hated the fact that her will was being tested again in this way.

So why the doubts now? How could Denise's silly tittle-tattle, and the discovery of an old set of bones, make her question herself after all this time? She'd been told when they joined that there would be periods of indecision, and that people were free to leave if and when they wanted. But the best thing to do during times of doubt – so they said – was to talk to one of the elders.

Fi entered a clearing. In the distance, she heard the sound of traffic from the main road. Yes, that was what she would do. She would return to camp and talk to Teresa Willow. It was the remoteness of the caravan that was getting her down. She would insist on a move, and that would change everything.

Reinvigorated by her decision, Fi headed back into the woodland towards camp, stopping as she approached Silas's caravan, where she saw the man in a full-blown argument with Teresa.

She had to admit that she didn't know Silas at all, but the transformation in him was staggering. He was screaming at Teresa, his body contorted in rage. Fi was worried he was about to lash out at the elder. She wanted to help, but found herself rooted to the hard ground as Silas grabbed Teresa by the shoulders.

Fi hated herself, but she couldn't move. It was as if Silas had grown in size. He towered over Teresa like he was about to devour her. Fi was impressed by the way the woman held her ground until Silas let her go and stormed off into the woods.

Fi felt as if she was intruding. She wanted to comfort Teresa, but something warned her off. She watched as Teresa wiped tears from her face with a savage swipe of her hand, before heading in the opposite direction to the main camp.

As Teresa walked off, Fi let out a deep sigh. Her heart was hammering and she wondered what she'd just witnessed. She moved towards Silas's caravan where the argument had taken place, wondering what could have caused such a fallout, and noticed that Silas had left his caravan door open.

She walked up the metal steps to the entrance, her pulse raising again as she looked about her, and before she considered what she was doing, she stepped inside.

# Chapter Eight

In the past, Louise had found it easy to separate her private and work life, but these days it seemed there wasn't a part of the south-west she hadn't been called to for one reason or another. Returning to Cheddar, she couldn't help but be reminded of the missing child investigation she'd headed up a few years ago, which had started with the disappearance of Madison Pemberton, a teenage girl who had been walking along the clifftops and had ended up a prisoner in the cave system.

Being here now with DI Pepperstone, at his invitation, sitting outside one of the tourist cafés on the main road bisecting the Gorge, she recalled those troubled days, which had included more than one visit to the environmental campaign group who had initially come under suspicion. It had been a tough investigation for so many reasons, none more so than the parallels between the missing girl and her niece, Emily. Louise wondered how much harder it would have been if Jack had been part of her life back then, and considered what the emotional toll of investigating Hugo Latchford's unexplained death might have on her now she was a mother.

According to Pepperstone, they were here to meet a former member of the group, Lyndsey Garrett, who had left the Verdant Circle last year.

Louise felt restless sitting in the sunshine, as if she was waiting for something to happen. Pepperstone had cemented the idea that Hugo Latchford's death was not accidental, and now she wanted to do everything in her power to find who was responsible.

'There she is now,' said Pepperstone, wiping his nose with an old tissue as he got to his feet.

A young woman in a flower-patterned summer dress stopped in her tracks as Pepperstone waved her over. A strand of straw-coloured hair fell over her face, and she blew at it as she studied Pepperstone and Louise, as if deciding whether or not to make a run for it. Eventually she walked over and nodded to Pepperstone.

'Hello, Lyndsey. Please take a seat. This is Louise . . . DI Louise Blackwell.'

Lyndsey nodded again, a half-smile forming on her face as she sat down. 'I've seen you before,' she said, as Pepperstone signalled to a waiter to order some drinks.

Louise searched for a memory of the woman but came up blank. 'I'm sorry, I don't remember,' she said.

'You found that girl, and the baby. You were in the papers.'

'That's right,' said Louise, who'd never been comfortable with any of the press she'd received due to her investigations. 'You were here then?'

'I was part of the environmental group protesting against the developments,' said Lyndsey, giving a big sigh. 'We lived on a site over in the hills, not far from here. You came to look at the caves.'

Louise recalled the location – the eerie manor house and the numerous mobile homes and tents that had littered the area. 'How was it, living there?' she asked, as the waiter placed their drinks on the table.

The sun was high, and Lyndsey shielded her eyes from the glare before opening a can of Diet Coke. 'Mostly good.'

'Mostly?'

'Believe it or not, the majority of us were there to make a difference. The developers were trying to ruin this place, more than they already have.'

Louise remembered feeling torn during their investigation into the group. As Lyndsey suggested, it had appeared from the outside that the group had positive goals. Their protests had been non-violent, though they had caused some criminal damage when they'd graffitied the outside of the caves. However, it was always imperative that she stayed impartial, and she hadn't allowed her own opinions to get in the way of any investigation. 'I understand that. But you were successful, weren't you?'

Partly due to the protests, although possibly helped by the publicity from the kidnappings, the proposed developments hadn't gone ahead. 'You could say that,' said Lyndsey. 'But there is always something. If you haven't noticed, the world is going to shit. Anyway, not long after you rescued that girl the group sort of fell to pieces and then we went our separate ways. I ended up with another group over towards Priddy.'

'The Verdant Circle,' said Pepperstone.

Lyndsey shrugged. 'I was there for a while.'

'But you chose to leave the group. Can you tell me why?' asked Louise, thinking of what Pepperstone had said about the occult beliefs within the group.

Lyndsey took her hand away from her face, lifting her chin as she looked at Louise as if in defiance. 'Just because I left, it doesn't change anything. My beliefs have stayed the same. I will do everything in my power to stop the destruction of this planet.'

'No one is questioning your principles, Lyndsey. I'm more interested in knowing why someone as passionate as you would be driven out.'

A cloud loomed over the sun, and Lyndsey visibly relaxed. 'I wasn't driven out. I left of my own volition.'

'And how easy was that?' asked Pepperstone.

'You know full well what I had to go through,' said Lyndsey.

'We're helping Lyndsey, as best we can, to gain some compensation from the group. Isn't that right, Lyndsey?'

Louise had to bite her tongue. It was information Pepperstone should have shared with her prior to the meeting, and the oversight was sloppy.

'And some job you're doing at that. I gave up everything,' said Lyndsey, turning her attention to Louise. 'My job, most of my friends, my house. Signed it over to them. I believed in it all. I still do, but . . .'

'Things changed?' asked Louise.

Lyndsey frowned. 'I was misled. The longer you're there, the more you find out. I chose to join the group. I wasn't coerced in any way. I sold my property because I believed it was for the best. They still do some amazing work, but some of the people there don't belong.'

'The people in charge?'

'Them as well, but I'm talking about some of the general members. Sometimes, we preyed upon the wrong people. The vulnerable, those at their lowest point. We would get them to join with promises of utopia, and they would do what I did, sell up and lose everything. I thought it was right at the time but now I'm not so sure.'

'It wasn't just that though, was it?' said Pepperstone.

'No. There was a sect within the sect,' said Lyndsey, taking another sip of her drink. 'I thought it was all rumours to begin with, but I guess I was a bit naive. You join something called the Verdant Circle, I guess you should expect some things out of the ordinary.'

'And what did this sect do which you didn't like?'

The sun had crept back out and Lyndsey shielded her eyes. 'Here,' said Louise, handing her some sunglasses.

'No, thank you,' said Lyndsey, sighing again. It was clear she didn't want to be here, sharing secrets about a group she still had regard for. Louise imagined it was a condition, implied or not, that Pepperstone had insisted on in return for his help. 'Some of the stuff made me uncomfortable. Don't get me wrong, I loved the ceremonies, the worshipping of Gaia. I long to return to a simpler time where we look after the Earth. But . . . some of the beliefs I couldn't align myself with.'

Louise studied Lyndsey. The frown lines on her forehead suggested she was going through some internal debate. Louise waited for her to continue speaking instead of pushing for answers.

'There were a few of them who thought we needed more. That we needed the help of Gaia, of Mother Nature. There were private ceremonies away from camp. I was never invited. These ceremonies . . . they offered gifts, do you understand?' said Lyndsey, under her breath.

'You mean sacrifices?' said Louise, catching a grin on Pepperstone's face.

Lyndsey nodded. 'From what I gather, it started small – rabbits, birds, that sort of thing. But I heard they were catching deer, sheep, cattle. I understood it in a way. The ritual beliefs ran deep through the group, and it's not unheard of, but I thought it was getting out of control.'

'And that is when you chose to leave?'

Lyndsey shook her head. 'No. I didn't like what they were doing, but I genuinely believed that they were trying to do some good. It was only when I raised my concerns that things went sour. There were some new people in camp, and they didn't take kindly to my interfering. I've shared this with him already,' she said, glancing at Pepperstone.

'We have some descriptions. Some names, if you can call them that,' he said.

'You know why we're here?' said Louise.

'The bones you found.'

'The human remains. What do you know about them?'

Lyndsey sucked in her cheeks, the sun still glaring in her eyes. 'There were always rumours.'

Louise's pulse quickened. 'Rumours?' she said, trying to hide her growing agitation.

'Before my time,' said Lyndsey, shaking her head. 'I never believed it, but there was talk about human sacrifice, particularly in the olden days, and the links to ancient occult practices. Some of the more extreme members thought this was why we were failing.'

'A lack of human sacrifice?' asked Louise, unable to hide her incredulity.

'Not me. Never me,' said Lyndsey, glancing around the terrace as if she were on trial. She lowered her voice to a whisper. 'Some of the older ones. In fact, not just the older ones. They thought animal sacrifice wasn't enough. That we had to offer more to appease Gaia.'

Louise had long ago stopped questioning the types of things people believed in. It never helped, deriding beliefs as being ludicrous. The only thing to take into account was how seriously people took those beliefs, and how far they were prepared to go for them. 'Did you ever see any of this happen?'

'Of course not,' said Lyndsey, indignant. 'Most of us didn't want anything to do with it. Only, I was the most vociferous. That's why they eventually kicked me out.'

'Who kicked you out specifically?' said Louise.

'We have the names and descriptions,' said Pepperstone, who'd been all but silent for the majority of their time there. Louise still wasn't sure how to take the man. He seemed to have an almost irreverent approach to the situation. 'What I would really like to know is what you know about Hugo Latchford and the bones recovered in Banwell Caves,' he said to Lyndsey.

For the first time since arriving, Lyndsey appeared taken aback. She leant back in her chair, her already pale skin losing colour. 'I had nothing to do with it,' she said.

'No one is suggesting it,' said Pepperstone.

'What do you know?' added Louise.

'As I said, there were rumours. Lots of them. It was impossible to know which to believe. One that always seemed to have a kernel of truth to it was the idea that the remains of a number of human sacrifices were scattered across the land in specific sites, and as long as these were kept in place, we would be safe.'

'Safe from what?' said Pepperstone, unable to hide his dismissiveness.

'The ravages of Mother Nature.'

'And you think Hugo Latchford was one of these sacrifices?' asked Louise.

Lyndsey shook her head. 'I thought they meant ancient sacrifices, people who had died years ago in pagan ceremonies,' she said, close to pleading. 'I hope that's still the case.'

'But you're not sure?'

'I'd always tried to dismiss the idea, as I didn't want to believe it could be real, but there were these legends that the sacrifices were more recent, committed by the group over the years, to keep us safe. I never believed it. I thought it was all talk. Then I read online that the bones you found belonged to Hugo Latchford, and I knew something was off.'

'Meaning?' asked Pepperstone.

'Meaning one of the legends was that Hugo's parents had sacrificed him twelve years ago, when they first joined us.'

# Chapter Nine

The caravan had a familiar manly scent, the air cloying as Fiona moved through the main room. She would have liked to open a window but didn't want Silas to know she had been there. She still wasn't sure why she was there. Maybe it was because of the fight she'd witnessed between Silas and Teresa Willow; maybe it was because of the portents and all the wild rumours spreading through camp like wildfire ever since Hugo Latchford's remains had been uncovered.

What she did wonder was why Silas had been so friendly with her when she hadn't once seen him in camp. Teresa had introduced him as if he was an important new addition to the commune, but as far as Fi was aware he'd spent his time holed up here.

She moved some clothes off one of the cushions and sat down, waiting for her pulse to drop. It was ludicrous being in here. But still, she didn't leave, the urge to look through Silas's things overcoming her.

Not that there was much to go through. It was clear, as she went into the bedroom, that he wasn't here for the long haul. Two bags took up space on the carpet, leaving all but no floor space, the bed scattered with dirty laundry.

It was like being detached from her body, as if she was watching herself ransack the cupboards and drawers of the small abode. She couldn't quite believe she was doing it, didn't really understand why she was doing it, but the illicit thrill was undeniable.

She froze as she heard the sound of rustling leaves from outside. How would she explain being here if Silas returned? She held her breath, waiting for the caravan door to open. *This is ridiculous*, she thought, as she waited a few more seconds.

*Right, that's enough*, she told herself, and was about to leave when she saw a broken wood panel at the far end of the living room.

The air seemed to be getting thinner as she dropped to her knees and crawled to the panel. The caravan was a replica of her own, but she'd never noticed anything like this before in hers. She jimmied the panel aside and peered inside the small gap. Her body was covered in sweat, the anxiety of being there almost too much to bear. She stuck her hand inside and felt two small packages with her fingertips. 'You'll regret this,' she said out loud, and groaned with effort as she reached to pull the packages free.

She stared in disbelief at what she saw. One bag was filled with tightly packed banknotes, the other a sealed bag of white powder. Hands shaking, she tried to put the bags back into the opening, in her desperation forgetting where each bag had originally been placed.

Shifting the bags into position, she tried to rationalise the discovery. The camp was awash with drugs, always had been. It was like a dirty little secret that everyone accepted. Fi had stopped some time ago, but had her own private stash locked away in the caravan. So it made sense that someone had to distribute it, and obviously that person was Silas. All she had to do now was get the hell out of there and hope he never realised she'd been snooping.

The wood panel was jammed in the opening and she had to stretch further in to retrieve it. As she did so, her hand alighted on another object.

'What are you doing?' she mouthed to herself, her hand still shaking as she withdrew the item. Also covered in a plastic sheath, it appeared to be a book of sorts. Old and fragile, it had a hardback cover decorated with ornate inscriptions, containing a number of loose papers.

Fiona checked her hands, wiping the sweat on her blouse before removing the book from its plastic covering, the smell of old paper and something akin to dampness tickling her nose. Each page was contained in its own plastic case, the parchment dense with handwritten words. To Fi's eyes they were illegible, the words tightly written in elaborate swirls, the letters impossibly small.

It was only when she looked further into the pages that it began making some sort of sense, with the addition of a number of hand-drawn images. These included various maps, national and local. She recognised the map for the Mendip Hills but was unable to decipher the scrawl of the headings. It was number three of twelve maps that encompassed the whole of the UK.

Things started to get strange after the maps. Fi flicked through the pages, mouth agape at the crude and realistic sketches, etched in perfect detail. They were mainly of adults in various states of disguise, wearing masks that made them look half-animal. In the drawings they were always dancing.

In each of the drawings, there was a child in distress.

Fi didn't want to see any more, but she couldn't help herself. She continued flicking through the books, until she saw the thing she feared most.

An image of the masked adults carrying a child into a cave.

Masked adults dancing around a frightened child.

Masked adults sealing a child within the cave.

It was too much. Her hands started shaking and she struggled to put the papers back in order, before shoving the plastic covering, along with the drugs and money, into the hidden compartment.

She felt like she was going to be sick as she stumbled outside, only remembering at the last second to close Silas's door behind her. The outside felt too bright, as if the sun was close to the Earth. She needed to get away, and she tripped through the branches into the woods, hurrying like a woodland animal, until she finally calmed down.

It didn't have to mean anything, but why have such a book, especially considering the recent discovery in Banwell? It sickened her to think that she'd initially been attracted to the man, when now she never wanted to see him again.

Max would be back from camp. Seeing him would make her feel better. She reorientated herself and began marching back to their caravan. She had to pass Silas's place again before reaching her own, and ran past it without looking, as if the book could somehow draw her in if she acknowledged it. She let out a sigh as the caravan disappeared from sight, catching the scream in her throat just before it was audible as she saw Max sitting outside her caravan – laughing and joking as if the man wasn't a threat at all – with the silver-haired Silas.

# Chapter Ten

Louise reported her meeting with Lyndsey to DCI Robertson later that day. They'd gone through so much together since she'd moved to Weston another lifetime ago, yet she sensed a distance between them that she hadn't felt before. It could be paranoia, but it was something she'd sensed in a lot of people since she'd given birth. It was subtle, and in some ways it was pleasant. People were more considerate, and patient, but Louise didn't want to be treated any differently. Of course, being a mother changed you, but it didn't change the person you were.

'Let me get this clear, this former member of the Verdant Circle claims that Hugo Latchford's parents sacrificed their own child?' said Robertson.

'She said it was a rumour, but I could tell from the way she told me that she hasn't completely dismissed it as a possibility.' A rumour wasn't anything to go on, and it sounded far-fetched even to her, but it wasn't something she could let go of yet.

Robertson puffed out his cheeks. 'We don't know where these parents are?'

Louise shook her head. 'We would have to go through the whole organisation from top to bottom. We're talking about thousands in the UK. Not that access would be easy or feasible. The cells act independently so it could be near-on impossible. And anyway, DI Pepperstone has been working on this for a number of years.'

'Someone must know the whereabouts of these people.'

'Sir, I'd like to go public. Get Mr and Mrs Latchford's pictures out there, see if we can get a response.'

'I don't like it when you call me *sir*,' said Robertson, his Glaswegian accent deepening. 'Our official stance on this is still suspicious death?'

'For now. I'd be inclined to make it a murder investigation, but either way we need to find Hugo's parents.'

Robertson nodded. 'I agree on that count. Do what you need to do. Speak to the PR department and get it sorted.'

'Thanks, Iain,' said Louise.

'Well?' said Robertson, as she reached the office door.

'Sir?'

Robertson gave her a hard stare, his brow furrowed. 'You know you haven't even shown me any pictures of the lad since you've been back.'

Louise laughed, loading pictures of Jack on her phone and returning to Robertson's desk.

'Sorry I'm late,' said Louise, as Yvonne handed Jack over to her.

The childminder smiled but Louise could tell she wasn't best pleased. She was over fifty minutes late picking Jack up after spending the afternoon liaising with the PR team about the campaign to find Hugo's parents, which would start in earnest the following day. 'I'll have to charge you the extra fee, Louise,' said Yvonne.

'I know,' said Louise, trying not to think about the eye-watering cost of the late fees.

'And I can't do this every day. I have a family too, you know.'

'I know. I am so sorry.' Louise couldn't blame the childminder for her response. She could have left earlier, or called her parents, but had been so wrapped up in the Hugo investigation that her mind had been distracted. 'It won't happen again,' she added, receiving a curt nod as Yvonne closed the door on her.

'I think Mummy is in trouble,' she said to Jack, as she carried him to the car.

'Mummy,' said Jack, agreeing.

Fortunately, Emily had already planned a play date with one of her friends so Louise still had time to pick her up.

'Hello, baby Jack,' said her niece, getting in the car and giving Jack a kiss.

Louise found herself welling up at the exchange. Emily had taken the new arrangement in her stride, and Louise was thankful for how well she got on with her cousin. She tried not to dwell on it, but her niece was only a little older than the age Hugo would have been when he'd gone missing. She understood that was part of why the investigation resonated so much with her. And although she'd seen some terrible things during her years in the force, the possibility that Hugo's parents had sacrificed their son seemed incredible to her; though sadly, not incredible enough to be dismissed.

Thomas's Surrey project was still ongoing, so he was going to be late home. Louise had never had to question her husband's commitment to family life, but it was unfortunate the new project had coincided with her returning to work. She made dinner for Emily and Jack and managed to get them both off to bed before 8 p.m. Louise had understood juggling both roles would be tiring, but hadn't legislated for the sheer exhaustion of looking after the children following a full day at work. Thomas had mentioned the possibility of hiring a live-in nanny, and although Louise had initially balked at the idea, she wondered now, as she made her way to bed at 9.30 p.m., if he was right. Work was likely to get more demanding, and there were bound to be times when developments meant the children would get picked up late.

She decided she would talk to Thomas about it over the weekend. Although it was difficult to imagine someone else living in the house with them, it would give her more time to focus on work. Though, as she climbed into bed alone, she wondered if that was really what she wanted. She was enjoying being back at work, and was motivated to find out what had happened to Hugo Latchford, but was it something she could see herself doing for the next twenty or so years? She'd enjoyed her maternity leave, and Thomas was doing well at work, so maybe it was time to think about a career change. Her parents weren't getting any younger, so maybe doing something less stressful and closer to home would be better for everyone.

She fell asleep with the thought in her head, and it was one of the first things she thought about in the morning as she rolled over to find the other side of the bed empty, and Thomas standing by the wardrobe dressing for the day ahead.

Louise drove through Weston on autopilot, dropping Emily at school before leaving Jack at Yvonne's; the childminder all smiles as if yesterday's crime had been forgotten. As she made her way along the M5 towards Portishead, she thought again about the toll juggling the roles of detective and mother was taking on her. Thomas had left that morning before she'd even got out of bed. After a tricky start, he'd made a success of leaving the force, so there was no reason why she couldn't. With the money he was bringing in, she wouldn't need to go full-time and would be able to give more of her focus to Jack and Emily.

That thought consumed her as she entered CID, noting the increased numbers of officers and civilian workers in the area, who were there in preparation for the media campaign they were launching that morning to find Hugo's parents. Did she want this any more? The constant battle with only the occasional reward? She sighed, telling herself she was just feeling negative because it was so early in the Hugo Latchford investigation. She'd been in this position before, feeling that she would never find justice for someone while having to sift through all of humanity's detritus to reach her goal.

'Louise,' said Robertson, sticking his head out from his office door and not waiting for a response before heading back inside.

Miles was at his desk and was about to say something to her when she mouthed the word 'coffee' to him before heading over to Robertson's room.

'Morning, Iain.'

'Shut the door, Louise,' he said.

Louise did as instructed, wondering if Robertson's curt tone meant he was in a bad mood. 'You had your morning coffee?' she asked, deciding to risk a rebuke.

'I wanted to catch you before you get started on all that,' said Robertson, ignoring her. 'I had a budget meeting with the chief last night.'

'Sounds ominous,' said Louise, wondering where the next cut in her team could possibly be placed.

'There's no easy way of saying this, Louise,' said Robertson, hesitating.

He appeared serious but Louise couldn't work out what he could possibly have to tell her that would be so bad. The department had just recruited Miles, so it was unlikely they needed to offload anyone at this stage. 'Spill the beans, Iain.'

'That's Detective Superintendent Iain to you,' said Robertson, with a slight upturn of his lips.

A wave of relief washed over Louise. 'You . . . Congratulations, Iain,' she said, as Robertson cracked a smile. 'You kept that one quiet.'

'It's not official-official yet. It's been going on for months now, long before you came back.'

'So what does this mean?'

'It means I'll be moving upstairs. More upstairs. Well, I will be once all the formalities are finalised. Taking over from Charlie. Might even get a new office.'

Charlie was Superintendent Charles Tyler, who Robertson reported to.

'Is he retiring?'

'Yep. And you know what this means?'

'The ruination of CID?'

'That as well, but we have a vacancy for a new DCI, and your name has been favourably mentioned by practically everyone.'

'Practically,' said Louise, with mock outrage.

'You'll have to go through the process. But you have the experience. A few interviews and the job will be yours. If you want it, that is.'

'I've never thought about it, Iain,' said Louise, taken aback. 'In truth, I never thought you'd leave us.'

'I'm hardly leaving you. If you become DCI, you'll see more of me than you do now.'

'I thought you were trying to convince me to go for it.'

'Very droll. Seriously, have a think about it. With the boy now, it could be the perfect time for you. It's a tough position but the hours are a bit more stable. Give it a think?'

Louise got to her feet. 'Definitely. Thanks for thinking of me.'

'Anything you get will be by your own merit, Louise. You more than deserve it, and you'll make a great leader.'

'Stop, you'll get me emotional.'

'That said, it wouldn't hurt your application if you sort out this bones case.'

Miles was waiting by her desk. 'That's more like it,' said Louise, accepting the hot cup of coffee from her colleague. Taking a drink, Louise felt the weight of change overwhelming her.

Miles was one of the new breed of graduate officers working in a system that would have been unrecognisable to her when she'd started. Robertson was effectively moving on, and she would have less day-to-day contact with him whether or not she ended up with the DCI role. She was used to change, but all this combined with the demands of her own life was sending her head into a spin.

She drank the coffee, deciding now wasn't the time to dwell on such matters. She ordered Miles to get her an update on the Latchford press release and started to map out a work schedule for the next couple of days.

# Chapter Eleven

Silas had been charm personified when Fi had taken a breath before approaching him and Max outside the caravan, as if nothing had happened. He must have noticed something was off, however, because he'd asked her if she was feeling OK. She'd batted the question away, blaming her flushed appearance on the weather, but he'd studied her for a bit longer than was necessary before apparently accepting her explanation.

She'd tried not to think about the drugs, the money and most importantly the book, as she'd watched Silas chatting to Max as if they were lifelong friends.

'What did he want?' she'd asked Max, the second the man left.

'What do you mean?' said Max, unperturbed.

'What was he talking to you about?'

'Nothing really. The solstice mainly. I told him about the celebration plans we've been working on in camp.'

Fi didn't want to scare the boy, and risked doing so by asking him more. And what exactly did she imagine Silas would have said to him? She decided to say nothing else about it for the time being but thoughts of the book continued playing on her mind. In and of itself, it didn't mean anything. The text had been impenetrable, and the images could have been nothing more sinister than illustrations for a story, perhaps a grisly fairy tale with some kind of dubious message of morality.

But it hadn't *felt* that way. She may not have been able to understand the text, but there had definitely been something wrong about the book. There was a reason Silas had hidden it. And with Hugo Latchford's remains being found around the same time as Silas had appeared in camp, it was way too much of a coincidence for her.

She got up and stretched, opening the caravan door and sitting on the step, taking in the morning air. Paranoid or not, she no longer felt safe in the camp. She wished Pete was still with her. He may have let her down in the past, but he would have had some idea about what she should do. As it was, Fi felt an urge she'd thought extinguished return. She had a hiding place of her own in her caravan, and in it her stash of drugs. Not as much as the bundle she'd seen in Silas's caravan, but enough for now. Would a little taste hurt that much?

But no, she couldn't do that to Max. She needed to keep her wits about her. Silas was a predatory threat and she needed to make sure he didn't get his claws into her son.

# Chapter Twelve

The first calls about Valerie and Jeremy Latchford came trickling in around lunchtime as the press and online campaign got underway. Louise's team monitored the responses, acting as best they could on anything that sounded like credible information. Louise was given a summary every hour as she worked through the rest of her caseload. All the while, she thought about Robertson's offer. Although very far from being a done deal, she knew Robertson wouldn't have mentioned the promotion if there wasn't a good chance of her succeeding.

In some ways, it was the perfect opportunity. Taking over from Robertson as DCI would make her hours more stable and her work more predictable, which would be perfect for her new family life. But although the former sounded perfect, it was the predictability that worried her. Gone would be the diversity of her current role. Not that it was always varied. The last decade or so had seen a great shift in police work that meant much of it was done from the office, making calls and analysing data on screens. But as a DI, Louise managed to escape some of the drudgery of the work – she'd spent over half her time, since being back, away at crime scenes and interviews – and she wasn't sure if she was ready to give that up.

Then there was the role itself. The constant policy meetings and paying lip service to superiors. Louise had already experienced that side of things, having once been demoted from her role in Major Crimes because of the collusion of those on higher pay packets. It was a world Robertson traversed with ease, but she didn't know if she had the energy in her to deal with the headaches of bureaucracy.

'Ma'am, we've just got a second hit on Valerie Latchford,' said Miles. 'Bideford, in North Devon,' he added, before Louise had a chance to read through the notes. 'Two separate accounts claiming that Mrs Latchford now goes by the name Amanda Warring. One has even sent through a photograph.'

'Thanks, Miles, I can see that for myself,' said Louise, taking a closer look. Miles looked rebuffed, and she realised she'd perhaps snapped at him for no reason. She understood his eagerness, and desire to impress, and remembered once being like that herself.

It was rare to get such an early hit in these circumstances. Appeals like this usually brought out the crazies, and hundreds of hours of investigation were often needed to come to the one positive outcome. But the picture was a good likeness of the images they had on file for Valerie Latchford. Although obviously a decade older, there was a clear similarity in the sharp contours of the woman's chin that suggested a match, or at least a likeness.

'Good work, Miles. Do some digging on this Amanda Warring. Give me a reason to travel to Devon,' said Louise, loading a file to do with another of her current investigations, a spate of house burglaries in the Winscombe area.

Despite the demands of her other cases, by lunchtime Louise had returned to the Hugo Latchford investigation. She didn't know if it was because it was her first case since returning, or the age

Hugo had been when he died, but it was all she could think of. She decided to do some more research on the Verdant Circle. It seemed the group had been formed by the Hawthorne family from Shropshire. The group still had charitable status, its stated goals at the time of incorporation being the preservation of the natural environment. Louise doubted the original goal of the organisation had been human ritual sacrifice, though she'd come across similar organisations in her past, including a suicide cult in Weston, so she couldn't rule out anything.

A couple of hours later, she caught Miles in her peripheral vision, hovering beside her desk. He was struggling to contain his excitement, all but jumping up and down on the spot as he waited for Louise's attention.

Louise wasn't sure if she wanted to laugh at his eagerness, or yell at him for behaving like a child. 'This better be good,' she said, looking up from her computer.

'We've had two more calls about Amanda Warring,' he said.

'That's not much of a surprise. She looks like Valerie Latchford, there's no denying that.'

Miles appeared momentarily crestfallen. 'I've spoken to the local nick,' he continued, undeterred. 'Said they would have a chat with her if we need them to.'

'I hope you told them to hold off for now?'

'I did,' said Miles. 'Could be a mistake, but there's nothing for an Amanda Warring on the electoral roll down there, and nothing is appearing on any of the databases.'

Louise rested her chin on her hand. In these situations, there was the danger of wanting a pattern to fit too much. The fact that there was a likeness was positive, as was the lack of records for the woman, but such things could be explained away. She could have recently moved to the area, or might simply live off-grid as some people did. 'Anything more?'

'From what I've discovered, she works part-time at a local café, Judy's in Westward Ho! No tax returns mentioning her name are showing, so I imagine it's cash in hand.'

'You have been busy. Let me see the images we have of her again.'

Miles passed over his phone. The similarities were striking. If the woman lived locally, Louise wouldn't have hesitated in going to see her. As it was, she could send the local police to question the woman, but if she was Valerie Latchford, and she was hiding something, it risked scaring her off. 'How far away are we?' she asked Miles.

'Two hours thirty-eight minutes at present,' said Miles, his eyes a mixture of triumph and excitement.

Louise recapped with the team before setting off for Devon. Sightings were still coming in nationwide for Valerie and Jeremy Latchford, but so far there had been nothing concrete for either. Tracey and Greg had both agreed that there was a definite likeness between Valerie Latchford and Amanda Warring, and with the other information Miles had uncovered it was agreed it was worth making the journey.

'Are you going to run it by your new friend Pepperstone?' asked Tracey.

'Not yet. Miles and I are going to make a quick journey to north Devon. I'd like to speak to this Amanda Warring face to face.'

Louise spoke to Thomas, who was still in Surrey, before calling her mother and asking her to pick up the children. She heard the weary acceptance in her mother's voice, and as she drove along the M5 towards north Devon, with Miles busy on his phone, she contemplated her choices, cutting them down to four paths she could take: stay as she was, hire some kind of nanny, live-in or not, apply for the DCI role and hope the hours would work out as promised, or leave the police.

She was surprised that the last choice didn't provoke a stronger response in her. Prior to Jack being born, it wasn't something she would have seriously considered. There had been many difficult times in her career, and she'd faced obstacles that would have tested the most seasoned of officers, but she'd always remained committed. She hadn't expected that giving birth would change her outlook so dramatically. She'd been all but a mother to Emily since her brother had passed away, but bringing Jack into the world had changed things whether she liked it or not.

'What made you apply for CID?' she asked Miles, trying to take her mind off things.

'It's why I joined the police in the first place,' he said, putting down his phone and sitting upright in his seat as if he was being interviewed.

'But why?'

'I guess I wanted to make a difference. Catch the bad guys, if you know what I mean? I know that sounds naïve, but I still cling on to that. Otherwise, it's not worth it, is it?'

Louise agreed. She'd always promised herself that the day she stopped caring, the day when she became accustomed and accepting of the atrocities she faced on a daily basis, would be the day she stopped. And it hadn't come to that just yet. She'd spent the last couple of weeks with thoughts of Hugo Latchford firmly in her head, and here she was making a near three-hour trip to speak to someone who might be nothing more than a mistaken identity.

'You keep clinging to that,' she said, taking the turning to Bideford, and promising herself she would take her own advice.

Bideford was a small town next to the estuary of the River Torridge, a few miles from Westward Ho!, where Amanda Warring worked. Louise battled through roadworks and curvy single-track lines until she reached the address they had for her, which had been supplied by one of the people who had responded to their campaign.

Louise parked outside the terraced house in the back streets of the small town. Crumbling paint flaked off the front of the house and the woodwork on the windows was chipped; dirty net curtains obscured the view within. 'Check around the back, just in case,' said Louise, waiting for a minute before knocking on the door.

She tried again when there was no answer before summoning Miles back. They were about to wait it out in the car when a door in the house opposite opened, an elderly man in a three-piece suit calling over to them. 'You looking for her?' he said.

Louise walked over and displayed her warrant card. 'Her, sir?'

'That woman that lives in there,' said the man, his voice full of distaste. 'Amanda.'

'We would like to talk to Amanda, yes,' said Louise. 'And you are?'

'Never mind me,' said the man. 'If you want to speak to her, you best hurry. Saw her leave thirty minutes ago. Looked like she was carrying everything she owned, not that that was much. Good riddance for me. Knew she was no good. What has she done?'

'What's your name, sir?' asked Louise.

'Kenneth Matheson.'

'You saw Amanda leave thirty minutes ago?'

'Give or take, that's right.'

'And what direction did she take, Mr Matheson?'

'Down yonder,' he said. 'If I was to hazard a guess, I would say she was off to the bus stop. There's a coach leaves for up country from there.'

◆ ◆ ◆

The nearest bus stop was a five-minute drive away, but a set of temporary traffic lights were causing chaos and the traffic was near stationary. Louise glanced at the satnav: 0.7 miles away. 'How are your running shoes?' she asked Miles.

'Shall I detain her if she's there?' asked Miles, who already had the car door open.

'If it looks like she's making a journey out of the county, I think it's fair to detain her. If there's time, wait for me to arrive.'

Miles shut the door and headed on foot towards the bus stop at a brisk pace. Louise checked her phone as she edged forwards in the car. The next coach heading towards Bristol wasn't for another twenty-three minutes, so they had time on their side; that was if Amanda hadn't already departed.

Louise buzzed down her window. The air was filled with the salt-tinged scent of the sea, which reminded her of Weston. She'd only made half the journey by the time Miles called.

'There's another set of temporary traffic lights further down, causing the hold-up. I'm at the bus stop. Only two others here, both male. Neither has seen anyone else.'

'Damn it,' said Louise, rounding a corner with a pasty shop on one side and a pub opposite. 'Hold on. I've eyes on her,' she said, spotting a woman in the beer garden of the pub, surrounded by bags and sipping a pint of lager. 'Get back to the Red Lion,' she said, turning into the pub's car park.

Buying herself a sparkling mineral water, Louise followed the woman into the beer garden as she waited for Miles. It was definitely the person they knew as Amanda Warring. Louise counted three large laundry bags and a battered old suitcase, and wondered if this was the woman's worldly possessions. She appeared calm, if strangely focused, her eyes gazing straight ahead as she occasionally took a sip from her pint glass.

Miles arrived, glancing over from the main road but not making direct contact. Louise got up, glass in hand, and walked over to where the woman was sitting. Deciding to take a chance, she sat opposite her and said, 'Hello, Valerie, do you have a second to talk?'

# Chapter Thirteen

Valerie looked too shocked to feign surprise. Her eyes darted around the beer garden, as if searching for an escape route, while Louise took out her warrant card and introduced herself. 'And this is DC Boothroyd,' she added, when Miles wandered over.

'I think you have me mistaken,' said the woman, her hand shaking as she took another drink. She appeared intoxicated, and Louise wondered what medications she was on at that moment.

'Things will go a lot easier for you if you tell the truth from the beginning, Valerie. You're not in any trouble, but lying to the police won't help you in any way,' said Louise.

'Who grassed me up?' said Valerie, her tone defensive and a little fearful.

'We've been trying to find you for a long time now, Valerie. Do you have any idea why?'

'You found my boy?' the woman said, her eyes reddening as she took another drink.

Louise nodded to Miles, who moved the pint away from Valerie. 'I know this must be very hard for you. I think it best if you came in to talk with us now, Valerie. Is that OK?' said Louise, who was keen to make sure everything was on record.

'My bags?' said Valerie.

'We'll take them with us,' said Louise, nodding to Miles again as she helped the woman to her feet.

◆　◆　◆

After a few calls, Louise managed to secure the use of CID in Bideford to interview Valerie. She was offered the opportunity of legal representation, which she refused. Louise made sure she was given water, and the coffee she requested, before heading into the interview room with Miles.

They could have been back at headquarters, such was the uniform design of the interview room with its nondescript white walls. 'How are you, Valerie?' asked Louise.

'I'm OK,' she said, nursing her cup of coffee. She appeared calmer than before, though her skin was still flushed, her eyes bloodshot.

'Thank you for agreeing to speak to us,' said Louise, before informing Valerie once more of her rights.

Valerie nodded, her eyes darting first to Miles then back to Louise as she drank from her cup.

'So, to confirm, your real name is Valerie Latchford?'

'I guess it was, once.'

'You haven't officially changed it, have you? Can we call you Valerie?'

'I suppose so.'

'Thanks, Valerie. As we discussed when I spoke to you earlier, we would like to question you about your son, Hugo.'

Valerie's body tensed at her son's name. 'Yes.'

'And we discussed the very sad news that his remains have recently been discovered in Banwell. Is that correct?' Louise tried to keep her words level and calm. She didn't want to upset Valerie, but she had to describe the facts.

'Yes,' said Valerie, staring into space.

'You'd already heard about the discovery, is that true?'

Valerie continued staring at the wall behind Louise, who wondered what terrible thoughts were going through her mind, and if those thoughts were laced with guilt.

'I saw it on the news.'

'And you didn't think to contact us?' asked Miles.

Valerie shrugged, her attention returning to the two police officers.

'When did you last see your son?' asked Louise.

Valerie placed her now empty cup down, a smudge of pink lipstick on its rim. 'When we gave him up,' she said, her voice catching.

'When you gave him up for adoption?' said Miles.

'He went to a foster family,' said Valerie. 'They lost him.'

'That must have been hard, giving him up like that?' said Louise.

'Of course it was hard. But if they had paid attention, he would still be alive.'

'You're speaking about the Jenkinses?' said Miles.

'Yes. They let him go to the woods by himself. What sort of people would do that?'

Louise noted a slight tremor running through Valerie, as if her blood was spiked with cortisol. She wasn't here to make moral judgements but wanted to know more about why the Latchfords had given up their child. 'Did you tell Hugo why you had to give him up for adoption?' she said.

'How do you tell an eight-year-old that? I wrote a letter for him for when he was older but I . . .'

'You never gave it to him?'

Valerie scrunched up her nose. 'I won't be able to now, will I?'

'And you haven't seen Hugo since that day you had to give him up?' asked Louise.

'No,' said Valerie. 'I thought about him every day. Every single day, but we never saw him again.'

'"We" being you and your husband?' asked Miles.

Valerie recoiled at the mention.

'We would like to speak to your husband, Jeremy. Do you know where he is?' asked Louise, ready to push Valerie now they were close to some answers.

'No, I haven't seen him in years.'

'You joined the Verdant Circle together, didn't you? Isn't that why you had to give Hugo up?'

The same faraway look as before reached Valerie's eyes, her concentration focused on something behind Louise's field of vision. 'Valerie,' said Louise. 'This is important.'

'I left not long after I joined. It was Jeremy who was really into that stuff. I got carried away, drawn into it. I was having . . . problems. Drink, drugs. They helped with that. And to begin with . . . it was amazing,' said Valerie, a dreamy look appearing on her features, making her look younger.

'And then what happened?'

'Things changed. Jeremy changed. I had to get away.'

'And you haven't seen Jeremy since?'

'No, thank God.'

'Valerie, I have to ask you. Did you or your husband have anything to do with Hugo's disappearance?' asked Louise, deciding to use the word *disappearance* rather than *death* at the last second.

Valerie shook her head, silently.

'You can see why I'm asking, can't you? It hasn't been easy finding you, and we have no idea where your husband is. And when we did find you, Valerie, you'd changed your name and you were about to leave town with some of your belongings. Why would you be doing that? Why didn't you want us to find you? What are you hiding?'

Valerie's face contorted into something approaching anger. 'You don't understand. It wasn't you I was running from, it was them. The Verdant Circle.'

# Chapter Fourteen

Louise had been unable to shake Valerie's story from her mind even after she'd returned home sometime after midnight. They had continued questioning Valerie but there hadn't been any reasonable grounds to arrest her. Yet Louise was convinced the woman was withholding something from them.

Valerie's story of giving up Hugo for adoption became more understandable following the revelation about her drug addiction at the time – something that had only been briefly alluded to in the reports of Hugo's disappearance – but Louise struggled more than ever to understand how a parent could do such a thing.

She knew this was blinkered thinking. She'd seen so much worse during her years on the force, and was aware that there was no accounting for the way addiction or mental illness could affect someone's judgement. Yet she found it incongruous that Valerie had chosen to give up all her worldly goods to follow her husband into the arms of a cult.

In the incident room the following day, she had to concede that her mind was clouded by thoughts of guilt regarding her own parenting. Last night had been the second time she hadn't seen Jack before he'd gone to sleep. Although she had known such a time would come once she returned to work, she'd felt lost last night entering the dark house, her only welcome the jubilant one from Molly.

Louise replayed her conversation with Valerie to Tracey, who was still helping with the investigation. 'I'm going to see DI Pepperstone again today,' she said. 'We need to get some more insight into this Verdant Circle group. I couldn't tell how much of it was for show, but Valerie appeared scared out of her skin, and her actions over the last ten years would suggest she's taking the threat of them seriously.'

'What does she think they're going to do to her?' said Tracey.

'That, she wasn't so clear on,' said Louise, who'd tried in vain to find out the answer. After confessing she was fleeing Bideford because of the Verdant Circle, Valerie had clammed up, spending the rest of the interview with her gaze fixed on the spot behind Louise.

'Does she think they killed Hugo?'

'Again, not clear, but she is spooked. It's a shame we have no leads on her ex. She seemed to be as scared of him as she was of the Verdant Circle itself.'

'Still lots of calls to work through, with more coming. Hopefully we'll get lucky,' said Tracey, blowing a loose strand of her wild curly hair from her eyes. 'Listen, I was meaning to ask you about Robertson. The rumour is he's moving upstairs.'

Louise had all but forgotten about the possibility of promotion. But now she felt bad about not sharing the information with Tracey. Although she'd only received her promotion to DI a few years back, Tracey was the same rank as she was, so would have a legitimate right to apply for any DCI vacancy. 'Sorry, I should have said. He told me yesterday. There'll be a new DCI role.'

'I see, taking your competitors out by withholding the information,' said Tracey, with a rueful smile.

'Sorry, Trace, I should have said earlier.'

'Don't be ludicrous. You're a shoe-in for that job. Should have happened years ago. Don't worry, you won't have any competition from me.'

'Robertson said I should go for it but I'm not sure.'

'It would probably give you more time at home, and I don't mind calling you ma'am if I have to.'

'Well, that's a relief. I'll give it some thought if I ever get the time,' said Louise, not sharing with Tracey that at that precise moment she was more likely to leave the force than go for any promotion.

Louise was staring hard at the crime board in the incident room when DI Pepperstone arrived in the afternoon. On the board, she'd arranged a photo of Hugo Latchford beneath the photographs of Hugo's parents and his two foster parents at the time of his disappearance.

'Old-school. I like it,' said Pepperstone. 'I come bringing gifts,' he added, handing Louise a cup of coffee.

Louise thanked him, glancing at the lanyard with his guest pass, his image blurry beneath the plastic. 'Sometimes the old ways work the best. Take a seat,' she said, walking over to the conference table at the side of the incident room.

'So I understand. Great result in finding Valerie.' Pepperstone sounded less wheezy than the last time they'd met, as if he was cured of his allergies.

'She says she was running from the Verdant Circle but couldn't quite say why.'

'Doesn't surprise me. They're secretive to a fault and they don't like their congregation talking. That's why we struggle to pin anything on them. You saw the way Lyndsey was the other day. I don't need to spell it out for you, do I? I have a file of missing people connected to the VC as long as my arm. I'm pretty sure if we went digging, we would find more than one set of bones.'

Louise was trying her best not to get irritated with her fellow DI. He had a way of speaking that made it sound as if he had the superior knowledge about everything. She'd grown accustomed to dealing with officers like that, and although it was grating it was usually counterproductive to pull them up on it. 'She was definitely scared about something,' she said, focusing on the case and trying not to let Pepperstone's attitude put her off her stride. She wondered if it was feasible to put Valerie Latchford in protective custody, but doubted the perceived threat was high enough to justify the resources.

'She's done well to avoid them all this time. You keeping a close eye on her?'

'As far as we are able.'

'She'll abscond as soon as she is able. I know there's little you can do about it, but I don't want it to come as a shock.'

Louise paused, holding Pepperstone's gaze for a couple of seconds. She didn't need to be told what to do, and needed him to understand that. 'It's Jeremy I need to speak to now. I was hoping you could help me with that,' she said, trying to play to his vanity.

'Good luck on that. The file of missing people I told you about. Jeremy Latchford is deep within it. His name comes up now and then, though we have at least three aliases for him. No sightings from all of this?' said Pepperstone, looking around at the officers and civilian staff still fielding calls from the press conference.

'None as positive as the sightings we had for Valerie.'

'They will be closing ranks with all this in the news. Anyone who is a potential danger will be monitored. If Jeremy is out there, he'll be locked away. Figuratively if not literally. He's probably fearing for his life just as much as his ex-wife is.'

It was frustrating that they couldn't do more about it, but as Pepperstone had stated previously, the group were well protected by a team of lawyers and were so vast that it was difficult to know where to begin. 'We need to speak to them. This is a suspicious death investigation . . . which may prove to be a murder investigation. I think we have the right to ask some questions,' said Louise.

'We have the right, certainly, but they have the right not to answer. Also, our investigation into them is still on delicate grounds. You would be impinging on us if you go in there all guns blazing.'

'No one was suggesting we do that.'

'Just wanted to be straight with you. I would appreciate a heads-up before you approach them in any way.'

'Here's your heads-up, Gerrard,' said Louise, amused by the confused look on the DI's face.

'Who are you planning to speak to?'

'The section Lyndsey told us about, out towards Priddy. You coming?'

Pepperstone frowned before getting to his feet. 'OK, I'll introduce you to them.'

Pepperstone drove as they headed further into the Mendip Hills, beyond Cheddar Gorge where they'd previously met Lyndsey, towards the small village of Priddy in the heart of the area. 'How long have you been investigating the Verdant Circle?' asked Louise.

Pepperstone didn't take his eyes from the road. They were close to Burrington, ten miles out from Priddy, driving through the heart of the Hills. 'About seven years now.'

'That's why you're taking such an interest in Hugo Latchford's death?'

'I would like to see you solve that, Louise, but my main concern is for my own investigation. I don't want anything getting in the way of it.'

'And here I was thinking you were here out of the goodness of your heart.'

They drove the rest of the distance without talking, the silence broken only by the sound of Pepperstone's laboured breathing.

He pulled into a parking area a couple of miles out of Priddy. The makeshift lot was overrun with vehicles, from small hatchbacks to camper vans, taking little or no notice of the parking lines on the ground. 'Been here for four years now. Despite the state of this, they actually look after the place very well. We get complaints from the locals but not as much as you would expect. They live peacefully, clean up after themselves, and in all truth probably make a positive impact on the local environment.'

'You sound like you're on their side,' said Louise, leaving the car.

'Maybe I am,' said Pepperstone, joining her outside. Louise could almost see his mind ticking over, and sure enough he couldn't contain himself. 'Unfortunately, that isn't my role. I don't care what they get up to as a group, as long as they aren't harming anyone. I care about the corruption at the top.'

'Thanks for clarifying,' said Louise, weary of Pepperstone's propensity for explaining the obvious to her.

A camp had been organised a half-mile into the woodland area. On the outskirts of the encampment were portable toilets and washing facilities that appeared to be in good order. Two young women, probably in their early twenties, were washing their hands in one of the sinks as Louise and Pepperstone approached. The women appeared momentarily startled, huddling closer, before one of them asked them what they wanted.

'Police,' said Pepperstone, showing his warrant card.

'Well, duh,' said the young woman. 'That much is obvious. Why are you here?'

'I'm DI Blackwell . . . this is my colleague DI Pepperstone,' said Louise, to stifled laughter from both women, which made Pepperstone grimace. 'We're here in relation to a suspicious death. The remains of Hugo Latchford were found in a caving system not that far from here. He was approximately eight years old when he died. You may have heard about it?'

The women disentangled themselves from one another, almost as if they'd relaxed. 'We've heard about that,' said the talkative one. 'It's very sad.'

'Would you be able to help us? His parents used to be – and maybe still are – members of your organisation.'

'Organisation?' said the talkative one.

'Your group. Your religion. Whatever this is,' said Pepperstone, his voice full of disdain, at odds with his earlier comments about the group's positive impact on the local area.

'We're just a bunch of like-minded individuals. But we will help if we can. I'm Lisa and this is Ange.'

'Louise and Gerrard,' said Louise.

'Nice to meet you, Louise,' said Lisa. 'Follow me and we can get some tea.'

Louise and Pepperstone followed the two women into the main camp area. Emptied firepits were surrounded by people sitting in deckchairs, reading books, drinking and smoking. It was close to a party-like atmosphere, but the police's arrival hadn't gone unnoticed. It was clear all eyes were on them as they moved through the encampment to a small brick building where Lisa showed them to an immaculately clean kitchen area.

'I'll put the kettle on,' said Ange. 'Tea or coffee? We only have instant for coffee.'

'Tea for me,' said Louise, as Pepperstone nodded in agreement.

'You own this property?' asked Pepperstone.

'We rent it.'

'Is that so?'

'Looks in good order,' said Louise, thanking Ange as she handed her some tea.

'You should have seen it when we got here. Wasn't even connected to the water or electric. We paid for the connection and have scrubbed this place to an inch of itself, haven't we, Ange?' said Lisa.

'Yes. I hadn't realised that I had signed up for that,' said Ange, with a grin.

Pepperstone took his tea. 'So what exactly did you think you'd signed up for?' he said.

Louise shot him a look, wondering why he was trying to antagonise the women.

'I thought you were here to ask about the boy?' said Lisa.

'We are,' said Louise. 'Here,' she said, showing Lisa the photographs of Hugo's remains on her phone.

'That's horrible, poor thing,' said Lisa, as they both looked at the images.

'As I said, his parents were members of your group,' said Louise, hoping to shame the young women into talking.

'That was a long time ago. I only found out when this all hit the news. We were told to expect potential trouble and a visit from . . . well, from you.'

'Who warned you that there might be trouble?' said Pepperstone, grimacing as he drank his tea.

'That's hardly important, is it?' said Lisa.

'I'll be the judge of that. How long have you been part of this group? You would have only been kids when Hugo went missing,' said Pepperstone.

'We only joined a few months ago,' said Ange, receiving a withering glance from her friend.

Louise was trying to work the pair out. Both were dressed in a similar way – low-rise combat trousers and cropped, tie-dyed T-shirts. Lisa's hair was coloured a drab red, whereas Ange was blonde. Both shared the same large brown eyes, and Louise wondered if they were related. She wanted to know what had brought them to the group, and what they'd left behind. But that wasn't the primary focus for now.

'But Hugo's story is well known within the group, isn't it?' Louise said, watching the two women exchange further glances before Lisa answered.

'We didn't know anything about him until the news came out about his . . . bones. We're still probationary members so not everyone shares everything with us. In fact, it might be helpful if you left now,' said Lisa, walking to the door just as someone else entered.

'Lisa, Ange,' said the newcomer, an older woman with plaited grey hair, wearing a longer tie-dyed T-shirt over cotton shorts and walking boots. 'We have guests?'

'Yes,' said Lisa, withdrawing into herself. 'This is . . . Sorry, I forgot your names.'

'DI Blackwell, and DI Pepperstone,' said Louise. 'And you are?'

'Zarah Tomlinson,' said Pepperstone, before the woman had a chance to answer.

'You know I don't go by that name any more, Gerrard,' said the woman. 'Teresa Willow,' she added. 'Pleased to meet you. Now, girls, off you go.'

Lisa and Ange bowed their heads and left, Teresa smiling as she waited for them to leave. 'Do you have a warrant to be here?' she said, the smile fading as the door closed behind them.

'You're honoured, Louise. Zarah here – or should I say Teresa? – is one of the VC's bigwigs. Former corporate lawyer turned environmental campaigner and embezzler. You might be a bit out of practice, Teresa, but we don't need a warrant to be here.'

Teresa bit her lower lip. 'I am still a lawyer. This is private property, and I would like you to leave.'

'This building?'

'We have a rental agreement on it.'

'Then we shall move outside, where I believe the world is free. Isn't that what the VC believes?'

'Please don't call us that. We have long since stopped using any motifs or terminology related to the Verdant Circle.'

'Moving with the times, you see, Louise. Pretending to shed their primitive ways, so no one looks at them closely,' said Pepperstone.

'Please leave,' said Teresa, opening the door for them.

The reception was a little more hostile as they left the building. The numbers from the group had grown, the majority of them waiting outside the entrance, standing in silence as Louise and Pepperstone went.

'What do you know about the death of Hugo Latchford?' Louise asked Teresa, as she squinted against the glare of the sunshine.

'If you'd like to ask me, or anyone here, about such things, then please feel free to go through our lawyers. Gerrard, I'm sure, will guide you in the right direction.'

Pepperstone was smiling, sweat dripping from his forehead. 'Let's go,' he said.

Louise stood her ground, looking at the bystanders one by one before setting off at a slow pace back to the car. 'What the hell was that?' she said, as they approached the car.

Pepperstone was out of breath as he reached for his keys. 'I don't know, but something is going on. I haven't seen Teresa Willow out in the wild before. She's one of their top lawyers. They must be scared of something.'

At that, Louise caught sight of a movement in the forest at the opposite end of the car park. She looked over to see a young woman peering from behind a tree. Louise took a cautionary step towards her, but the woman darted back behind the tree like a startled deer, and by the time Louise walked over, had disappeared from sight.

# Chapter Fifteen

The last few days hadn't been easy for Fi. She'd only seen Silas once more, catching him leaving her caravan one day after talking to Max as she'd returned from a walk. He never came to the main camp, and when she tried to talk to Denise about him, she clammed up as if she couldn't recall seeing him the other day.

On Thursday, Fi had been in the caravan after a long day in the kitchen and had grown worried when Max hadn't returned on time. She'd been about to walk back into camp to find him when there'd been a knock on the door. 'Denise,' she'd said, her friend drenched in sweat, her face cherry red.

'There you are,' said Denise.

Fi's heart began to hammer. 'What's the matter? Where's Max?' she demanded.

'No, don't worry, he's fine. I've been sent round to tell you that we have visitors.'

'Visitors?'

'Police.'

'So what?'

'Teresa sent me. They want us to stay away from the main camp for the time being.'

'Oh, OK,' said Fi, wondering what they were trying to hide. 'Is that all it is?'

'The Hugo Latchford thing is spooking everyone. You'll be OK here for now, won't you? I'll let you know when there's an all-clear.'

Fi nodded, wondering what the hell was going on as she watched Denise rush away back towards the main camp. When she'd gone, Fi walked in the opposite direction towards the other static caravans dotted around the outskirts. There were no signs of life, the occupants presumably at the protest in Hampshire or working in the main camp. She stopped near Silas's caravan, wondering if he was hiding, but decided not to check.

Instead, she walked towards the perimeter of the camp through a route rarely used, battling her way through trees and vines, and on more than one occasion having to change direction when her pathway was blocked. *This is ludicrous*, she thought to herself, crawling on her hands and knees to get beneath a fallen tree that had created an archway on the track. Why the hell was she snooping around like a criminal? Maybe this was the chance she needed. If she could catch the police as they left, tell them what she'd seen, maybe they would search Silas's caravan. Surely the drugs and the money would be enough to get him, at the very least, off camp.

Eventually, the pathway cleared and Fi was able to walk through the woodland. She stopped by a giant oak tree, a hundred yards from a second pathway that led to the main camp. She was considering joining the camp when two figures emerged, a man and a woman, from the way they were dressed clearly not members of the commune.

Fi watched them as they walked by. They weren't speaking, the woman walking ahead as the man followed. Not wanting to be seen, Fi tracked them through the trees for another few hundred yards where they stopped by a car, the man getting in first. The woman stretched before getting in the car, and turned towards Fi as if she knew she was being watched.

Startled, Fi hid behind the tree. She wanted to approach, but fear got in the way. What if Silas knew she'd been in his caravan and had moved the drugs and money? He would know it was her who had spoken against him, and where would that leave her at the camp?

In the end, she'd waited for the police to drive off before heading back to her caravan. The look of the policewoman had stayed with her into the weekend. There had to be a reason for them to have visited, and the more she thought about it, the more she believed that reason had to be Silas. The police visit was all the talk in camp, but no one was mentioning Silas, and Fi began to doubt her sanity. She didn't want to speak about him, as only Denise and Teresa seemed to know of his existence.

She needed to do something. She'd caught sight of Silas in conversation with Denise and Teresa by Silas's caravan. It was hard not to think they were talking about her and Max, and by the time she reached home her paranoia was definitely getting the better of her.

Max was in a foul mood, refusing to say more than the odd utterance, and clammed up when she asked him about Silas.

When he'd gone to sleep, she returned to the hiding place in the rear of the caravan and held the small baggy of drugs in her hands, debating whether she could safely use again. In the end, she left them where they were and instead took out her phone and charger.

Pete had told her to keep it. Phones were frowned upon in the camp, but he'd insisted she keep it for emergencies. She charged it in her room. The pay-as-you-go handset was still in credit.

She must have held it in her hands for over an hour, turning it over and over, debating whether or not she should call the police. She thought about the kind face of the policewoman and was sure she would understand. Fi might not be able to make sense of what

Silas was up to, and the strange images she'd found in his caravan, but maybe the policewoman would.

She poured herself some home brew, downing a glass in two savage gulps, before filling it again. What exactly did she think was going to happen? She took another gulp, things not feeling as ludicrous as before. Silas was a danger, that was a definite. And if he was a danger, then that meant Max was in trouble.

That was enough for her. She had no other option but to call.

# Chapter Sixteen

Louise spent Thursday and Friday analysing the countless documents on record for the Verdant Circle. The majority of the material came via Pepperstone and highlighted what he had been telling her about the numerous cases in progress against the group as a whole, such as money laundering and the illegal financial control of its members.

Louise switched off her computer, exhausted at the end of another week. Despite the PR campaign and its wide reach, she didn't feel they were any closer to finding out what had happened to Hugo Latchford. The only positive she could take was the discovery of the location of Valerie Latchford. Before leaving for the weekend, she made a call to her contact in Bideford to make sure the woman was still under surveillance.

'Nice and early,' said Yvonne, as Louise arrived in Weston an hour later. She ignored the passive-aggressive greeting, and wrapped Jack in her arms, only for him to struggle and start to cry.

'It's been a tiring week for him,' said Yvonne, as if Louise didn't know her own child.

'Thanks,' said Louise, taking Jack's bag from her as her son stretched his body and tensed in her arms. 'Come on, you. Thanks, Yvonne,' said Louise, struggling to balance the bag and her child in full tantrum mode as she walked back to the car.

'Do you want to go to the beach after we pick up Emily?' she said, as she tried to squeeze him into the child seat and pull on the restraints.

'No,' he screamed, tears streaming down his face as Louise clicked his harness into place.

Thrusting a snack bar into his hands, she switched on the air conditioning and drove to pick up Emily, feeling guilty that at that precise moment the only place she wanted to be was back at work. When she'd returned to being a detective, she'd presumed there would be some push and pull between her career and family life. She had experienced that division in a different way even while her brother was alive, but this was new to her.

She loved the children more than anything, but couldn't deny the desire to solve the Hugo Latchford investigation was taking precedence in her thoughts at that precise moment, and she wasn't sure how to deal with that insight.

The guilt stayed with Louise over the weekend. Jack's foul mood continued into the Saturday, and Emily wasn't her usual happy self. Taking into account the addition of Noah, Thomas's eleven-year-old son from his first marriage, who was currently going through a rebellious phase and ignoring everything his father said to him, the house was not the most relaxing of places to be.

Things improved on the Sunday with lunch at Louise's parents' house, taking some of the pressure off them, but that only made Louise feel worse. All she could really think about was the Hugo

Latchford investigation, and when the time came for her to drop Emily and Jack off on Monday morning, she couldn't deny that in some ways she had been counting down all weekend.

She tried to convince herself that it didn't make her a bad mother, and she wondered, as she made the familiar journey to Portishead, if Thomas had been having the same reservations as he made his way to work earlier that morning.

The conflict remained within her as she entered CID. She'd already formulated a plan of action for the week ahead, which involved meeting with former, and hopefully the odd current, members of the Verdant Circle. The focus was still on finding Jeremy Latchford, and she planned to do some digging on the two young women she'd met at the Mendip Hills, Lisa and Ange, in the hope that they knew more than they'd been willing to tell.

'Hi, boss,' said Miles, as she set up at her desk.

'You're eager, Miles, but I like it,' said Louise, taking the offered coffee from him and wondering how she'd survived her pregnancy without the drink.

'Something came in from the night shift. I was going to call, but I know you have to drop your kids off.'

Louise was taken aback, not recalling ever sharing such information with the newbie, but decided to let it ride. 'Don't leave me in suspense.'

'No,' said Miles, shaking his head as if waking himself up. 'I have a copy here,' he added, walking over to his desk.

Louise took the headphones connecting to the computer and put them to her ears as Miles pressed play.

*Police, how may I help you?*

*It's about the bones you found. That young boy, Hugo Latchford.*

The sound from the caller was crisp and clear. It seemed to Louise as if the caller, young and female, was outside when she called.

*Can I take your name, please?*

*I think I may know who is responsible.*

*Your name, please, madam.*

*But I'm scared. I think he's coming for us next.*

*Are you in danger, madam? Please can you tell me your name and location?*

Silence followed, Louise feeling a tremor in her chest as she waited for the caller to continue.

*I have a son. He's only ten. I think he's coming for him. I think he wants to take him for the solstice.*

*Please, madam. Tell me where you are. I can send help straight away.*

*I . . . I think he's coming.*

*Please, madam, your name . . .*

The line went dead at this point. 'Do we have a location for this caller?' said Louise, her pulse still pounding through her body. Sometimes it was hard to spot the fake from the genuine, but

Louise had heard enough to be sure this was authentic. There was terror in the caller's voice, a candid fear for her child's life.

Miles frowned. 'No. We have a phone number, but no location as of yet.'

Louise called Pepperstone, and later that afternoon they played the recording for Robertson. 'The call came from a prepaid SIM card, unregistered,' said Louise.

Robertson frowned. 'It should make it easier to justify a trace. Play it once more,' he said.

The more Louise listened to the distressed woman, the more she grew convinced it was a genuine call. The panic was heightened in the last words she uttered – *I think he's coming* – where her breathing became erratic, as if she were being pursued.

'What is the relevance of the solstice?' asked Robertson, turning his attention to Pepperstone.

'The solstices, winter and summer, have been an important part of the VC since its inception. Obviously, they're not unique. It's a big thing for those interested in ancient practices, *spirituality*, and the environment,' said Pepperstone.

Louise noticed how difficult the DI found it to hide his cynicism, and wondered if that was a result of his frustrations in bringing to justice the criminal elements of the Verdant Circle, or if it was more of an inherent prejudice. 'I've seen the gatherings at Stonehenge, that sort of thing. Never noted any child sacrifice though.'

Pepperstone laughed, despite Robertson remaining stony-faced. 'They call the summer solstice Litha, or more commonly midsummer,' said Pepperstone. 'As you say, there are often gatherings at places sacred to such groups, such as Stonehenge. They celebrate life, fertility, nature, that sort of thing. The VC has its roots in ancient druidry. As I mentioned to DI Blackwell, we have believed for a long time now that they have been taking some of those ancient and less common practices to heart. We've found evidence of animal sacrifice, particularly during times of festivities, but nothing concrete when it comes to human sacrifice. To be honest, as I've said to DI Blackwell, our focus is on the corruption side of things. We've heard rumours of an internal subset more aligned to the ancient ways, but it has never been a priority for us.'

'So, we're looking at a potential child in danger, and a potential sacrifice in two weeks' time?' said Robertson, shaking his head. 'I agree that the call sounds genuine, but it's not much to go on. I can arrange a warrant to track that number, but if it's unregistered . . .'

'We could release the phone call?' said Louise.

Robertson pursed his lips. 'I don't think that would be helpful at this stage. Could create a panic.'

'We need to go back to the group and speak to the members one by one. Make it official,' said Louise.

'You think that would work, Gerrard?' asked Robertson.

Pepperstone looked skywards. 'Very doubtful. You saw how Teresa Willow was, Louise. If she's still on site, she'll close everything down. Stop anyone talking to us.'

'We need to at least try,' said Louise.

Pepperstone sighed. 'There could be another way,' he said.

Louise looked at Robertson, who held his hands out in front of him. 'Well?' he said.

'We have a UCO in the area.'

'You have an undercover officer in Priddy? Why didn't you mention this before?' said Louise.

'I didn't say they were in Priddy. They're in the area. And anyway, I didn't think it was relevant.'

Louise was incredulous. 'You didn't think it was relevant?'

'We're making a lot of assumptions here. Even if there is a child in danger, we have no concrete link to the Mendip Hills group,' said Robertson, trying to play peacekeeper.

'I agree,' said Louise. 'But with the solstice only two weeks away, we could be running out of time. The UCO could help us to find Jeremy Latchford or help with finding out who killed Hugo. I presume your UCO has been questioned on this already?' said Louise, not hiding her anger at Pepperstone.

'They'll be aware, I imagine. But there hasn't been direct contact for some time. These guys can't just pop into town for a quick chat, you know.'

Louise's body tensed. She'd had enough of patronising policemen in her years in the force, and Pepperstone's tone and seeming disregard for what they were trying to achieve was pushing her to a confrontation.

'That'll do,' said Robertson. 'Louise, this is your investigation. You make the call. I'm sure DI Pepperstone will give us the courtesy of his resources. If there is nothing else.'

Louise held her tongue, appreciating the way Robertson had defused the situation. 'Sir,' she said, not waiting for Pepperstone as she left.

Miles must have thought twice about approaching her as she left Robertson's room, doing a quick double take and changing direction to the kitchen area. Louise could feel the heat in her face. She didn't usually let people affect her in such a way, but Pepperstone had been getting under her skin ever since they'd met, and his latest behaviour had pushed over the edge. It wasn't just the fact that he had undercover officers he hadn't mentioned before that bothered her; it was the total disregard for her and the patronising way he talked to her. He'd had a big opinion of himself since that first day, but it was clear to her now that he thought his work was of more importance than her own, and that wasn't conducive to a positive working relationship.

Not that she could let him see the effect he had on her. She poured a cup of water from the water fountain and took it back to her desk where Pepperstone was waiting, blowing his nose. 'Let's see if we can get your UCO to Priddy. I take it you can't give me a name?'

Pepperstone shook his head. 'I'll get on to him now. Anything else for me, boss?'

Louise rolled her eyes. They were both the same rank, so Pepperstone was being deliberately obtuse. If she hadn't thought the UCO was a good idea, she would have told him where to go. As it was, she needed his assistance, at least for the time being. 'That's all for now, Gerrard,' she said with a forced smile, and waited for him to leave before calling over Miles.

'How are you with dogs, Miles?' asked Louise.

'Um, fine, why?'

'Because we're going for a dog walk. Do you have anything to change into?'

'I have some spare clothes in the lockers.'

'Great, try not to look like a police officer, and meet me in the car park in fifteen.'

An hour later, Louise had picked up Molly from home and was driving the dog and Miles towards Priddy. Once more, she'd been forced to call in her parents. She'd heard the reticence in her mother's voice as she'd agreed to pick up Emily and Jack. Her mother loved both her grandchildren, but Emily moving in with Louise had been supposed to herald a new chapter in her parents' lives, and that all seemed to be changing now Louise was back at work. It was already clear things couldn't go on like this, but Louise couldn't dwell on it too much.

'So, why are we going on a dog walk?' asked Miles, looking back towards Molly, who was sitting upright in the boot, watching the traffic go by.

'I want to take a closer look at the camp. What better way to go undetected?'

'But they've seen you?'

'Yes, but I wasn't dressed like this,' said Louise, who'd changed into less formal clothes when picking up Molly. 'And I have a cap to wear.'

'That should be fine, then,' said Miles, with a smile.

'Hopefully everyone will be too interested in Molly to bother with us.'

They pulled up at the outskirts of the camp thirty minutes later, accessing the woods from the road, where Louise let an excited Molly off the lead.

'Are we searching for anything in particular?' asked Miles, looking around at the endless trees and the narrow dirt track.

'We'll know it when we see it,' said Louise, thinking about the woman she'd spotted in the woods when she'd visited the camp with Pepperstone. It was probably too much to hope it was the same woman who'd called in fear for her child, but she couldn't shake the thought that they might be the same person.

As Louise traipsed through the dry mud, she thought how unusual the investigation had become. It was still a cold case – the continuation of the unsolved disappearance of Hugo Latchford – but the anonymous call had changed everything for her, and she was certain there was more to unravel in relation to Hugo's death. She knew she shouldn't read too much into it, but everything about the call rang true to her and she was convinced it was genuine. Which made it all the more frustrating to be out here, searching for someone who was unknown to them at the moment.

They moved deeper into the woods, Molly having the time of her life, disappearing with a jump into the woodland before appearing further down the path, having taken her own secret route.

'Look,' said Miles, pointing through a mass of vines to a glimpse of bright material in the distance.

They walked further along the path until the flash was clearly visible. Thirty yards in they stumbled across a mini campsite, the bright material belonging to a two-person tent.

'Hello,' called Louise.

The tent was zipped up.

'Fresh firepit, and drinking water,' said Miles.

Louise called out again but stopped short of opening the tent, not wanting to intrude on anyone's privacy. 'Let's move on. If someone is staying here, it's on a temporary basis,' she said, wondering if the woman she'd seen that day with Pepperstone was staying in the tent, and if so how alone she must feel at night in the remote area.

They came across three more tents as they moved further into the woodland, each seemingly empty. 'Probably members of the VC,' said Miles. 'How far is the main camp area?'

'Not that far,' said Louise, who was thinking along the same lines. She could understand how some of the members might prefer time away from the large collective, though didn't envy them camping out every night.

Soon the pathway narrowed. Louise was about to turn back when Miles found a secondary route that went further into the woods. This pathway appeared to be man-made, the foliage and low-hanging branches cut away to create a zigzag path around the trees. Molly already had her nose down and was following the new path with great interest.

'Here,' said Miles, following the dog, his own head bent as he rushed through the trees after her.

'I'm too old for this,' said Louise, already out of breath as she walked around the trees. Finally, she came to a small clearing, which held a static caravan. The caravan was surrounded by trees, as if they had grown around it over the years.

They walked over to the home, Miles using his height to peer through the windows at the front of the caravan. 'Definitely someone living there,' he said. 'Look, it's connected to electricity and water.'

A broken wooden gate led to a small garden area in front of the caravan. Louise took the four metal steps to the caravan's door and knocked. 'No one is home,' she said, as Molly began to bark.

Louise stepped down and followed the sound of the dog. Another two hundred metres down the path they came across three other caravans, this time with people outside, one Louise immediately recognised.

'DI Blackwell. Having an interesting walk?' said Teresa Willow, approaching her.

'Yes, thank you,' said Louise to the lawyer.

'You may not be aware, but once again you are on private land,' said Teresa, handing Louise a set of papers. 'Deeds of land ownership. We own sixty acres, as you will see. Usually, we're quite open to anyone using our land, but I'm not sure about your reason for being here so will have to ask you to leave.'

'Do you live in one of these?' asked Louise, nodding towards the static caravans.

'Sometimes.'

'And who else lives here?' Louise looked at the gathered people – seven others in total – and tried to commit their faces to memory.

'We don't like to give out that information. Now, if you don't mind, Sam and Ainsley here can show you back to your car.'

Louise laughed as two burly men dressed in camouflage fatigues walked over to them. 'That won't be necessary,' she said, putting Molly on a lead. 'At least we know where to find you now,' she added, signalling to Miles that now was the time to leave.

# Chapter Seventeen

Fi woke with a jolt on Monday morning, her first instinct to look over to the other bed where Max was soundly asleep. Her head was thudding, her mouth as dry as sand, but she was too tired to move and go searching for water.

It couldn't have been a coincidence that, a few seconds after calling the police, there had been a knock on the door. Panicked, she'd hung up and answered the door to find Denise and Teresa, who said they'd happened to be out walking and had wanted to check in on her.

That was last night. They'd shared a few drinks, and after they'd left Fi had finished off the home brew and hadn't felt the same since; though she'd had enough wits about her to know her phone was missing.

Finally, she made it out of bed and stumbled to the sink, where she doused herself with water. How her hangover was this bad, she didn't know, but she didn't feel right at all. The doubt and paranoia remained, and although previously she'd trusted Teresa and Denise, seeing them in conversation with Silas had thrown her.

She let Max sleep as she watched the sky gradually lighten. Her dreams had been plagued with images of Hugo Latchford being buried alive, and the same thing happening to her boy. It was only when she'd got through to the emergency services that she'd fully understood her fears.

Someone knocked at the door. It was all Fi could do not to scream.

'Hey, sleepyheads, I've got some breakfast for you,' came Denise's voice.

Fi looked down at her baggy jogging bottoms and sweatshirt, both decorated with stains, and ran her fingers through her greasy hair. 'Coming,' she mumbled.

Denise was all smiles as she held out two paper bags. 'Feeling rough?' she asked, her voice edged with pity.

'I've felt better. I'd invite you in but . . .'

'Oh, don't be silly,' said Denise, barging past her and opening the blinds in the main room. 'Little man still sleeping?'

Fi nodded.

'I'll get him up,' said Denise, disappearing into the bedroom.

Fi put her hand on her chest, which felt tight. Why all the interest in her and Max all of sudden, she thought. Was it because they knew she'd phoned the police?

Her heart rate returned to something approaching normal as Denise came back followed by Max, who was already tearing into the banana from his breakfast bag.

'I can take him to camp today,' said Denise, under her breath. 'You get some rest.'

Fi nodded, disgusted with herself for still feeling unwell as she sat down and drank the milk Denise had given her, while her friend helped Max get ready. Her addictions had been one of the reasons she'd been keen to join the group, and although she'd fought the urge to take the stash of drugs, she'd overindulged in the alcohol when she should have known better. 'I'll join you,' said Fi, getting her to feet, the blood draining from her as she reached out to the sideboard for balance.

'That's OK, you rest up here,' said Denise, something approaching sympathy in her eyes.

Fi crashed back down, wondering if her energy would ever return. Max came over and hugged her goodbye, and she could smell her own foul breath as she kissed him. This time, she did manage to get to her feet as Denise left the caravan with her boy.

Fi told herself she was just being silly. Denise would never do anything to hurt Max. But as she propped herself against the window pane, her fingers slipping in the grime, and watched her best friend and son walk hand in hand towards camp, she thought once more about her missing phone, and the book she'd found in Silas's caravan, and tried to fight the fear that she would never see her boy again.

# Chapter Eighteen

After leaving Priddy, Louise managed to collect Jack and Emily from her parents before it was Emily's bedtime. Emily was playing in the garden, as Jack went to sleep on his grandfather's lap.

'It's like she never left,' said Louise's mother, looking out at Emily, who was chasing the dog around.

Louise tried to ignore her mother's passive-aggressive comment. 'Sorry, Mum. This has all taken me by surprise,' she said, wondering why, after all her years working abnormal shifts, she'd ever thought it would be any different. 'It will be easier when Thomas's project in Surrey ends. He'll be able to get back at a more normal time and we can share the childcare more evenly.'

'I don't mind. Honestly, I don't, Louise. But it would be easier for us if we knew where we were every day. If it is easier, I can pick them up from school and the childminder, and they can come here for their tea. At least then you won't need to worry about rushing home every day.'

'I thought the idea was for you and Dad to have more time to yourself,' said Louise, glancing over at her father, who'd fallen asleep with Jack snug in his arms.

Her mother walked over and took Jack from him. 'It's fine. I kind of miss having them around. It won't be forever. We could try for the next six months and see how we go?'

Louise hugged her mother, trying not to wake Jack, who looked so peaceful in her arms. 'That would be fantastic, Mum,' she said, feeling like a failure.

The following day at work, Louise called a meeting in the incident room and updated the team about her run-in with Teresa Willow in the Mendip Hills the day before, and the possibility of Pepperstone's UCO helping them.

She glanced at the images on the crime board, admitting to herself that they weren't much further along than they'd been in the beginning, beyond having located Valerie Latchford. Assigning duties, she left the team and went to speak to Robertson.

'I know what you're going to ask me, but we can't go in there heavy-handed,' said Robertson, before she had the chance to speak.

'Something odd is going on there, Iain.'

'No doubt. They're a relatively secret community living off-grid. I'm sure lots of odd things are going on. But there is no way we can get a warrant to start searching the place. Believe me, I've sounded it out already.'

Louise thought of Teresa Willow, and the self-satisfied way she'd dismissed her in the woods yesterday. It was clear the group were heavily lawyered up, which in some ways seemed to go against their beliefs. 'Where does that leave us?'

'At the moment, this is still a cold case. The focus has to be on finding explanations for what happened to Hugo Latchford.'

'And the call?'

'We treat it like we would any other call of its nature.'

'Oh, come on, Iain! The call came through as a response to our PR campaign. We have to treat it as if it's linked,' said Louise.

'I'm afraid I don't agree. It was an emergency call that came in during the same period. You know as well as I do how often we get similar calls. You also know the danger of skewering unconnected evidence to fit into the case. At present, we have no proof linking that call to the historic case of Hugo Latchford's disappearance.'

Louise knew that he was right but it was still hard to hear. 'I guess this is the type of decision DCIs have to make,' she said.

'On that point, the assistant chief constable wishes to speak to you.'

Louise frowned. 'About the position?'

'Just an informal meeting. But I would treat it as seriously as if it was the final interview itself. He needs to see you want the position, and naturally what you can bring. He already knows how I feel about it, and I believe you have a decent relationship with him, so you should be OK. Friday, two p.m.'

'I see it's already booked.'

'Do your preparation. We can do a mock interview together on Thursday.'

'Thanks, Iain,' said Louise.

'Think nothing of it. The sooner I get you promoted, the sooner I can get out of here.'

Louise would rather not have thought about her meeting with the assistant chief, but if she wanted to make the sort of impression that Robertson expected then it would take some thought and effort.

Although Assistant Chief Constable Brightman was a much more supportive and approachable assistant chief than his predecessor – ACC Morley, who had tried his best to get her kicked off the force completely – they hadn't always seen eye to eye. Although generally not her own fault, Louise's past at her job had been plagued by trouble with fellow officers who in the main had since left the police; including her former direct boss, Tim Finch, who was currently serving time for numerous charges, including sexual assault.

Louise knew such controversy stuck, and at some point during the interview process it would be mentioned. Furthermore, she needed to convince herself she truly wanted the promotion. If Brightman, or any of the others, spotted even a hint that she wasn't one hundred per cent behind the role, then she would be bypassed. That meant another few nights of soul-searching ahead of her, and she wasn't sure she had the energy at present.

Back in the incident room, she worked through the daily reports from the PR campaign. The calls were drying up, and there had been close to nothing regarding Jeremy Latchford. The team had conducted more interviews with local caving groups, and anyone with links to Banwell Caves, but Louise knew that the only chance they had of finding out the reasons for Hugo's death lay in the past. She had to treat the investigation as if Hugo had just gone missing, and that meant returning to his life prior to his disappearance.

She uploaded the original missing persons file report from that period. She'd read it many times over and had the majority of the information stored in her memory, but she started from the beginning in case she had overlooked something.

She read through Hugo's school reports from his time with his natural parents, and latterly with the Jenkinses in Shepton Mallet. The reports were quite general, but Hugo sounded as if he'd been well adjusted, if a little withdrawn, following his move into foster care. Louise made a note of the teachers' names and matched them to police interviews from when Hugo had gone missing. It highlighted just how many people had been affected by the boy's disappearance, and Louise added the teachers' names to a list of people to speak to.

Next, she went further back into the Latchfords' lives. They had married two years prior to Hugo being born. Jeremy was from the West Country, but Valerie was originally from Leeds and had moved to the area when her father was posted to the RAF station in Locking when she was a child. After marrying, they'd moved in to Jeremy's farmhouse in Frome together.

Louise brought up the address on the system, and searched for it in a maps app. From what she could see from the images online, the building was still standing, and when she cross-checked it with the Land Registry, she discovered the property belonged to Maize Developments Limited.

She ran a search on the company and found they were currently under investigation by the Met, specifically Pepperstone's department. From what she could see, Maize had direct links to Ella Gosling, who was the chairwoman of one of the charitable foundations linked to the Verdant Circle.

Louise called Pepperstone. When he didn't answer, she decided that she needed to pay the Latchford house a visit.

# Chapter Nineteen

The house that had once belonged to Hugo Latchford's parents was an isolated building on the outskirts of Frome, only twenty minutes from where Hugo's former foster parents – the Jenkinses – lived in Shepton Mallet.

From the outside, the property appeared to be dilapidated. The front garden was overgrown, with vines and moss spreading over the property and blocking the entrance to the front door.

'Try the gate,' said Louise, pointing towards a barely visible metal door in the fencing at the side of the house.

Miles battled through the vines and grabbed hold of the frame with his giant hands. 'Won't move,' he said, pulling at the door.

Louise looked through the opening. The backyard of the property was a replica of the front garden on a much larger scale. The place was otherworldly, with a rusted swing set where Hugo might once have played poking through the long grass that sprouted three feet in the air. She reached in through a small hole in the fencing and found a latch on the metal door. 'Try now,' she said, stepping back.

Miles frowned, clearly embarrassed, and waited until she was clear before attacking the door with renewed vigour and pulling it open in one attempt. 'Not a pleasant smell,' he said, stepping over the threshold.

Louise followed, the stench of fox urine and something unidentifiable – ammonia-like – filling the air.

They walked to the rear of the property. The windows were all boarded up, and a familiar uneasiness came over Louise. She'd been inside a similar house a few months before her maternity leave – a family home where the parents had kept their children locked up in the cellar. She had no desire to enter and find something similar, but peered through the gaps in the boards anyway, the interior dark and uninviting.

'What a waste,' said Miles. 'Why go to the bother of obtaining the property only to leave it in such disrepair.'

The same thought had crossed Louise's mind. The house was seemingly owned by the Verdant Circle, whose modus operandi appeared to be recruiting people and fleecing them of their money. So why had they left the property vacant?

'Can we go in?' asked Miles.

Louise took a deep breath. 'It would be hard to justify,' she said. 'No one appears to be in danger.'

'Does that mean no?'

Louise shone her torch through the gaps in the boards. All she could make out was discoloured carpets, and the remnants of old furniture. She knew the true nature of the house would be found within, possibly below ground, but she couldn't risk entering at present even though the chance of obtaining a warrant was all but zero. 'For now, it means no. I need you to do some digging when we get back. Find out the full history of this place. If it's been put to use at all since the Latchfords sold it.'

'I'd love to have a sneaky look,' said Miles, displaying all his youthful enthusiasm with a beaming smile.

'Next time,' said Louise, stumbling through the weeds towards the front garden, moving faster than she'd intended, eager to return to the car and get away from the house.

◆ ◆ ◆

Louise knew better than to read too much into the condition of the old Latchford house. There could be numerous innocuous reasons why it was in a state of disrepair and the Verdant Circle had failed to make a profit from it. But it did make her keen to speak to Valerie Latchford again, and she called her contact in Bideford to make sure the woman was still where she'd said she would be.

Louise wanted to know what state the house had been in when the Latchfords had given it away. It was more than possible that the place had always been that way. She didn't know how the family had lived before Hugo was given up. One of the misunderstood presumptions about the people that groups like the Verdant Circle attracted was that they were often poorly educated with few resources. Quite often, the opposite was true. From what she'd researched and Pepperstone had told her, the Verdant Circle tried to target wealthier patrons, and had different processes in place to appeal to different demographics. Although Valerie Latchford's life appeared to be in disarray at present, it didn't mean it had been at the time, and Louise wanted to know more.

Miles's phone rang as Louise was nearing headquarters.

'Going to answer that?' said Louise, noting her colleague's cheeks were slightly flushed when he checked the number.

'Ah, no.'

Louise smiled. 'Not that pretty little bone lady, is it?'

'It is.'

'Answer it. It could be about the investigation,' she said, enjoying the light relief of gently teasing the young officer.

'Hi, Chloe,' said Miles. 'I'm in the car with DI Blackwell,' he added, before any conversation could begin.

'Don't mind me,' mouthed Louise, as Miles went silent listening to the pathologist talking to him.

'OK, I understand,' he said, after a long pause. 'You're there now?'

Louise slowed the car as Miles hung up. 'It was about the case?'

'Yes. She'd like to see us straight away. Some new information has come to light about the bones.'

Dr Chloe Baker was waiting for them at reception. If Louise hadn't known beforehand, she would never have been able to tell that the forensic pathologist and Miles were seeing each other. The pair acted as if they had never met, Chloe's face unreadable as she led them to an office that had the feel of a police interview room.

Louise and Miles each took a seat as Chloe set up the whiteboard in the room. 'As I mentioned, I sent the bones for further analysis,' she said, getting straight to the point as images of Hugo Latchford's remains appeared on the screen. She looked uneasy, and Louise immediately wondered if she'd made some kind of mistake.

'The isotope testing and microbial analysis of the bones and teeth suggest that the boy may have been held captive prior to his death,' said Chloe, uploading close-up images of the bones. 'See here,' she added, pointing to the screen. 'Microscopic lesions found on the joints and sites of muscle attachment.'

'What does that mean?' asked Louise.

'It would indicate he was regularly bound and chained up. Likely for extended periods. His bone growth was impacted.'

Louise thought back to the cave where the remains had been discovered, where there had been no signs of captivity. 'And what else?'

Chloe loaded another slide. 'Examining the bones under high magnification, we discovered parallel micro-abrasions indicative of cuts with a serrated blade.'

'He was tortured?' asked Miles.

Chloe sighed. 'I would say it was highly likely.'

Louise buzzed down her window as she drove back to headquarters. She'd known it was a possibility that Hugo had been tortured in some way, but the confirmation was hard to stomach. She pictured the last years of his life.

First, being abandoned by his parents, then kidnapped, and eventually entombed within the caves. She was reminded again of the tragic parallel between Hugo and the girl, Aisha Hashim, who'd suffered her last agonising moments in the airless shipping container. It made no difference to Louise that Hugo had died a decade earlier. She needed to get him justice, and to find those responsible.

At headquarters, she presented her evidence to Robertson. 'I need a warrant to search the camp in Priddy,' she said.

'What are you hoping to find? This was a long time ago, Louise.'

'I know that.'

Robertson scratched the back of his head. 'It's not enough. The only link between Hugo Latchford's death and the Verdant Circle is the fact that Hugo's parents gave him up for care to join the group. That is tentative at best.'

'And the rumours about pagan rituals and sacrifice.'

Robertson lowered his tone. 'You're answering your own question there, Louise. Rumours are meaningless.'

'I'm convinced they're involved somehow, Iain. Plus, that call. What if it happens again?'

'It's not enough.'

Louise held her boss's gaze. He was right, but her understanding that didn't make it any more palatable.

'Thursday,' said Robertson, as she stood to leave. 'Don't forget.'

Louise shook her head. 'How could I?' she mumbled under her breath, wondering how she would ever make such decisions if she became DCI.

Returning to the incident room, she caught sight of Miles with his head in his hands. 'What's up?' she asked.

Miles looked up, his face ashen. 'More bad news,' he said. 'Valerie Latchford has gone missing.'

# Chapter Twenty

Fi sat in the gloom of her caravan, picking at the meal Denise had given her as Max talked about his day in camp. She should have been pleased that he was thriving so much, but she couldn't ignore the pang of fear, or possibly jealousy, as he told her how Teresa and Silas had taken him for a walk in the afternoon.

'Just the three of you?' she asked, trying to hide her panic, sipping at the milk and wondering if the sickness would ever end.

'Denise was there for a bit.'

'Where did you go?'

'I told you, into the forest. They showed me these old stones. Silas told me about our ancestors, how we were much more . . . connected to the Earth,' said her son, struggling to recall the exact words he'd been told.

'Isn't that nice,' said Fi, drinking the warm milk that Denise had said would help her feel better. It was hard not to think that she was being monitored – that Teresa and Silas had taken Max for a walk as a warning to her. That they could take her child whenever they wanted. They could do anything with him. She had no idea what had happened to Hugo Latchford all those years ago, but she was growing more and more convinced the same thing was going to happen to Max, and she couldn't let that happen.

Later, as she put him to bed and was kissing him on the cheek, she saw a glimpse of Pete in her son's eyes. It had been her boyfriend who had first mooted the idea of joining the Verdant Circle, and where was he now? Fi had tried to do as much research as possible before making the decision to join. It had seemed such an idyllic way to live, and the group had shown them round one of their other camps, a more built-up compound in the Midlands, and had answered every question they could think of without once putting any pressure on them to join. That had clinched it for Fi. If they were this deranged cult, then why had they let her and Pete move so freely without once asking them to join?

In the end, it had seemed like a no-brainer. They'd sold their little terraced house to help fund their life with the Verdant Circle – the group holding the money for them, and deducting a little each month for expenses, as was shown to them on their monthly statements – and life had been nearly idyllic. Sure, people came and went from the group, usually leaving without warning, but Fi hadn't thought anything of it.

Pete had grown suspicious, however. He'd started putting doubts in her mind. Why were people here one minute, gone the next? Why were some people invited to select meetings and ceremonies, when they were left in the camp? She'd always found it a little strange how quickly his mind had been changed, and how desperate he'd been to leave. He'd wanted Max to go with him, but she'd told him in no uncertain terms that would never happen. And yet he'd still left them, and had never returned.

Even after he'd gone, they'd managed to get on with their life in camp. Max missed him of course, and although they rarely talked about him, she knew from Max's occasional silences that Pete's departure had taken its toll on her son. But he'd adjusted well. There were lots of other children in camp and he'd made lots of friends, and she felt that they'd both moved on. The only anomaly she still struggled with was the fact that she'd had to stay in the caravan and wasn't allowed to move into the main camp. That aside, things had been fine, or at least bearable, until Silas had arrived.

Fi felt worse than ever, jittery and self-conscious, and until she felt better she wouldn't be able to think straight.

Feeling herself succumbing to sleep, she forced herself off the couch and made a half-hearted attempt at cleaning some of the junk that had piled up around the small metal sink. Sniffing at the milk bottles set aside for recycling, she winced at the smell, her stomach tightening. Paranoia returning, she collected the other three bottles Denise had brought over during the last couple of days. She sniffed each, responding in the same way. Then she thought back to the meals she'd had since she'd called the police. Denise had prepared them all, but Fi had been the only one to drink the milk. There was also the matter of her missing phone.

Were they drugging her? She'd known Denise ever since she'd joined, and had trusted her with her life. But that didn't mean it wasn't happening. She'd seen the concern on her friend's face that night when she'd called the police. Maybe she'd known what Fi was doing – that she was spiralling, feeling out of control – and was doping the milk to help her rest. God only knew how tired she'd felt recently. If that was the reason, then Fi could forgive her, but for now she needed a clear head.

She rinsed out the bottles and went to bed, determined to rejoin the camp the following morning.

# Chapter Twenty-One

Louise had spent the rest of yesterday in conversation with her contact in Bideford, and after asking her parents if Jack and Emily could stay with them for a couple of nights had decided to make the journey south with Miles. By the time they arrived in Bideford in the morning, a CCTV image had appeared of Valerie Latchford leaving the train at Taunton station the previous evening, so no sooner had they arrived than they were on their way back.

They arrived at Taunton police station at 10 a.m., where they went through the footage. Valerie had left Taunton train station at 8.32 p.m. and was last seen walking along Kingston Road. Louise liaised with Taunton's CID team, and requested that all officers be put on high alert for sightings of Valerie, before leaving with Miles.

'Where are we going?' asked Miles, when they were back in the car.

It was only just gone 11 a.m., but Louise had already been up for six hours. What she really wanted was a nap. But instead, she instructed her colleague to make a quick detour to the petrol station for some coffee before they did a circuit of Taunton on the off-chance, and then made the short journey back to Portishead.

In the incident room, she called Pepperstone, but the DI wasn't answering. She got the distinct feeling that he was avoiding her. It was clear he had little interest in her cold case unless it benefited his own investigation, and if she was going to get any assistance from him, she needed to prove how it would benefit him.

Louise left him a message before turning her attention back to Valerie Latchford. She checked for any friends or relations known to the woman in Taunton and the surrounding areas, but nothing about her history suggested a connection.

Louise tried not to dwell on the possibility that Valerie had been responsible for Hugo's death, and the signs of torture preceding it. The horrific implications aside, Louise had spurned the chance to arrest her, and even though that hadn't really been an option, she knew the guilt would weigh heavy if Valerie managed to escape justice because of her.

Pepperstone finally got back to her in the late afternoon. 'Not surprising,' he said, as she told him about the pathologist's findings and Valerie's disappearance. 'I'm sure she'll show up.'

'I need to speak to someone high up in the Verdant Circle,' said Louise, ignoring his dismissive manner.

'Wouldn't that be lovely.'

'I'm serious, Gerrard. If it isn't enough that we've found the remains of a boy with links to the group, we now find out he may have been tortured.'

'There is nothing linking him directly to the VC.'

'Except his parents.'

'His parents were members, he was not.'

'I don't think you quite get it, Gerrard. This is a murder investigation,' said Louise, stressing the reality of the situation.

'I don't think you quite get it, DI Blackwell. I have spent the best part of seven years monitoring this organisation and I will not have you coming in on a whim and spoiling things.'

'A whim?' said Louise, her raised voice carrying through the office, causing a few people to look her way. 'It's a dead boy,

Gerrard. That not important enough for you? I will speak to someone in that organisation with or without your help.'

She heard Pepperstone's laboured breathing on the other end of the line and decided to temper her approach. 'Work with me, Gerrard. This could be the in you want. We link the Verdant Circle with Hugo Latchford's death, then we have them. I don't care about the financials. That's your thing. Help me find out what happened to Hugo, and I'll help you take them down.'

The breathing continued. Louise imagined Pepperstone weighing up his options, deciding how much her involvement would risk the level of his success. She waited for a few more seconds until he eventually said, 'Leave it with me,' and hung up.

Louise sat back in her chair, as everyone else returned to their work and pretended to ignore the fact they'd heard her heated conversation. She downloaded the files Pepperstone had initially sent her on the Verdant Circle. She understood in part why the DI was so protective about his investigation. It was a mammoth undertaking, currently with thirty-five open cases against the organisation. She ran through the names on file, which included the lawyer she'd met in the Mendip Hills, Teresa Willow, and the assumed current leader of the organisation, Ella Gosling.

Ella Gosling was a direct descendant of Wilfred and Sarah Hawthorne, the founders of the Verdant Circle. Little was known about Ella – but if, as suspected, she was in charge of the group's financials, then she was likely to be a very wealthy individual, at least on paper.

What really interested Louise was what was missing from the files. The open cases against the group were already in the public domain, but Pepperstone hadn't given any details on the extent of the rest of their investigations. Louise had no way of knowing if Ella Gosling was under surveillance, or what larger supposed crimes the group were considered guilty of.

'Ma'am, we've got her.'

Louise turned sharply, trying not to jump. 'Jesus, Miles, for someone so big you're able to move around very quietly. Who have we got?'

'Valerie Latchford. Just got pinched for shoplifting in Taunton.'

Louise glanced at her watch. It was 4.25 p.m. 'Why don't these things ever happen in the morning, Miles? You ever wonder that?'

'Constantly.'

'You know the drill. Get the car, and I'll meet you downstairs in five.'

At Taunton police station, Valerie Latchford looked in more of a state than the last time Louise had seen her. She'd been passed fit to speak to them, but her eyes were bloodshot and she was shaking as she sat opposite with her duty solicitor on her left.

'Why did you run away, Valerie?'

'Free country, ain't it?'

'I guess it is, Valerie. But you may remember I'm investigating your son's death. I asked you not to leave Bideford.'

'I got spooked.'

'By what?'

'By everything. I felt like a sitting duck. I was sure they were going to come for me.'

'The Verdant Circle?' asked Louise.

Valerie didn't answer, staring through Louise as if she weren't there.

'I told you we can help you, Valerie. You need to speak to me.'

'There's nothing I want to say.'

Louise sighed and took out her phone. 'Here – I didn't want to show you this, but it's best you see,' she said, handing the phone over with the updated images of Hugo's bones.

'What's this?' asked the duty solicitor.

'We have had further analysis of Hugo's remains. We believe that, prior to his death, Hugo was a victim of torture and was possibly kept in captivity.'

Valerie shrieked, and pushed the phone away from her.

'I know there's something you aren't telling us, Valerie. Now would be the time. Help me and I will help you, I promise,' said Louise.

'Let me see those pictures,' said Valerie, tears in her eyes as she took the phone from Louise. 'They did this to my boy.'

Louise didn't know if it was a question or a statement. 'You think the Verdant Circle were responsible for Hugo's death?' she asked.

'He never liked him, did you know that?' said Valerie, handing the phone back.

'Who? Your husband?'

Valerie started nodding, as if willing herself to speak. 'I never told anyone this, but he wasn't Hugo's father.'

Louise glanced sideways at Miles, who was busy taking notes. 'Jeremy Latchford was not Hugo's paternal father?'

'Nope.'

'Was he aware of this?'

'Eventually. Don't get me wrong, the decision to give Hugo up was a joint decision. We both felt the Verdant Circle was the right place to be for us, but we weren't sure about Hugo. We knew the adoption process would take some time, and that he would be fostered first. We told ourselves that we were going to get him back before it came to that, but that was before Jeremy found out.'

'How did he find out?' asked Louise.

Valerie chuckled to herself. 'I told him. Can you believe that? There are different levels in the Verdant Circle, and Jeremy was keen to push himself as far up the chain as possible. With that came some sacrifices. One of them was a kind of couples counselling. Crazy, I know. But during that period, we were made to share secrets about our lives . . . things we'd never spoken about before. We were told we had to be fully open to progress with the group. Jeremy was all for it. I don't know how they got it out of me, but by the end I was telling them and Jeremy everything. And that was when he found out he wasn't the father.'

'Who was?' asked Miles.

'That isn't important,' said Valerie.

Louise frowned, annoyed that Miles had interrupted Valerie when she was speaking. 'How did Jeremy take it?' she asked, shooting Miles a look that warned him not to speak again.

'Not very well, as you can imagine. Not that he didn't have his own fair share of secrets to tell, believe me. But that was it for him, as far as I was concerned. We were living separately as it was, and from that day he just ignored me. He flourished within the group, I faded. When Hugo went missing, I was sure he was responsible but I didn't have the courage to speak up. What sort of mother does that make me, I wonder?'

Tears streamed down Valerie's face, but she tried to fight them as if she thought she didn't deserve the release.

'You think Jeremy could have killed your son?'

'You don't know the half of it. They were up to some weird shit, out there in the wilds. I didn't get to see it, but I knew it went on. Could have been Jeremy, could have been one of the others.'

Louise wanted to grab the woman and shake her, to find out why she hadn't spoken up at the beginning when her son had gone missing, but it was too late for that now. 'Where can we find Jeremy?'

Valerie shrugged her shoulders. 'I have no idea, but he'll still be with that lot. They meant the world to him, much more than I or Hugo ever did.'

Louise turned to Miles and raised her eyebrows. Miles looked away, subdued after her earlier warning. She realised he'd just been trying to help, and made a mental note to go easier on the young officer, and not to take out her frustrations with the investigation on him.

'One more quick question, Valerie. The house you lived in with Jeremy, do you know what happened to it?'

Valerie shut her eyes. 'Don't you know? That became one of their meeting places. It's close to one of their sacred places – that's how they got to speak to us in the first place. It had been in Jeremy's family all his life and the Verdant Circle wanted to buy it.' She opened her eyes. 'Isn't that funny, we ended up giving it to them. I haven't been back since we left, but I imagine they still use it.'

'What sacred place?' asked Louise.

'Close to the quarry. There's a druid's altar. A ruin of course. They like to meet up there and play make-believe.'

# Chapter Twenty-Two

Her resolve to rejoin the camp had faded by the time Fi woke on Wednesday morning. The chime of the clock alarm felt like it was inside her head, and it took all her effort just to reach out and turn it off. She lay in bed, the sound of birds chirping as bright sunshine assaulted her eyes. She needed to fight this feeling, but the sickness was still within her.

'Mummy?'

Max was standing by the doorway, already dressed.

'What are you doing up, honey?'

'Denise and Silas said they were going to take me on a walk before school,' said Max, his body wedged behind the door as if he feared something on the other side.

'Let's eat first,' said Fi, groaning as she got herself into a sitting position and pulled on a threadbare dressing gown.

Despite having done the dishes last night, the living area was rife with the smell of decaying food. Fi stumbled over to the sink, searching for the source of the smell before opening the window. They had no food in the caravan. Usually, Fi would walk into the camp, but she had grown reliant these last few days on Denise.

'Shall we walk down?' she said.

Max looked doubtful. 'Denise will be here soon,' he said, with a smile. 'She said she would bring us breakfast.'

Fi collapsed on to the sofa. Even if she had wanted to, she wouldn't have been able to make the walk. She was beginning to think something was seriously wrong, in a way she had never felt before, yet when Denise arrived a few minutes later she didn't say anything.

'Still feeling poorly, hun?' said Denise, breezing through the caravan, opening the blinds and windows, tidying the place as if it was her own.

'A bit better,' said Fi, not recognising her own raspy voice.

Denise placed two brown paper bags on the counter. 'That's great,' she said. 'We can keep Max out of your hair for today. I've left some food for you over there, and I'll pop back later when Max is finished for the day.'

Fi went to object, but Denise and Max were already leaving. 'See you later, Mum,' said Max, not making eye contact as he shut the door behind him.

Fi glanced out of the window, her heart pounding as she caught sight of Teresa and Silas joining Denise and her son, before the four of them headed into camp.

Her mind was swamped with images of adults in animal masks; of Max being tied up and trapped forever in some unknown cave. She wanted to run after them, to beg them not to hurt him, willing to humiliate herself if it kept her boy safe. But she had let them lead him away, and she looked around in disgust at the mess of the caravan.

She did her best to tidy before settling down to eat the breakfast of fruit, cereal, and milk. She bit into a hardened pear and opened the bottle of cold milk. 'A great source of protein and fat,' Denise had told her.

Fi sniffed at the bottle, reminded of the sour smell from last night. It seemed OK to her, but her gut instinct told her not to drink it. She chuckled to herself, fearing she was at peak paranoia, as she poured the milk down the sink.

She opened the paper bag Denise had prepared for lunch, pouring away a second bottle of milk. She had no idea why her friend would want her doped up, and maybe it was all in her head, but she needed to find out for herself.

If the milk had been tainted these last few days, then it would need time to leave her system. Fi took a book from her shelf and forced herself outside into the fresh air.

Now it was just a waiting game.

# Chapter Twenty-Three

Despite everything Valerie had shared with them, there was nothing that Louise could hold her on. She was sure Valerie had had nothing to do with Hugo's death, at least directly, but she didn't want her to abscond again until everything was resolved. Valerie was charged with shoplifting, then released. Louise told her to return to Bideford, but Valerie gave them an address for her friends in the Taunton area where she said she would be staying.

When Louise returned home that night, Thomas was waiting up. 'Hello stranger,' he said, switching off the television as she entered the living room.

Louise sighed and sat down on the sofa, collapsing into him. 'It's good to see you,' she said.

'We're like ships passing in the night,' he said, pulling her closer.

It felt good to be next to him. But it dawned on her that she couldn't remember when they'd last had time like this, alone. Since she'd returned to the station, it had felt like they were rarely in the same house, never mind the same room or the same bed. 'How's the Surrey thing?'

'Going a bit longer than I anticipated, but I don't have to go in tomorrow.'

'It was much easier when I was on maternity leave,' said Louise, looking up at him.

'We knew it would be hard. It's Sod's Law that I've had to work away at the same time. It's only been a few weeks. Give it time, we can get into a routine that works. I'll be able to help out much more when I'm back at headquarters on a daily basis.'

Thomas was an ex-copper so knew the shifting demands of time that Louise was under. He'd also worked with her before, so understood her dedication meant that once she was involved in an investigation she had to give it her full attention, and that it often took over her thoughts and actions.

'What sort of routine involves me working all hours, and never seeing the children?'

'It's not every day, is it? We knew there would be times when this happened. As I said, I'll be able to pull my weight soon, and I'm earning enough now that we could look at getting an au pair. That would make it easier for both of us in the morning, and after school. And the weekends for that matter,' said Thomas, yawning. 'And there's the DCI thing.'

Louise lay her head on Thomas's chest. Sometimes she forgot the comfort he brought her, just by being a constant presence in her life. 'So, Mr Moneybags, if we have enough for an au pair, do we have enough for me to give up work?'

Thomas laughed, playing with her hair.

Louise pushed his hand away and sat up. 'I'm being serious,' she said. 'I already feel things changing between me and Jack.'

'What do you mean?'

'Oh, I don't know. It's as if he doesn't need me any more.'

Thomas smiled – cautiously, as though he feared her response. 'He's not even two, Louise. You see him every day. It's going to be a long time before he doesn't need you any more.'

She frowned. She knew she was being oversensitive, but being back at work had thrown her and she didn't know the best way to handle it. 'But if I was serious. If I really wanted to leave. Could we do it?'

'We could afford it, but that isn't the question.'

'What is?'

Thomas scratched the day-old stubble on the side of his cheek. 'The question is whether you could live without it, Lou. It didn't go unnoticed how twitchy you were, going on maternity leave.'

'Twitchy?' said Louise, feigning indignation.

'No, I don't mean it like that. Listen, you were born to be in the police. I've never met anyone so dedicated. Me, I could take it or leave it. And I left it. You? It might sound dramatic, but it's in your blood.'

'But I can't carry on doing what I'm doing, and I can't see myself sitting behind a desk like Robertson.'

'I think you're misremembering Robbo's input into things, Lou. You've said yourself how vital he's been in your investigations. He was there on the pier with you that day, remember? The thing is, you can make the role work for you any way you want it to. With the bonus of being able to send some poor sucker off to a crime scene when you're home in bed.'

Louise thought about Thomas's last words as she arrived at the Latchfords' old house in Frome the following morning with Miles. He'd been right in saying that Robertson wasn't always desk-bound. Maybe it would work, but if so, she needed to get her act together as she was supposed to be meeting the assistant chief tomorrow.

After interviewing Valerie yesterday, Louise had called Pepperstone to find out what he knew about the so-called sacred site near the Frome property. The DI had sent over schematics for the area but hadn't given her any update on arranging for her to speak to the Verdant Circle's leaders.

'Right, let's go,' said Louise, as they walked around the back of the house towards a woodland area a hundred yards in the distance.

The solstice was just over a week away now, and the hot weather remained relentless. Louise felt sweat drip down the back of her neck, and before they reached the woods she was coated.

'Compass ready,' said Miles, his phone held out in front of him. 'This is like being in the scouts.'

'I didn't take you for a former scout, Miles.'

'Once a scout, always a scout,' he said, heading off into the trees with something approaching glee in his eyes.

Miles found the spot ten minutes later – a secluded grove with moss-covered stones arranged in a circular pattern. 'Is this it?' she asked, running her hand over the stones, which were intertwined with the roots of the surrounding yew trees. 'Stonehenge I can kind of get, but this?'

Miles sat next to the stones. 'Looks like this has been used as a firepit,' he said, pointing to the middle of the circle. 'I guess they believe in the historic power of these things.'

'You can believe anything if you're prepared to suspend your disbelief. One thing is clear: the Verdant Circle must have a hell of a lot of money if they're prepared to leave a property such as the house back there vacant just so people can come visit this place now and then.'

Louise walked around the area, hoping some truth would reveal itself, but it wasn't long before they returned to the car.

Back at headquarters, she drew a circle around the photograph of Jeremy Latchford as she explained to the team what Valerie had told them yesterday. 'Hugo wasn't his son. That may have made it easier for him to kill him or to assist in doing so. Either way, I want all our efforts put into finding this man.'

Louise had hoped this revelation would change things, making Latchford the prime suspect so that all resources could be focused on him. But in reality, it hadn't. She'd wanted to speak to Jeremy Latchford from the beginning and still did. She issued a wanted notice on him nationwide, meaning all forces would be on the lookout for him, but that would probably make no difference if he was holed up in one of the Verdant Circle's camps.

Pepperstone called and they arranged to meet later in the afternoon. He turned up an hour late, Louise dismissing his apologies as they entered the incident room.

'I see Jeremy Latchford has been promoted to chief suspect?' he said, glancing at the crime board.

'You knew he wasn't Hugo's father, didn't you?' said Louise, not prepared to waste any time.

Pepperstone shook his head. 'I know little about the man, beyond the fact that he is still active within the group. I've told you before, we looked into Valerie and Jeremy when Hugo went missing, but that side of things isn't my priority.'

'What side of things?'

'If he isn't stealing money from innocent people, then he isn't a concern of mine.'

'Even if he has killed his son?'

'I think you may be jumping to some wild conclusions there, DI Blackwell. Even so, that is your priority, and not mine.'

Louise didn't react. She'd encountered such blinkered thinking before in the police – but Pepperstone seemed more single-minded than most. 'Is there a reason you're here?'

'Listen, my UCO has infiltrated the Priddy camp. If anything is going down there, they'll manage to get a message to us.'

'And Ella Gosling?'

'I can't let you speak to her, Louise. It would risk our operation.'

Louise took a deep breath. She'd hoped Pepperstone would have come round to her way of thinking, but it was clear he was intent on remaining stubborn. 'I believe this is a murder investigation, Gerrard. And if it is, it's possible other people are in danger. I will be speaking to Ella Gosling.'

Pepperstone smiled, and in the gesture, Louise saw every condescending male officer she'd had to suffer over the years. 'That won't be happening, believe me,' he said, getting to his feet. 'You'll be hearing from my superiors in due course.'

Tracey walked over as Pepperstone left the office. 'What the hell was that about?' she asked.

'Little boys' power games. I need your help, Trace.'

'Of course.'

'I need an address for Ella Gosling. I need to speak to her before Pepperstone stops it happening.' Tracey had more in-house contacts than anyone Louise knew on the force. If anyone could find the information Louise needed, it was her.

'Leave it with me. I'll see what I can do.'

'You're a star.'

'Any news on the promotion?' asked Tracey, under her breath.

'Seeing the assistant chief tomorrow. My mind's not in it at the moment. I was supposed to meet with Robertson today to go through a practice interview but there hasn't been time.'

'Why don't you pop home now. Get prepared. Nothing much is going to change today. And if it does, I'll keep you updated.'

'I appreciate that. Let me finish up here, and I'll go,' said Louise.

But two hours later she was still in the incident room. She'd spent the time undertaking more research on the Verdant Circle, and Ella Gosling. There were a couple of official addresses for the woman in the UK, but it wasn't clear where she was actually residing. Maybe Tracey would have better luck, but the more Louise read, the more her desire to speak to the leader of the group grew.

As usually happened, she felt herself becoming more and more absorbed by the investigation. She reread the report from Dr Baker, her mind scarred by the magnified images of the abrasions on Hugo Latchford's bones. It was easier now she knew Jeremy wasn't the boy's biological father to believe he had something to do with Hugo's death. Not that paternity meant that much. Louise had learnt that early in her career. She knew that the wider public would be amazed, as she had once been, at the way some parents, biological or not, treated their children. She'd dealt with abuse cases, one way or another, since her days on the beat. It was terrible to have to accept, but the possibility that Jeremy Latchford had tortured and killed Hugo was something Louise had no difficulty in imagining.

She tried not to think about Emily and Jack, but with investigations such as this it was impossible not to do so. She fought the urge to call the childminder to check how Jack was doing, knowing that once she made that call it would set a precedent that would be hard to resist. Instead, she wondered about Jeremy Latchford's past and if there was anything in it that would explain any dysfunctional behaviour.

Jeremy's mother was still alive. Evelyn Latchford was a resident at the named care home in Somerton, just a few miles from where they had interviewed Valerie Latchford the day before.

Louise was about to phone the care home when Miles walked over carrying his laptop, a grin broadening on his face. 'What are you so happy about?' asked Louise.

Miles reeled in the smile, as if he'd been caught out. 'May I?' he said, turning the screen to show Louise. 'I was thinking about those stones we saw this morning and thought I'd do a bit of digging. There's no mention of them, and it could be a coincidence . . .'

'Get to the point,' said Louise.

'Oh, sorry,' said Miles, pressing a button on the keyboard. 'As I said, it could be nothing, but I found out there was a missing persons case in the area fifty years ago. Around the time Jeremy Latchford was born.'

Louise read through the case file on Miles's screen.

'Ben Carter. Ten years old. Body never found,' said Miles.

'So I see.'

'See where he lived?'

Louise scrolled down to the address, which was less than four hundred yards from the Latchford house.

# Chapter Twenty-Four

Louise felt conspicuously overdressed the following day at work, wearing a more formal business suit than usual in preparation for her meeting with the assistant chief. She was pleased she'd talked things through with Thomas. It felt like they would be able to get things at home sorted once their workloads settled down, and with the children staying with her parents for the week, she'd been able to spend the evening researching the disappearance of Ben Carter fifty years ago.

Why the case didn't appear in the notes of Hugo Latchford's disappearance was a bit of a mystery. She put it down to the fact that Hugo had gone missing in a completely different area, but she was surprised the investigating officers at the time either hadn't found out about Ben Carter, or hadn't thought it a link worth investigating. It was even more strange considering the boy had disappeared in a similar fashion, having gone out to play one weekend, albeit alone, and never returned.

Louise had been unable to uncover any direct link between the Carter family and the Verdant Circle, but the proximity to both the Latchford house and the druid's altar meant she wasn't about to give up on the theory anytime soon.

'Sorry I'm late, ma'am,' said Miles, out of breath as he arrived in the incident room.

Louise noted he was wearing a well-fitting suit, shirt and tie, which was better than his usual attire. She wondered if he'd heard the assistant chief was stopping by that afternoon. She'd been very impressed with the young man in the last couple of weeks, and it was clear he was very ambitious.

Louise had arranged to meet Jeremy's mother, Evelyn, at the care home in Somerton later that day. Prior to that, Miles drove to the address in Taunton that Valerie had given them yesterday. But there was no answer as they rang the doorbell at the terraced house. Louise peered through the front window, the remnants of a mini house party clear through the net curtains. Louise rang the bell again, but if there were any occupants in the house they were still in bed and not moving.

Louise had wanted to quiz Valerie about Jeremy's childhood, hoping to find out if she had any knowledge of the Ben Carter disappearance, sure that such a thing would have left a lasting impression on the area, even if it had happened in the distant past. After a third try on the doorbell proved unfruitful, she left a message on Valerie's phone asking her to get in contact at her earliest convenience.

The drive to Somerton took fifteen minutes. The heatwave was continuing, and Louise left her suit jacket in the car. The care home was a red-brick building that had been converted from a number of residential properties. Louise had visited many care homes over the years. It was hard to know what to expect. Many of the places she'd visited, especially since the pandemic had caused so much damage, felt understaffed. She'd always had a deep respect for the care workers who manned these places, and it felt criminal how so many were undervalued for the work they did.

The care home's duty manager, Janet Thornton, greeted them. Louise had spoken to her yesterday and arranged the appointment. She'd explained how Evelyn suffered from dementia and was often not very responsive. 'I think you've caught her on a good day . . . But be warned she can turn just like that,' said Janet now, as she guided them to a room on the ground floor. 'You have some guests today, Evelyn,' she said to a woman who was sitting in an armchair watching television.

'Hello, Evelyn. My name is Louise, and this is Miles.'

Evelyn looked them both up and down. 'Well, don't just stand there,' she said, her voice a deep rasp. 'Take a seat.'

'I'll leave you to it,' said Janet. 'You know where we are, Evelyn.'

'Yes, yes. Treats me like a child, that one,' said Evelyn, once Janet was out of earshot. 'Police, aren't you?'

'That's right,' said Louise.

'Is this about my Hugo?'

'In part, yes.'

Evelyn's eyes were downcast. 'I've seen the news. Surprised none of you came to see me sooner.'

'It must be hard, going through all this again.'

'It's like nothing has changed. I was sitting in this very same seat when I was told he'd disappeared, and I was sitting here when his name came up on the television. At least he can rest now, I suppose.'

Louise nodded. 'Who told you he'd gone missing the first time?' she asked, trying to keep her questioning light.

'Jeremy.'

'Your son?'

Evelyn squinted, her rich blue eyes studying Louise with interest. 'They think I'm doolally here, and I think I am half the time. It's a bit like being drunk. My memory comes and goes. I couldn't tell you how long ago it was when Jeremy told me Hugo had gone missing, but I can see it crystal clear in my head. Ask me what I was doing last night, I couldn't tell you. It will happen to both of you, mark my words. You're young, you think it won't, but it will. And let me tell you, it's the worst of all worlds.'

Louise could relate. She'd seen similar changes in her parents, particularly her father, these last couple of years. Small things like forgotten sentences, and mispronunciations, more impactful due to their insignificance. 'When was the last time you saw your son, Evelyn?'

Evelyn sat up straight. 'I don't know. Not long after, I think.'

'Not long after?' said Miles.

'You're a big 'un, aren't you? Not long after . . . Hugo.'

'That was twelve years ago,' said Louise.

Evelyn looked away. 'Was it?'

Feeling the conversation drifting, Louise asked Evelyn what she knew about Ben Carter.

Evelyn looked confused, and Louise was wondering if the conversation was over when she said, 'I remember. Strange family. Lee, that was my husband, used to call them hippies. Guess you can't call them that now, can you. They were a bit odd, but I didn't have a problem with them. The parents used to dress funny. Flower clothes, colours in their hair before it became a thing.'

'And the boy?' said Miles.

'Hugo?' said Evelyn, wide-eyed.

'No, Ben Carter,' said Louise, softly.

Evelyn looked at them both, her mouth open as she struggled to recollect. 'Oh, yes, the Carter boy. Mute. Never said a word. Different times then, of course. He used to go out into the woods. One day he never came back.'

'What did you think when it happened?'

'What do you mean, what did I think?'

'Did you think there was more to it than him simply disappearing?'

'I was pregnant with Jeremy then. I felt sorry for them, but I just guessed those things happened. It was very sad.'

'How did your husband feel about it all?' asked Louise, something changing in Evelyn as she asked the question, as if the colour had faded slightly from her eyes.

'I'm feeling very tired now,' said Evelyn, looking at Louise and Miles as if she didn't know who they were.

Louise thanked her, and called on Janet, who sent in one of her assistants to tend to Evelyn.

'Sounds like you got a lot out of her. Sometimes they get like that, all the excitement wears them out.'

Louise understood how Evelyn felt she was being infantilised, but she didn't comment. 'You obviously keep track of everyone who visits. Would you be able to give me a list of who has visited Evelyn recently?'

'No need, I'm afraid. I've worked here for the last nine years, and in that time she's never had a visitor.'

# Chapter Twenty-Five

The meeting with Evelyn Latchford had left Louise with more questions than answers. But for now, she took that as a positive. Both the Carter parents were dead, and it was as if Evelyn Latchford was the sole carrier of the memory of Ben Carter. Louise couldn't help but wonder if there was a cave somewhere holding Ben Carter's remains, and if the Verdant Circle were responsible.

'Imagine putting your mother in care, and never seeing her in all this time,' said Miles, as they headed back to headquarters.

'Happens a lot more than you'd imagine,' said Louise, checking the time. 'I want you to look into Ben Carter's disappearance when we get back. See if you can speak to anyone from that time. I know the file is threadbare at present, but let's see if we can find any link to the Verdant Circle.'

Miles nodded. 'From what I can ascertain, they were formed two years prior to Ben Carter going missing. Beginning to feel like a hell of a coincidence.'

'Let's not jump to any conclusions,' said Louise, though she couldn't deny it had crossed her mind.

As they arrived back at headquarters, she thought further about the impact Ben Carter's disappearance would have had on a young Jeremy Latchford. It had happened before his time, but he would surely have known that Ben Carter had disappeared in the same area where he'd played as a child. Could Carter's disappearance have given him nightmares, or provoked his imagination enough that he had tried to recreate the disappearance as an adult?

Louise understood she was getting ahead of herself, but there was no harm in thinking along these lines. It gave her another reason to speak to Valerie Latchford. If anyone would have insight into Jeremy's thinking, it was her. Though who Louise really wanted to speak to was Jeremy himself, and the silence on that front, coupled with the anonymous call they'd received the other night from the scared woman, was increasingly making her uneasy.

Assistant Chief Constable Brightman was already in CID. He was with Robertson, the door shut, and Louise was surprised to feel herself getting nervous. Even so, it felt like a distraction she could do without. Her workload was bigger than ever, and she wanted to make some more inroads in locating Ella Gosling before the day was out.

She added Evelyn Latchford's name to the crime board, and adjacent to Hugo Latchford wrote the name Ben Carter, accompanied by a giant question mark.

'Ah, Louise, how are things progressing?'

Louise turned around to see Brightman, who'd crept up on her with Robertson. He was all smiles, and Louise was reminded of how supportive he'd been ever since taking up the position following the departure of Morley and the imprisonment of her former colleague Tim Finch.

'We're making headway, sir,' she said.

'Ben Carter?'

'Another missing person, from fifty years ago. He lived a few doors down from where Hugo Latchford eventually lived.'

Robertson's eyebrows darted up high on his brow, and Louise had to stifle a laugh. 'News has just come to light,' she said, for his benefit.

'Intriguing,' said Brightman, walking off.

'We'll be ready for you in fifteen,' said Robertson. 'Conference room three.'

The interview was less formal than Louise had anticipated. For the majority of it, Brightman talked about his plans for the restructuring of the department. Louise quizzed him over her potential role and voiced how she would be keen to keep a more hands-on aspect. Brightman didn't raise any objections. Everything remained professional, and Louise was pleased there were no questions about her family beyond a polite inquiry as to how Jack was getting on.

'Yours to lose,' said Robertson, when she met him later in his office.

'They must be interviewing other candidates?'

'Naturally, but you've got everyone's vote. Even mine.'

'Heartening to know.'

'Let's make the application official, shall we?' said Robertson.

Louise gave out a mock sigh. 'If it will get you off my back, then fine.'

After completing the formal application for the DCI role, Louise returned to the Hugo Latchford investigation. She studied the crime board, searching through all the connections, willing her brain to find something among the names and incidents.

The Ben Carter disappearance was still at the forefront in her mind. As Miles had mentioned, the disappearance had occurred two years after the believed start date of the Verdant Circle. The lead investigating officer had passed away, and after trawling through the archives of news stories it appeared there had been little about the disappearance in the press.

Louise thought about Evelyn Latchford, alone and unloved in her care home. If Ben Carter's disappearance had had any effect on Jeremy Latchford years later, then what had Evelyn thought at the time? Pregnant with Jeremy, the disappearance of a neighbour's child must have played on her psyche. Had it also affected the way she had brought Jeremy up? Had she become overprotective, not giving him the space to flourish? Had this eventually impacted on his development? And what about when, nearly forty years later, her grandchild went missing? It must have been like all her nightmares coming true, a cruel example of history repeating itself.

Flicking through her notebook, Louise stopped at the entry in which she'd recorded how Evelyn had discussed her husband's dismissive description of Ben Carter's parents as hippies. She did a preliminary search of Lee Latchford in the database, to find that Jeremy's father had a long criminal record. The entries stopped three years after Jeremy was born, his convictions all violence-related, including a six-month stretch for GBH involving a nasty incident at a local bar when an intoxicated Lee Latchford had hospitalised a local man.

It was another indication that Jeremy Latchford's childhood might not have been ideal.

Louise rechecked the notes on the investigation into Ben Carter's disappearance. She was staggered to discover that Lee Latchford hadn't even been questioned. Here was someone with a long history of violence, who lived a few doors down from the family, and he didn't appear anywhere in the report. It wasn't the first oversight she'd seen in a police investigation, and it was possible that Lee had been interviewed, or ruled out for a simple reason, but it left more unanswered questions for her.

Miles walked over from his desk and told her he'd made contact with another of the Carters' neighbours from that time. Marion Parker was a widow who now lived in Weston. She'd lived next door to the Carters at the time Ben had disappeared. 'She can see us tomorrow. That's where you live, isn't it?'

'Don't get too familiar now, Miles,' said Louise, teasing.

'Sorry, I just thought I could drive and meet you there.'

'I'm kidding, Miles. That sounds like a plan. Before you leave, I need you to do one more thing,' she said, showing him the file on Lee Latchford. 'I want to see inside the house Jeremy Latchford was brought up in. Get on to Legal, see if they can make contact with the Verdant Circle team. If they've got nothing to hide, then there's no reason to stop us searching the place.'

'Sure thing. You really think they'll let us look around so easily?'

'Probably not. But make sure we drop in Ben Carter's name as well. Let them think we could potentially have enough to get a warrant. See if that makes them spring into action.'

Miles nodded and walked back to his desk.

'And don't be late tomorrow morning,' said Louise, logging off.

# Chapter Twenty-Six

By Friday evening, Fi was already feeling better. Denise brought her more food when she dropped Max off early evening. Fi tried to fight the feelings of paranoia, but hadn't she caught a questioning look from her friend as she'd handed the paper bag over, as if she were surprised Fi was feeling more herself?

'How was your day?' Fi asked Max, who barged past her and into the caravan, pouring himself a drink of water. It was good to see her son thriving, but it would have been nice if he'd at least given her a hug. She watched him drink, and tried to banish thoughts of the images she'd seen in Silas's book.

'He's had a great time. He stayed on with us afterwards and helped around camp,' said Denise.

'"Us"?'

'Silas and some of the others.'

Fi held her tongue. Denise's initial reservations about Silas had seemingly disappeared. Fi wanted to scream at her friend that Silas wasn't the man they thought he was, that she'd been right to be scared of him, but it wasn't the right time. Denise was standing by the front door, as if she expected to be invited in, but Fi didn't want any guests. She needed to see what a clear night's sleep would do for her. To see if it would make her re-evaluate exactly what was going in camp. 'You seem to be getting friendly with this Silas,' she said, hoping Denise didn't read too much into what she was saying.

'He's a great guy. He's really helping. Lots of ideas, you know. He was asking after you.'

'That's nice. Hopefully I can come with you tomorrow and chat to him some more.'

'That would be fantastic. I thought you were looking better. I'm sure Silas would love that.'

Fi noted the smile on Denise's face but wasn't sure she could trust it. She wondered if Denise had seen the book, or if she was working with Silas selling drugs in the camp. 'So, I'll see you in the morning?' she said, still blocking the path into the caravan.

'Oh, OK. Yes, see you in the morning,' said Denise, walking off.

Later, with the milk poured down the sink, Fi picked at her food. Was it coincidence that more than forty-eight hours after taking her last drop of milk, she felt so much better? It was hard to believe that someone was trying to poison her, and more so that Denise was involved, but it wouldn't be the strangest thing to happen at the camp. They were technically a collective, but all groups had leaders. She and Pete had accepted that from the beginning. They'd managed to all but mess their lives up, so it was no hardship to accept that others could do a better job of organising them.

The leaders were subtle. They made you think you were doing things because you wanted to. But there were rumours. Members left all the time, some by choice, others by force. Fi had been told that those who didn't want to leave were often *persuaded*.

And then there were those other rumours, the ones she tried not to think about; the ones that linked to what she'd seen in the

155

book. The hierarchical structure meant there were divisions within the camp. Fi had always thought she would slowly make her way up that invisible ladder, but it appeared she was where she'd always been, while Denise had seemingly moved on and was hanging out with Teresa Willow and the other elders. Why this had happened, she wasn't sure, and maybe her time was coming, but at that moment she doubted anything would change for her.

Those higher up in the pecking order usually had more freedom to move from camp to camp, and were invited to secret ceremonies and events that people like Fi never got to see. Fi had never been bothered by it before, but after seeing the images in Silas's book, she couldn't help but imagine what went on at these events. It was risky to talk about such things, but gossip was rife, and ever since the news had reached the camp about the bones being found in Banwell Caves there had been an edge. She knew some people had left since then, and she wondered what would happen if she tried to leave with Max. She was supposed to be able to leave at any time, but what if they stopped her?

Fi watched Max gently snoring. She'd been so sure this was the right life for him, and perhaps it still could be. Maybe what she needed to do was test the limits of the group. Make up some story about wanting to visit a family member and see how they responded.

She pulled Max's blanket over his shoulders, realising her hand was trembling, and kissed him on the forehead. She shouldn't be feeling this way. If the thought of asking to leave was making her this nervous, then this couldn't be the right place for her. And if that was the case, she needed to find a way to leave without being detected.

# Chapter Twenty-Seven

Thomas arrived home early, and it was the first time since Louise had returned to work that they'd eaten together as a family.

'I miss this,' she said, as she watched Jack joyfully shovelling food into his mouth.

'Me too,' said Thomas. 'How was the meeting with Brightman?'

'Bit strange, really. Very informal. Robertson says it's mine to lose.'

'Glad to see he's keeping the motivational speeches going. So, what do you think?'

'You know me, I've been giving this investigation all my attention.'

Thomas had worked with her on a number of investigations during his time on the force. He understood how focused, border-line obsessed, she could become during an investigation. One of the things she loved him for was how well he understood that, and the fact he'd never tried to change her in any way. 'I'm sure you'll make the right decision,' he said, picking up a beaker that Jack had dropped, the boy frowning until he handed it back to him.

'It's our decision to make, Tom.'

'I know, I know. You know I'll support you either way.'

*Would leaving the police mean more evenings like this?* she thought, as she bathed Jack and put him to bed, then read Emily a night-time story before her niece fell asleep. It felt idyllic, but it wouldn't always be like this. Life would naturally change as both children got older, and the thought of being out of work, out of a role she'd been in since graduation, made her nervous, and so she forced it out of her mind as she spent the rest of the evening watching mindless television on the sofa with Thomas.

In the morning, things were more of a rush. Thomas left early for work, and she only just managed to drop Emily off at school in time before heading to Yvonne's with Jack. Thirty minutes later, she was in Worle, next to Castle Batch park, where Miles was already waiting for her.

'I got you a coffee on the off-chance,' Miles said, joining her in the car, ten minutes ahead of their scheduled meeting with Lee and Evelyn Latchford's former neighbour, Marion Parker.

'Just what I need,' said Louise, taking a drink. 'I'd like you to take the lead today, Miles. Keep it light, but let's find out a bit more about that time when Ben Carter went missing. I want to know about the Carters, but I'd also like to know what Mrs Parker knew about the Latchfords.'

Miles couldn't hide his smile as he left the car. It was great to see his enthusiasm, and Louise hoped it was something he could maintain through his career.

Marion Parker lived in a well-positioned semi-detached house next to the park. A dog started barking as they rang the doorbell, a tall striking woman in her seventies answering the door, a wriggling Jack Russell in her arms. 'Yes?' she said.

Louise nodded to Miles. 'Mrs Parker? DC Miles Boothroyd and DI Louise Blackwell. We spoke yesterday on the phone.'

Mrs Parker studied their IDs in turn before allowing them access. 'Come on through, it's not much, but it's home,' she said, placing her dog on the ground as she walked towards her living room.

'Quite a collection,' said Miles, his eyes wide as he looked at the shelves covering every wall in the room, each packed with dolls of various shapes and sizes.

Mrs Parker frowned. She had striking features, with high cheekbones and large brown eyes. Louise noted the wear on her skin, patches of discolouration below a mole underneath her right eye. 'I'm not crazy, if that's what you think. I'm a collector, and I repair and restore for other people. I don't think they're my babies or anything,' she said, staring straight at Miles as if issuing a challenge. 'At least, not all of them,' she added, winking at Louise. 'Take a seat. Can I get you something to drink?'

'We're fine, Mrs Parker,' said Louise, easing down on the sofa and nodding to Miles to do the same.

'New, is he?' said Mrs Parker. 'You scared of the dolls?'

'Only a bit,' said Miles, with a nervous laugh. 'Thank you for taking the time to speak to us, Mrs Parker.'

'This is about those bones found in the caves? Terrible business.'

'Yes, in a way. The remains that were found belonged to Hugo Latchford.'

'I know,' said Mrs Parker, defiantly. 'The Latchfords were neighbours of mine. Never met the boy though. I left that place before he came along.'

'Did you get on well with them?'

'Lee and Evelyn Latchford? Long time ago now. The dad was a drunk, that I do remember. Always getting into some sort of bother. Never understood what Evelyn saw in him. I felt sorry for her when she was pregnant, but then I never had kids so what do I know?'

'You lived next door to the Carters?' said Miles.

'You asking or telling?' said Mrs Parker, shaking her head and smiling at Louise. 'Yes, they were my neighbours. Odd bunch, but very nice.'

'Odd in what way?' asked Miles.

'Into the environment in a big way, before it all became so popular. They did their best to recycle, even got me involved. It was devastating what happened to them.'

After a shaky start, Louise was pleased to see Miles taking control of the interview. 'Did you know the boy – Ben – well?' he said.

'Not really. He was very shy. I mean very. You would say hello to him and he would cower behind his parents.'

'But they let him go out on his own?'

'Like them, he loved nature. His mother said that was where he was happiest. That's what happened back then. Kids had more freedom. Parents would let them roam, and see them when they got home. Feel sorry for them now. I go over to the park nowadays, and if you see any kids over the age of ten, they're all on their phones. Back then they were free.'

'I know it was a long time ago, but what can you tell me about the time when Ben went missing?'

For the first time since they'd arrived, Louise noted the confidence drain from Mrs Parker's features. 'Such a terrible thing. They left it so late. It was dark when they knocked at my house, and they hadn't even called the police. We searched the hills as best we could but we never found anything, not a trace of clothing, nothing.'

'You were questioned by the police at the time?'

'Yes, told them what I'm telling you. It was a long time ago,' said Mrs Parker, once more turning towards Louise.

'What do you think happened to him?'

'I think he was taken. Don't know by who or what, but I couldn't get out of that place quick enough. I felt bad for those poor parents, but I couldn't live there any more. When I found out about that Latchford child the other week, I just didn't know what to think. Too much to hope it was a coincidence.'

'Did you ever suspect Lee Latchford had anything to do with it?'

Mrs Parker's face was scrunched in concentration. 'I think he had an alibi if memory serves. Been in the pub all day, for a change. He's not still alive, is he? I thought his liver would have killed him by now.'

Miles shook his head and looked at Louise. There was no mention of an alibi in the reports. But if Lee Latchford hadn't been a suspect, then it wouldn't necessarily have been included. 'Lee Latchford died ten years ago,' he said.

Mrs Parker nodded. 'Before or after his grandson disappeared?'

Miles didn't respond.

She shrugged. 'I'll be honest, I never thought about him having anything to do with it, but now you mention it, it's something I can certainly imagine. I guess that's not much use to you now, is it?'

'Did you ever hear about any groups in the area?' asked Miles.

'Groups?'

'From what we understand, the area where you used to live in Frome has attracted a lot of environmental groups over the years.'

Mrs Parker nodded. 'Yes, that's right. I do remember a few times when there were lots of people in the area. They would sometimes camp in the summer months. Locals didn't like it but I always found them very respectable.'

'Was there ever any suspicion that they were involved?' said Miles.

Mrs Parker shot the young officer a look that bordered on the condescending. 'I don't know, son, I wasn't running the investigation, and that was fifty years ago.'

'But nothing you heard at the time. Nothing the Carters said to you?'

'I didn't really speak to them much after their boy went missing. I offered my help, but how do you help a family in that situation. The last time I spoke to them was the day I left. I said sorry and never saw them again. Always felt bad about that.'

Miles glanced at Louise, who nodded. 'You've been very helpful, Mrs Parker, thank you.'

'And you've been charming company,' said Mrs Parker, glancing at Louise with a sly grin. 'Do come again.'

# Chapter Twenty-Eight

That evening, Louise took Emily and Jack to the Grand Pier. As Jack dozed in his pushchair, Louise guided her niece around the noisy machines with their flashing lights and wondered how anyone could sleep in the presence of such a cacophony. She even let Emily try the grabber machine, and was surprised when she managed to win a cuddly Dumbo on the first go.

'I've been coming here since I was your age, and I've never won anything, do you know that?' she said, delighted to see the joy in the young girl's face.

Thomas was due late home that night, so she took the children to a local Greek restaurant, the Kalimera, owned by her long-term friend Georgina. Georgina was impossibly glamorous, her hair and make-up faultless, and she picked Emily up in her arms. 'Nice of you to pop by,' she said, glaring at Louise.

'I know, it's been a while, sorry. Back at work now.'

'Ah, the beautiful busy police lady. Sit – I will send someone over to take your order.'

For the second day in a row, Louise experienced a sense of normality, eating in the restaurant she'd visited on a daily basis when she'd first moved to Weston, and more recently for much of her maternity leave with a fractious group of mothers in her

NCT group. Despite this, her thoughts soon returned to the Hugo Latchford investigation.

After speaking to Mrs Parker, she'd added Lee Latchford to the crime board. It was less than ideal, having the deceased man as a potential suspect for both Hugo and Ben Carter's disappearances, but his criminal record and proximity to both boys when they'd gone missing meant he had to be considered.

Louise reread his testimony from the time Hugo had gone missing. He'd moved to Keynsham by this point and had claimed to be estranged from Jeremy and Valerie, having accused his son of robbing his house from him. He'd told the investigating officer that he hadn't seen Hugo in two years, and had a verified alibi for the time Hugo went missing.

Louise discovered that Evelyn and Lee had sold the house to their son when Jeremy and Valerie got married, Lee having moved out three years previously.

The rest of the afternoon was taken up with requests to gain access to the old Latchford house, but no one from the Verdant Circle was responding. Louise had checked with Legal, and they were sure there was no chance of getting a warrant at the moment. What Louise expected to see there, she wasn't sure, but the connection between Hugo Latchford and Ben Carter was obvious, and she needed to see the house that both Jeremy and his son had been brought up in for herself.

'Party next week. We're doing a barbecue on the beach,' said Georgina, handing Louise a flyer.

'Next Saturday.'

'The solstice. Longest day of the year.'

'Something tells me we won't be able to make it, but I'll do my best. Now, I need to get these two sleepyheads home,' said Louise, hugging Georgina goodbye as she wondered what, if anything, was in store for her this coming week.

◆ ◆ ◆

Louise was reminded of the solstice when she glanced at the flyer from Georgina the following day. She checked the date Ben Carter had gone missing, noting it was three weeks before the summer solstice of that year. Hugo had gone missing two months after the summer solstice, so that didn't give them anything to work with. If he'd been held in captivity for some time after his disappearance, as the remains would suggest, then it was feasible he had been held in captivity until the following solstice, but that wasn't something Louise was going to even consider at present. The idea that the Verdant Circle could be involved in human sacrifice still seemed far-fetched, and for now she felt it best to focus on the connection between the father and son, Lee and Jeremy Latchford, and the first missing boy, Ben Carter.

Louise felt guilty going to work on a Sunday, and it was a wrench leaving everyone during breakfast. Miles was the only officer in the incident room when she arrived at headquarters. 'Any news from the Verdant Circle?' she asked.

'I've left messages again. I'll keep doing it. I could always pay their headquarters a visit. But it's all the way up in the Lake District.'

Louise frowned. 'Keep trying. If they're not answering then I doubt their offices are manned. I'll get on to DI Pepperstone, see if he's willing to help.'

Pepperstone continued being elusive, only returning her call in the late afternoon. She updated him on the Ben Carter disappearance, noting the pause before he answered.

She could hear his nasal breathing down the line as he considered his response. 'Any record of this family having links with the VC?' he said.

'Not from our end.'

'I didn't even know about this before. Bit of a tentative link?'

'Two boys from the same street disappearing?'

'Come on, Louise, it was forty years apart, and Hugo Latchford wasn't living there when he disappeared.'

Louise knew he was right, but the connection between the two incidents meant she couldn't rule anything out. 'Do you have a name for anyone in the Verdant Circle we can speak to? We've been trying to get access to the Latchford house but there's no response.'

'You've been trying their headquarters?' asked Pepperstone, laughter in his voice.

'Sham?'

'Sure is. The best person to speak to would be Teresa Willow, but I understand she's not your number one fan.'

'No, we're not the best of friends.'

'Leave it with me, I'll see what I can do,' said Pepperstone, hanging up.

Louise wasn't holding her breath. She made some calls and searched for more phone numbers for the Verdant group but felt like she was being sent in circles. She considered returning to the site in Priddy to speak to Teresa Willow, but as Pepperstone had stated she wasn't on good terms with the lawyer, who wouldn't give her any help without being forced.

Louise stared at the crime board as if willing answers from the photographs and names. The date of the solstice had already been added, and again she wondered about its relevance. Making one more failed attempt to contact the Verdant Circle hierarchy, Louise eventually decided to change tack.

If they wouldn't let her speak to them, then she needed to get them to come to her. The connection between Ben Carter and

Hugo Latchford wasn't public knowledge, but it could be. Working with the press was a dicey game at best. Sometimes it could be beneficial, but Louise had had more than one negative experience involving journalists in the past. For now, however, she could see no other way. She'd built up a number of contacts over the years, and so she decided to call Giles Manning, a senior reporter for one of the national broadsheets.

'Louise, good to hear from you,' he said, answering on the second ring. 'How's your bag of bones case going?'

Louise was impressed but not surprised that he knew about the Hugo Latchford investigation. It may not have made the national news, but Giles wasn't a chief crime reporter for no reason.

'It's why I'm calling,' said Louise, telling him about the latest developments with Ben Carter.

'Could be intriguing. But why are you really calling me, Louise?'

'No pulling the wool over your eyes, is there? I was hoping you could help me . . . In exchange for exclusive access, obviously.'

'I'm not sure there's enough here for me to run anything. Not yet.'

'I think there could be a longer piece in the pipeline for you, Giles. There is something going on with the Verdant Circle. I don't need much, but it would be great to get their name out there. Even if it meant embarrassing them into speaking.'

'But what exactly is it that you have?'

Louise knew she had to be careful. 'I'm sure you're aware of where Hugo Latchford used to live as a child. Less than a stone's throw from Ben Carter,' she said.

'OK . . .'

'And I'm sure you're aware of the significance of that area to the Verdant Circle with the druid's altar.'

'I see,' said Giles, as if the significance was only now dawning on him. 'OK, Louise. I'll try and join the dots.'

'And you'll remember how I've helped you in the past?'

'Of course, leave it with me,' said Giles, hanging up.

# Chapter Twenty-Nine

The camp was busier than Fi could remember it. It was the first day she'd been in the main section of the camp since the night she'd called the police, having been all but confined to her caravan. She was sure everyone's eyes were on her, and did her best to ignore them as she dropped Max at his school and headed back through the woods.

'Glad to see you're feeling better.'

Fi turned to see Silas approaching her. 'Much better, thank you,' said Fi, looking around, only to find they were alone. She felt her blood pumping through her veins, and knew how important it was to act like everything was fine.

'Things are in full swing for the solstice celebrations,' said Silas, holding his ground.

The mention of the solstice turned her stomach. Both the solstices were important times in camp. She remembered the fevered celebrations last summer, the singing and dancing going on for days despite the continued rain, and it made her recall the images she'd seen in Silas's book. If the weather continued as it was, it would be much different this time.

She couldn't recall the last time she'd felt the rain on her body. Heaven knew, the land needed it. The woodland was tinder-dry, and it was as if an invisible weight was hanging over the place. 'Max is very excited about it.'

'Wonderful to hear, speak to you soon,' said Silas, standing stock-still so she had to walk around him.

If Fi had her way, it would be the last time they ever spoke. She'd spent every waking moment of late thinking about everything that had happened over the last few weeks. She'd come to the conclusion that it didn't matter if she was being paranoid. Even if she was completely wrong about what was happening, and the danger she perceived when it came to Silas, she needed to get out.

Not that she doubted the man was a predator of some sort. To her, it was like an aura he was shrouded in. She hated knowing he'd been near her son, after seeing that hateful book, and never wanted to see him again.

But it wasn't just him. She realised now that she'd been so desperate for this place to work, that she'd remained blinkered to its reality. Even when Pete was here, she'd sensed something was off. He had been more vocal about his concerns, whereas she had tried to make it work, knowing that if it didn't work here, there was nowhere else to go.

That was her main concern now as she took her place in the kitchen, trying her best to ignore the sly glances and hushed conversations as she pulled on her apron and hairnet.

'I didn't know you were coming back today,' said Denise, rushing over to her as if she wanted to get her out of the place.

'I thought I'd surprise you,' said Fi, thinking how much better she'd felt since she'd stopped drinking the milk.

'Great, great. Well, just take it easy. Let me know if you need a rest.'

Fi nodded and began preparing the day's vegetables. It was all but impossible now to consider anyone here a true friend, someone she could trust. Most in the camp were in the same situation as she was. They'd given up everything to be here, and in doing so had made themselves vulnerable. Fi was sure they'd all joined with good intentions, and the majority still thought it was the right place to be. But there had always been a number dissatisfied with their life here, and Fi understood now that she'd chosen to ignore those obvious signs.

The day passed slowly. If it had been as easy as getting up and leaving, then she would have done just that, but she would be leaving soon, one way or another.

The sly looks continued through the day. She fought the feeling that everyone knew her plans.

After work, she went to the school area to find that Max had already left, one of the ad hoc teachers telling her he was out playing with his friends in the woods.

She walked back alone, the track that had once filled her with joy now provoking nothing but dread. She was reminded of how isolated they were out here in the woods. She thought again about Silas's book and – despite her best efforts – pictured Max as one of the helpless children being taken to the cave. She blinked the image away, and decided she could use her isolation to her advantage.

She dropped her bag at the caravan, and checked that no one was watching before heading out into the woodland. It truly was a wonderful part of the country here, and not for the first time Fi wished things could be different. Life was far from comfortable as part of the group, but it was a way of living she could have accepted. It was amazing to be so close to nature, and she would miss that the most.

And they did make a difference. Only recently, one of their groups had helped stop a planned fracking development in the north-east. But the cost was too much. Paranoid or not, she needed Max out of there, and escaping seemed the most sensible route.

She walked deeper into the woods. In the distance she could hear traffic, and she marked a number of trees, positioning stones by the trunks every twenty or thirty yards, until she reached the clearing where she had seen the policewoman the other week.

Drenched in sweat, she continued on, fearing that any second Silas or Denise would appear and stop her. But she reached the road without incident, and froze as a car rushed by inches from where she stood.

It was ludicrous to feel this way. She wasn't supposed to be a prisoner, yet that was how she felt. The rumours and folklore had got to her, and the book she'd found in Silas's caravan had convinced her that now was the time.

She walked further along the road, the tarmac softening beneath her feet in the blazing sun. It crossed her mind to keep on walking, to reach the nearest police station and share her concerns. Even if they laughed her out of there, surely they would come for Max. The group had no hold over him, and child safety was always a priority.

But she couldn't take the risk. She jumped back on to the verge as a lorry swept around the corner, and hurried back into the woods. At least she now knew the route. If she could make her way back to camp unnoticed then she would have a plan, a way to get her and Max out of here for good. And then it would just be a case of putting that plan into action.

# Chapter Thirty

Louise was a little surprised the following morning to see that the journo, Manning, had been true to his word. A small article had been posted on the newspaper's website, and he had dropped her a line to say the story would appear in the print run later that day. Louise's name was mentioned as the lead investigator in the report, which she hoped would be enough to prompt some sort of response.

At headquarters, she tried the numbers for the Verdant Circle, still with no answer, and the first response she received to the article was from DI Pepperstone at the station later that morning.

'Can I have a word?' he said, walking over to the desk in the incident room Louise had been using of late, as if he were in charge of the whole investigation.

Louise continued looking at her laptop for a few seconds until she was ready to speak to him. His unhappiness was obvious, and more than one person was sneaking a look at them. 'Good to see you, Gerrard. Give me five minutes and we can speak in my office. It's through there,' she said, pointing towards the main CID.

Pepperstone's breathing was erratic, as if he'd run up the stairs to the room. 'I'd rather speak now.'

'Just finishing off something. Help yourself to a drink from the kitchen. Mine's a black coffee.'

Pepperstone hesitated before heading off, Louise keeping her eyes on her screen until he'd left the room. Ten minutes later she joined him outside her office, noting he hadn't made her a coffee. 'Come through,' she said.

'What the hell is going on?' said Pepperstone, before she'd even sat down.

Louise noted the glances heading their way and closed the office door. 'I don't know how it is where you work, but here it's considered bad form to come into someone else's nick and start mouthing off.'

Pepperstone sat without invitation. 'Oh, get over yourself, Louise.'

'No, you get over yourself, Gerrard. I don't care what your current grievance is, I will not have you speaking to me like that in front of my colleagues.'

Pepperstone's face reddened. Louise stared at him, listening to his laboured breathing. 'Fine, I apologise. I hope you will give me the same courtesy.'

'What are you talking about, Gerrard?'

'Don't try that one. You know fine well. Your little article in the paper today.'

'I'm not a journalist.'

'I know you're behind it, so drop the charade.'

'What is your exact issue?' asked Louise.

'Do I have to spell it out to you? Seven years I've been working on this case, and here you are a few weeks in, jeopardising everything.'

'By a small article in a newspaper?'

'Yes. It wasn't your call, Louise. Who knows how the VC will respond to this. We have things in place to bring them down, but this could cause them to close ranks.'

'I think you're being a tad paranoid.'

'So, you didn't get that journo to publish your story simply to get a response from the VC?'

'Even if I did, so what? I'm working on a possible murder investigation. I have tried my best to cooperate with you, but I need results as much as you do. Possibly more so. There could be others in danger.'

'Seems like we're going around in circles here.'

'I'm open to working with you, Gerrard, but I need to speak to the Verdant Circle.'

Pepperstone stood. 'I hear you might be going for a promotion,' he said, making it sound like a threat.

Louise laughed. 'You'll need to do better than that, DI Pepperstone. Now, how about you get the hell out of my office?'

Louise spent most of the afternoon fielding calls from other media outlets, as well as having a terse conversation with the head of the constabulary's PR team, who tried to instruct her that all interactions with the national press should go through them. Even DCI Robertson had a quiet word with her later in the afternoon, and Louise had to bite her tongue when he suggested that going against protocol could have a detrimental effect on her promotion chances.

Although she hadn't admitted anything, she began to think that she might have made a mistake. The article had done nothing to provoke a response from the Verdant Circle, and as patronising and full of himself as Pepperstone was, it would probably have made more sense to have kept the DI on her side for the time being.

That all changed when a phone call came in for her as she was leaving for the day.

'DI Blackwell, this is Taylor Betancur. I am Ella Gosling's personal assistant,' said the man on the other end of the line.

'How may I help you, Mr Betancur?' said Louise, unable to fight the surge of adrenaline in her system.

'I understand from your numerous phone calls that you would like to speak to one of the patrons of our charitable trust.'

'I was beginning to think you didn't exist.'

Betancur replied as if he hadn't heard her comment. 'Mrs Gosling will be at home tomorrow morning and has agreed to meet you to discuss any questions you may have.'

'Thank you, when would—'

'Nine thirty a.m. I'll text you the address,' said Betancur, before hanging up.

# Chapter Thirty-One

Jack and Emily were both asleep as Louise left early the next day. She kissed them and Thomas goodbye before heading out into the dark morning. She took a sip of coffee from her Thermos flask, then started her car and drove into Weston, which was glorious in the quiet of the early morning, the town still sleeping as she made her way up the Locking Road towards Worle, where she'd agreed to meet Miles in the supermarket car park.

Ella Gosling lived near Ironbridge in Shropshire. They had a long journey ahead of them if they were to get there in time. Miles squeezed himself into the passenger seat of Louise's vehicle. A quick glance suggested he hadn't long been up. His face was puffy, and his eyes were downcast as if he was struggling to stay awake. 'I'm happy to drive,' he said, putting on his seat belt.

'You're fine,' said Louise, driving off towards the M5.

They drove straight through, the roads relatively quiet until they reached the outskirts of Ironbridge, and pulled up outside Ella Gosling's house with plenty of time to spare. The large detached property was part of a gated community, and a further set of gates surrounded the entry to her house.

'Not bad for a charity,' said Miles.

'Let's not jump to conclusions,' said Louise, despite agreeing with her colleague.

Miles was the only person she'd told about the call from Taylor Betancur yesterday evening. She knew Pepperstone would be furious if he found out, and could even manipulate it to prevent Louise from attending, so she'd decided to keep it between the two of them for now.

'Ready?' she asked.

Miles nodded.

'My turn to do all the speaking,' said Louise. Although she'd thought about little else since Betancur had called, she still wasn't sure what she hoped to achieve from the meeting. In a perfect world, she wanted permission to search the old Latchford house as a start, but she wondered if there was more to be unearthed. The fact that Ella's assistant had contacted her directly after the story appeared in the press suggested there might be something she was prepared to share with them. Though the opposite was equally possible, and the invitation could be a way of trying to shut them down.

Louise pressed the button outside the property, and as the steel gates pulled apart the front door opened. 'DI Blackwell and DC Boothroyd,' said Louise to the man standing at the threshold.

'Taylor Betancur,' said the man, who was dressed in an immaculate, tailored suit. 'I believe we spoke on the phone. Please come through. Mrs Gosling is waiting for you in the library.'

Miles suppressed a laugh at the mention of a library, and together they followed the PA through a high-ceilinged lobby area to a wood-panelled room lined floor-to-ceiling with books, where two people were sitting in leather armchairs.

Ella Gosling stood and shook hands with them. 'Ella Gosling. Thank you for coming. This is one of my lawyers, Alan Kettlewell,' she said, the man getting to his feet and offering his hand.

They all sat, Mrs Gosling requesting that Betancur fetch coffee. She smiled at them in turn before saying, 'So, I understand from the article in yesterday's press that you are looking into the discovery of human remains in Banwell Caves, as well as the disappearance of Ben Carter fifty years ago?'

'That is correct,' said Louise.

'I certainly wish you luck, but I did wonder why you chose to mention the name of my charity in your article.'

'It wasn't my article,' said Louise, taking a cup and saucer from Betancur, who had returned with the coffee.

'Come, now, DI Blackwell,' said Kettlewell. 'You wanted our attention and now you have it.'

'It's true I have wanted to speak to you. Lovely coffee by the way,' said Louise, placing her cup back on the bone china saucer.

'I believe you have already spoken to one of our team, Teresa Willow?' said Kettlewell.

'In a manner of speaking. I don't want to waste anyone's time here. You'll be aware that the remains we found belong to Hugo Latchford, and that Hugo's parents were – and in the case of Mr Latchford, are – members of the Verdant Circle?'

'We were questioned as an organisation when that poor boy went missing. I believe Jeremy and Valerie were very cooperative,' said Mrs Gosling.

'Well, you would expect that, as he was their son.'

Mrs Gosling edged back, as if recoiling from Louise's response.

'You can understand why we would be keen to speak to Mr Latchford now that news of a second missing child has come to light. A missing child who lived in the same area as the Latchfords.'

Kettlewell smiled, the gesture a mixture of contempt and confidence which Louise had seen so many times before. She already knew what he was about to say before he formed the words. 'Jeremy Latchford wasn't even born when Ben Carter went missing.'

Louise decided not to match the lawyer's condescension. 'No, but his father was alive, and now, as a group, the Verdant Circle own the property where Jeremy Latchford, and Hugo for a time, was raised.'

'I am sure this is all a terrible coincidence,' said Kettlewell.

'I am sure you must understand that we need a little bit more than that to go on, Mr Kettlewell.'

'What is it you would like?' asked Mrs Gosling, with a humourless smile.

'For starters, we would like to look inside the Latchford house,' said Louise, noting the look of disdain on the lawyer's face.

'And?' said Mrs Gosling.

'We would like to speak to Jeremy Latchford.'

Mrs Gosling conferred with her solicitor. 'The first I can help you with. I can get someone to show you around the house tomorrow if you like. As for Mr Latchford, he is his own person and I am sure he'll contact you when he finds out about all this.'

'But I believe he is still a member of your organisation?'

'We're a charity, DI Blackwell, not a prison. People are free to come and go. We don't keep records in that sense. Mr Latchford could be in any of our collectives, or none.'

Louise looked around at the opulence of the Goslings' personal library, which was bigger than the whole of the ground floor of her own house, and at her expensive lawyer and PA, and doubted that the Verdant Circle had such a lax approach to their membership. 'We're close to elevating this case into a murder investigation. In which circumstance, we would insist on speaking to Jeremy Latchford and it would be an offence to block that anyway.'

'Mrs Gosling has already told you she doesn't know where Mr Latchford is,' said Kettlewell.

Louise took another drink of coffee. 'It was your parents who formed the Verdant Circle, the Hawthornes?'

Mrs Gosling looked momentarily taken aback. 'That's right.'

'Did they live here when they started?'

Kettlewell went to speak but Mrs Gosling stopped him. 'No, we had quite a humble upbringing. All this is from my husband's side of the family,' she said, pointing towards the shelves.

According to Pepperstone's reports, Rupert Gosling was an international banker who spent his time in the world's major financial centres. He certainly had the type of wealth to afford a place such as this, but that didn't explain the numerous fraud cases outstanding for the group. 'Where is Mr Gosling now?'

'Frankfurt,' said Kettlewell, a little too quickly.

'If you don't mind me asking, Mrs Gosling. I've been to one of your camps, and I must say the life I saw being lived there is far removed from the splendour of this house.'

'I'm not here to explain anything to you, DI Blackwell. Now, I have told you I am happy for you to see the house in Frome.'

'Which you now own?'

'I don't own it. The charitable trust owns it. I am happy for you to view it, for whatever strange reason you may want. But I am not sure how else I can help you.'

'Were your parents into druidism? Am I pronouncing that right?' said Louise, not ready to end the conversation.

Mrs Gosling sighed. 'My parents were people of the Earth, Inspector. They set up this glorious organisation to help the Earth. Their work in environmental circles is well documented.'

'But there has always been an element of ritual in their work. What would you call it, paganism perhaps?'

Mrs Gosling grinned, the gesture an almost faultless replica of her lawyer's earlier smile. 'No need to try and label everything. Our group incorporates many beliefs, and yes many of them are not mainstream, but what of it? I would imagine it might be a little bit more useful worshipping the land we live on, than some imaginary being that rules over us, don't you?'

'But isn't it the case that some of your group may have taken things a bit too far?'

'In what way?' said Mrs Gosling, her lips tight as if she was holding her breath.

'There have been incidents of animal sacrifice, you must be aware of that?'

'As I said, Inspector, we have a diverse and very large membership. We don't manage anyone, and can't be held accountable for their behaviours.'

'And what about human sacrifice?' asked Louise, deciding to take a risk, figuring that they were only moments away from being asked to leave.

'Don't be so ludicrous,' said Kettlewell.

'It's fine, Alan. When you do difficult work, people are always putting obstacles in your way. I imagine you have found that during your career, DI Blackwell. These sorts of accusations pop up every now and then. Of course, we have nothing to do with them.'

'It's a little bit more serious than an accusation popping up,' said Louise. 'The remains of a boy have been found, whose parents belong to your group.'

'That doesn't mean anything,' said Mrs Gosling, getting to her feet. 'I admire what you are trying to achieve, but believe me, you will not find what you are looking for here. Now, if you don't mind, I have a number of other meetings today.'

# Chapter Thirty-Two

True to Ella Gosling's word, permission to visit the old Latchford house was granted later that afternoon. Louise hadn't long got back, and agreement was made with one of Ella's lawyers to visit the house the following morning, the stipulation being that no more than two officers would be present. As it was a voluntary search, Louise had no option but to accept, even though it would severely hamper her ability to properly search the place.

Louise was still trying to process everything about her conversation with Ella Gosling, the story of maintaining an environmentally concerned charity, and the juxtaposition with the luxury she lived in.

What had troubled her the most was the easy dismissal of any potential link between Hugo Latchford and Ben Carter's disappearances. Although there was nothing concrete Louise could prove, she refused to believe the two incidents were isolated.

Back at headquarters, she and Miles had started the all-but-impossible task of looking into local disappearances in the last fifty years, and to try and make a link, however tentative, to the Verdant Circle.

Louise knew from her previous work on missing persons cases how difficult such a task would be. Numbers on missing people were difficult to maintain, but it was believed that over 5,000 people nationwide had been missing for one year or more, 1,700 of which were children, and as the Verdant Circle were a national organisation, each missing person was a potential link. When they took into account the fact that not all missing persons were reported, and that cases such as Ben Carter's had long since been filed as cold cases, then the full extent of the job became apparent.

They ran what searches they could, prioritising either cases where the missing person had lived near a believed Verdant Circle subset, or where the organisation itself was specifically named. Louise knew she was looking for the proverbial needle in a haystack, and that a full investigation would require resources they could never hope to have, but for now it felt like time well spent.

'Louise,' bellowed Robertson, sticking his head in and out of the incident room before she had a chance to answer.

'I wish you wouldn't do that, Iain,' said Louise, a few minutes later in his office.

'I have to take every opportunity to undermine you while I can, Louise,' he said, deadpan in response.

'I'm sure you'll continue to do that when you're hobnobbing with the top brass. How can I help you?'

'You went to see Ella Gosling today?'

'That's correct.'

'I know we've been here before, and you know that I trust you implicitly, but this is putting us – and by that, I mean me – in some hot water.'

'I don't really know how, Iain.'

Robertson made a gesture resembling something between a smile and a grimace. 'I could tell straight off that you didn't get on with the mouth-breathing DI, but we need to be working with his department in the spirit of cooperation.'

'I'm not getting this talking-down because of Pepperstone?' said Louise, incredulous.

'Higher, much higher. The sort of height that stops DIs becoming DCIs, if you understand me.'

'It's this kind of nonsense that makes me question whether I should be looking for promotion. You know they contacted me, don't you?'

'Who?'

'The Verdant Circle. Ella Gosling's PA called me yesterday. They invited me to her house. What was I supposed to do?'

'You kept that quiet,' said Iain. 'Conveniently.'

'What can I say?'

'Was it at least useful?'

'You know how these things are.'

'You found nothing, then. Listen, Louise, you're not going to like this, but all further correspondence with the Verdant Circle has to be shared with Pepperstone's mob.'

'I need their permission?'

'I didn't say that, did I? The scope of their operation is huge. Bigger than I think Pepperstone has let on. You just need to share the information.'

'It's all about money, Iain.'

'Yes, money, but lots of it. We can't jeopardise it, and we can't be seen to be at risk of jeopardising it.'

'You can't expect me to go cap in hand to Pepperstone every time I need to speak to someone.'

Robertson made the same half-smile gesture as before. 'You can't speak to anyone senior, especially the leader of the whole bloody operation, without sharing it first.'

'You know I'm seeing the Latchford house tomorrow. What if Ella Gosling attends?' said Louise, standing.

'Don't be flippant, DI Blackwell,' said Robertson, his attention already back on his computer screen.

Louise was still reeling from her conversation with Robertson the following morning as she headed towards the old Latchford house in Frome. She understood Robertson's position, and held nothing against him, but the incident only sufficed to highlight how frustrating police work could be. Pepperstone had obviously had a word with a superior officer at his station, and they in turn had got on to Robertson.

Her boss wasn't generally one to bow down to anyone, but he had to toe the line as much as anyone else, and if he was warning her then she had to take it seriously. He hadn't come out and said it, but with a promotion on the cards, it was obvious the top brass were watching her more closely than normal, and it wouldn't do not to be seen as a team player.

She'd thought that with Tim Finch out of the way, things would get easier, but it was just a different form of harassment stopping her from doing her job. Not that she couldn't concede how unusual an investigation this was becoming. At present all they had was the twelve-year-old remains of Hugo Latchford, and a missing persons case from half a century ago. Although there was physical evidence suggesting Hugo had been mistreated, there was nothing definite to suggest his death was anything other than misadventure. Once they got to speak to Jeremy Latchford, the whole investigation could come to a juddering halt, but with the solstice only days away, Louise was determined to get some answers.

A slight woman who looked as if she was in her early twenties greeted them by the front of the house. Louise caught her giving Miles an approving look before the woman addressed her. 'Hi, I'm Jackie Barr. I've been asked to show you around by the owners,' she said.

Louise displayed her warrant card, wanting to keep everything formal. 'May I ask what your relationship with the owners is?'

'I am with the firm Taylor and Taylor,' said the woman, handing Louise a business card.

'Pleased to meet you,' said Louise, wondering how many lawyers Ella Gosling and the Verdant Circle had on their books.

Jackie opened the door and led them through to the hallway. Louise wasn't sure what she'd expected to see. There was never going to be anything incriminating at the scene, but she'd wanted to get a feel for the place where Jeremy Latchford and Hugo, for a much shorter time, had lived.

The smell of fresh paint lingered in the air as they walked through the house, which was empty of furniture. Any character had been eliminated by a job lot of white paint spread unevenly over every wall and ceiling.

'What do you think we'll find if we scrub all this away?' said Miles, under his breath, as they moved upstairs.

It was a clever move by the Verdant Circle. It was all but impossible to imagine Hugo being brought up in the house. They walked through to one of the bedrooms, Louise wondering if it had been Hugo's old room. Valerie Latchford had shown remorse for what had happened to her son, but Louise had to wonder how much love the boy had experienced in his short span on Earth. She imagined the room decorated in more child-friendly colours, pictured a duvet set with superheroes on it, Hugo snuggled in his bed surrounded by numerous cuddly toys, but it didn't ring true. There was a coldness to the room, and the house in general, and she wasn't sure if the shoddy paint job had made it worse or not.

'Anything else you'd like to see?' asked Jackie, as they reached downstairs.

Louise glanced to her right. 'Cellar?'

'Yes. Not much down there except old boxes.'

'If we could.'

The young solicitor opened the door, a wave of fetid air rushing at them.

'Damp issues,' said Miles, leading the way down the narrow staircase.

During the Aisha Hashim investigation, Louise had uncovered two adjoining cellar rooms in Avonmouth where a brother and sister had been kept intermittently throughout their youth. This place was much smaller, full of old boxes and newer paint tins, but Louise had to consider if at any point Hugo had been kept down here. Was this the place he'd been held in captivity for so long it had impacted his bone growth? As she moved the boxes aside, searching for signs of captivity she knew couldn't be there, she wondered if Jeremy Latchford had also suffered the same fate. As the Hashim case had demonstrated, these things often proved to be cyclical, and maybe Lee Latchford had been the catalyst for everything.

'Thank you,' she said, moving up the cellar's staircase a little faster than she would have liked, until she was in the relative openness of the kitchen. 'If we could see the garden before we go?'

The solicitor nodded, opening the creaking kitchen door, which led out to a long narrow garden, overgrown with brittle dry grass and pointed weeds. Louise didn't let that put her off, brushing the weeds aside until she reached the back gate, which was securely fastened. 'Can you see over?' she asked Miles, who went up on his tiptoes.

'It's where we were the other day. A pathway directly to the druid's altar,' said Miles.

'I can see why they let us look around the house,' he said, as they headed back to headquarters a few minutes later.

'They literally whitewashed the walls for us,' said Louise.

'You think that was symbolic?'

Louise took a deep breath. 'Who the hell knows. I feel like we've been chasing our tails on this since the beginning. Maybe they were trying to distract us from something.'

'I can't help thinking about the woman who called last week.'

'You and me too,' replied Louise. The woman had sounded confused, possibly high, but her terror had been real. 'Maybe I should speak to Lyndsey Garrett again.' Lyndsey was the only former member of the Verdant Circle who was willing to talk, and had first mooted the idea of human sacrifice. Again, Louise was forced to try and ignore the nagging feeling that they were clutching at straws. Something was definitely off about the Verdant Circle, but getting to the bottom of it was feeling more and more like an impossible task. The experience of DI Pepperstone was testimony to that, and unfortunately in order to meet Lyndsey again, he was just the man she would have to contact.

She was about to formulate a plan to get the DI back on her side when her phone rang, Yvonne's name popping on to the screen. 'I need to take this,' she said, putting the childminder on to speakerphone. 'Hi, Yvonne, everything OK?' she asked, a burst of adrenaline pumping through her veins as her mind played out her worst nightmares – all of them involving Jack being in danger.

'Nothing to worry about, Louise, but Jack has had a series of vomiting incidents this morning.'

Louise was stunned into silence. She pulled the car over, taking a deep breath before answering. 'Is he OK?' she said, not recognising her own voice.

'I've spoken to the NHS careline. He has a slight temperature, and he doesn't want anything to eat or drink at the moment. He hasn't been sick again in the last thirty minutes, but I thought you'd want to know.'

The adrenaline was making Louise dizzy. Yvonne knew what she was doing, but it didn't stop the stab of fear that the sickness could escalate into something more serious. It put everything into perspective, and she knew what she had to do without hesitation. 'Thanks, Yvonne. I'm on my way. Let me know if anything changes,' she said, hanging up and heading back to Weston.

# Chapter Thirty-Three

Fi tried to sleep as soon as it was dark. In the past few days she'd made the journey through the woods to the road three times, and had left markers so she could travel safely in the dark. Tonight she'd packed a small holdall, and put Max to bed an hour earlier than usual. Everything was in place, and if they were ever to leave, now was the time.

But sleep wouldn't come easy. She wanted to rest so she was prepared for the track through the woods. Although she felt more herself, the vestiges of her illness, enforced or not, lingered in her bloodstream. She knew if she was to successfully escape – and how sad it was to think of it in those terms – then she had to be rested and at full strength, but all she could do was lie there and listen to the sounds of the woodland.

Leaving now would be too risky. It wasn't even 10 p.m., and people would still be awake. She'd read somewhere that in warfare the optimum time for attacks was 4 a.m., the time when nearly everyone was asleep. And although this wasn't a military operation, she knew it gave her the best chance of leaving undetected.

She got up and made some tea, deciding she was too pumped to fall asleep and hoping that the energy would still be there later. She double-checked the holdall, trying to ignore the taunting voice in her head telling her that this was all she was worth – a bag full of old clothes and what little cash she'd withheld from the Verdant Circle. She knew she was more than that, and everything that she really had was currently sleeping in the other room. They'd taken a chance moving here, and they'd made a mistake. She'd made a further mistake not following Pete out of the camp, but all that could be rectified.

Fi's heart skipped as there was a knock on the door. Panicked, she threw the holdall under the foldaway table in the kitchen. 'Who is it?' she said.

'Hi, Fiona, it's Silas.'

Pain rushed into Fi's stomach and chest. 'Hi,' she said, creaking the door open an inch.

'Oh good, you're still awake,' he said. 'Sorry to bother you so late, I've just come back from a get-together with the solstice committee. May I come in?'

'It's a mess,' said Fi, feeling helpless.

'Don't be silly. It's fine. I'll only take a few minutes of your time.'

Fi opened the door further and allowed Silas to enter, knowing that refusing would cast more suspicion on her. 'Would you like some tea?' she asked.

'That would be wonderful, thank you,' said Silas, taking a seat.

Fi's hand trembled as she made the tea. It wasn't natural to feel this way. She barely knew the man, but every time she was with him all she could think about was the book. He accepted the tea with his usual cold smile, pretending to warm his hands on the cup. 'Such a beautiful night. I love this time of year, don't you?'

Fi shrugged. Her relative solitude precluded her from enjoying anything at the present. 'How can I help?'

'Oh yes, sorry, I forgot myself. As I said, I was talking with the solstice committee tonight and we have decided to invite Max to take part in the celebrations. He would be part of a select group who would perform in the ceremony. I am sure he must have mentioned the preparation he's been doing in class.'

Fi nodded, though she'd heard nothing about it from Max. 'What would that entail exactly?'

'Nothing too much. Some of the children have been working on some routines to show everyone. As a thank you, Max has been invited to camp out with other members of the group on the eve of the solstice, at the druid's altar in Frome.'

Fi could feel her heart beating hard in her chest. 'Camp out?'

'Just something we put together for some of the better-behaved children. Obviously, there'll be plenty of adult supervision, and they'll get the adventure of two nights out under the stars.'

'Max hasn't left here before. Not since we joined,' said Fi, wondering to herself why she was arguing when she planned to leave anyway.

'All the better for him then. Have you been there before? It's a magical place.'

'I'll speak to him tomorrow. See what he says.'

Silas nodded, his head moving slowly as if he was annoyed at her indecision. 'OK, Fiona. Remember, this is a great honour for him, so best to sign him up as soon as you can.'

Fi got to her feet, Silas following suit. 'Goodnight,' she said, showing him to the door and watching him make his way from the caravan. When he was out of sight, she collapsed on to the sofa.

Her whole body was shaking. She was sure she was overreacting – it seemed unfeasible that Silas would invite Max for a camp-out so openly if something untoward was planned – but everything Silas had said, and the way he had said it, unnerved her.

She thought about that poor little boy who'd been found only a few miles away, and wondered how he'd ended up in that position. Had his parents been offered the same proposition? From what she knew, the boy hadn't been a member of the Verdant Circle, but his parents had. It had taken too long for her to fully realise, but it was finally hitting home that there were things she didn't understand about the organisation she was so intrinsically involved in. Pete had been right to leave. She regretted now more than ever that she and Max hadn't left with him, and resolved to get away from there immediately.

◆ ◆ ◆

By 2 a.m., she couldn't wait any longer. She made a last check of the holdall and pocketed a small kitchen knife, before waking Max. 'Where are we going? It's dark,' said her son, rubbing his eyes.

'We're going on a little adventure,' said Fi. 'I need you to get changed into some nice warm clothes and then we're going for a midnight walk. How does that sound?'

Max was tired but the idea of a midnight adventure seemed to energise him. Fi urged herself not to rush, when all she wanted to do was grab Max in her arms and run. They were still ahead of time, and she managed to get him to eat something – half a banana and a handful of raisins – before they were ready to head out.

Despite the sounds of wildlife, the woods felt quieter than usual as she eased open the caravan door. She winced as she heard the metallic screech of the door creaking, even though they were a good few hundred yards from anyone else.

'It's so dark,' said Max, yawning.

'Don't worry about that. I have torches. Here,' said Fi, placing a head torch around his head. 'We'll keep the lights off for a bit though, shall we. Just look up at the big moon and the stars. We don't need much more than that for now.'

Max adjusted the strap around his head. He looked so angelic wrapped in his winter coat, even if it was overkill for the summer night, the woods having retained much of the day's heat. She felt so guilty for having to put him through this. Worse still for having placed him in this position in the first place. She had no real idea of whether or not he was in danger, but she was convinced this was no longer the right place for him.

She led the way around the back of the pathway, trying to avoid the main route, replaying the journey she'd mapped in her mind hundreds of times that day. The main cause of concern was avoiding the attention of the other residents in the caravans dotted around the woodland, but they passed the last of them without incident – including Silas's, who had his lights switched off.

'OK, we can switch on our torches now,' said Fi, as they entered the woodland proper.

Max switched on his headlamp, a beam of light piercing the darkness and causing Fi to look around in panic. 'What is it, Mummy?' said Max, confused and excited by what was happening.

'Nothing, darling, I'm just glad I changed the batteries for that thing. You're going to be able to see where you're going properly now, aren't you?'

'Where are we going, Mummy?'

'You'll see, come on,' said Fi, heading in the direction of the first tree she'd marked earlier that day.

Max was choosing not to match her pace and she was forced to hasten him along. 'I'm tired,' he said, as they came across another tree Fi had marked.

She knew the woodland well, but it was a different beast at night and she was glad to see the collection of stones by the trunk. 'Not that far now, darling,' she said, as she heard the sound of a lone vehicle in the distance.

She didn't feel the panic she'd experienced the time she'd called the police, but her pulse was still racing. She'd thought beyond reaching the road itself, but not much. Even from the road, it was too long a walk to reach civilisation so she knew they would have to hitch, and that would bring with it unavoidable jeopardy. The Verdant Circle didn't go so far as to send patrol cars out during the night – at least none that she was aware of – but there was a risk that someone from the camp could be driving along the road. But that was a risk she had to take.

Five minutes into the journey and the heavens opened. The rain wasn't something Fi had planned for – though the land definitely needed a downpour – and she saw the hesitation in Max as the water started dripping from the covering of trees. 'We should go back,' he said.

Fi tried to laugh it off. 'What? You love adventuring, Max. I didn't think you'd be put off by a little warm rain.'

'I'm tired.'

Fi continued walking. She would have told Max where they were going and why, but he wouldn't understand. This was his world now, and leaving it was going to be difficult for him. 'Come on, you'll wake up soon.'

Max hesitated before following. The rain was heavy but they were protected from the worst of it now, and Fi could only hope that it would stop by the time they reached the road.

Progress was slow and Fi kept sneaking glances behind her. 'What is it?' said Max, picking up on her paranoia.

The rain drowned out all other sounds in the woodland, but in Fi's imagination she could picture Silas and the others chasing after them. She thought about Silas's twisted book, and told herself that would not happen.

Her hand reached into her pocket for the knife she'd taken from the kitchen earlier. She'd never hurt anyone in her life, but she would not allow anything to happen to Max.

'Mum, I'm tired.'

Fi stopped, only now hearing her heavy breathing accompanying the sound of the falling rain. 'Sorry, are we going too fast?'

'I want to go home.'

'Not long now, come on.' He was too big to carry and had a stubborn streak in him that would make it all but impossible to urge him on if he chose not to walk.

'I have solstice practice tomorrow.'

'I know. We'll get you back in time,' said Fi. She hated lying to him, but he wasn't moving, and every second they remained was an extra chance for Silas and the others to discover they were missing. She took a risk and grabbed his hand. He winced and she softened her grip. 'Please, Max. I wouldn't be doing this if it wasn't necessary.'

He held her gaze, and she feared what was going on behind his eyes. He was becoming a true son of the Verdant Circle. She hadn't attended any of the classes since they'd joined, and it was only now dawning on her that she had no idea what information he'd been fed in his makeshift school. Deep down, she had always suspected Pete had been right to leave, and now here was the real test. 'Please,' she urged, relieved when she felt give in his grip, and he followed her.

She tried not to rush. They were minutes from reaching the road, but that was when the real work would begin. The rain continued bouncing off the ground as they reached the last checkpoint. 'We're going down this little hill now, be careful,' she said, still holding Max's hand.

His grip tightened and, for a second, she thought he was going to pull away and run back to camp, but he kept hold of her as they shuffled down the hill and reached the road. Rain battered the tarmac and she was reluctant to step out of the shade.

'What are we doing by the road?' asked Max, as a lorry drove by, the driver oblivious to their presence.

'I told you, we're going on a little adventure,' said Fi, holding on a little tighter.

'Away from camp?'

'Yes, for a bit.'

'What about solstice?'

'Let's not worry about that now,' said Fi, trying to fight her fading resolve. All of a sudden, it felt like a ridiculous plan. It was clear Max didn't want to be away from camp, and now it didn't seem feasible that they could simply walk away. 'This way,' she said, stepping on to the verge, the rain hitting them with full force as another car passed them by.

'How far are we going to walk?'

Fi continued to drag him along. The only saving grace of their situation was the day's residual heat, which meant the rain wasn't uncomfortable.

'Are we leaving the camp forever?'

Fi couldn't deny the hint of panic in her son's voice. 'Please come on, Max. I'll explain everything later.'

Maybe if it had been a year or two down the line, he might have denied her, but for now he did what he was told and they continued down the winding road, battling through the rain, stopping only when a car began approaching from the other direction.

This was what it had come down to. It was too late to second-guess herself. Fi stuck out a hand, and the car slowed, the driver winding down the window, only for Fi to realise too late that she recognised the person behind the wheel.

She grabbed Max and tried to scramble up the bank, back into the woodland. But despite the weeks of drought, the downfall of rain had made the path slippy and she lost her footing as the car came to a stop. She fell back down the hill and landed on her back, Max managing to stay on his feet.

Fi went for the knife, heartbroken by the shock on Max's face. 'It's OK,' she mouthed, as a man left the car and approached her.

'Are you OK? You're Fiona, right?' he said.

He was new to camp. Fiona thought he might be called Neil. He was in his thirties, athletic-looking, and she'd never seen him hanging around with Silas or the others, but she wasn't about to take any risks. 'Keep away from us,' she said, scrambling to her feet and brandishing the kitchen knife.

'No need for that. I just wanted to check that you're not hurt. My name is Neil. I'm from the camp. I think you've seen me before. What are you doing out here at this time of night?'

'I could ask you the same question.'

Neil nodded. 'Are you OK?' he asked Max.

'We're having a midnight adventure,' said Max, his attention flitting from Neil to the knife in Fi's hand.

'You're trying to leave?' asked Neil.

Fi kept the knife in front of her. 'And if we were?'

'I'm not here to stop you, if that's what you think.'

'So, you'll let us go?'

'Of course, I'm not trying to stop you. What do you think is happening?'

Neil looked so genuine and full of concern that Fi wanted to trust him. 'I just want me and my son to get the hell out of here.'

'You think you're in danger?'

'I know we are.'

'OK, let me help.'

'How?'

'Let me give you a lift. Do you have anywhere in mind?'

'The nearest police station,' said Fi, deciding it made no difference to tell him her intentions.

Neil nodded. 'I can help with that.'

'If you think we're getting in your car, you're mad,' said Fi, brandishing the knife as the rain began to ease.

'Wait there,' said Neil, returning to his car.

Fi looked at Max in panic. She didn't know what to do. She was rooted to the spot. There was no time to make a run for it, and Max appeared to be on the verge of tears. Before she knew it, Neil had returned and was holding something in his hand. 'Here,' he said, handing her what appeared to be a small leather phone case.

Fi opened the case to see a police badge inside.

'My name is DC Maddox. I'm working undercover at the camp. If you're in danger, I can take you to safety,' he said. 'But I'll need you to give me the knife.'

It felt too elaborate to be a ruse, but it still took a few seconds for Fi to lower the knife. It felt like a risk, but she handed it to the man calling himself DC Maddox, and together with Max they got into the car and hoped the man truly was who he said he was.

# Chapter Thirty-Four

After picking Jack up, Louise spent a few uneasy hours waiting for his temperature to return to normal. It wasn't the first time Jack's temperature had rocketed since he was born, but she hated seeing him in distress and only felt content when he started eating again.

As Jack lay on the sofa next to her, Louise's thoughts turned to her visit to the Latchford house. The house had felt off to her, and she was sure there was more to it than what they'd seen in the whitewashed building. Unfortunately, feelings and hunches were useless to her, and her mind teased at the various threads of the investigation until they stopped making sense and she crashed to sleep.

Jack's temperature was back to normal by the morning, so she dropped him at Yvonne's before heading to headquarters. In an ideal world, she would have spent the day at home with him, but she couldn't give up the time on the investigation. There were other parents out there suffering way more than her, and it was her duty to help them. It was harder than ever saying goodbye, but she felt that she had no choice. She was still coming to terms with juggling this extra responsibility and her job. It wasn't exactly harder than she'd imagined, but on days like yesterday it had taken more of her headspace than she would have liked, and she was already feeling exhausted by the time she arrived at Portishead to see DI Pepperstone waiting for her.

'Gerrard.'

'Louise,' said Pepperstone, checking his watch as if she was late for a meeting.

'Can I help you with something?' she said, walking towards the lift.

'On this occasion, it's something I can help you with,' said Pepperstone, as she was about to press the button.

Louise gestured for him to continue, not prepared to play any games with the man this early in the morning.

'A UCO's cover was blown yesterday evening. He was travelling back to the camp in Priddy when he saw a woman and a child on the roadside.'

'I'm sorry to hear about your UCO. Is he the one you got transferred?' said Louise, who understood the amount of work and time undercover officers had to dedicate to their roles.

Pepperstone nodded. She could see it pained him that his officer had been compromised, but he hadn't stooped to blaming her just yet. 'The woman and child were residents at the Verdant Circle camp. They told my officer that they were trying to escape.'

'Those were the exact words they used?'

'The very same. The mother recognised my officer, and believing the threat to be real, he had no option but to show his identification and take them to a place of safety.'

'Thanks for coming to me, Gerrard. When can I see them?'

'I can take them to you now. They're effectively homeless. They're staying at the station in Wells and we're looking into finding them temporary accommodation.'

Louise was waiting for the catch but didn't want to pre-empt. 'I'll get my colleague and head over now.'

'I can take you, Louise. For now, it would be better if you went alone. My UCO is compromised, but only by the mother and the child. I'm hoping speaking to her will help us both, so perhaps we can work together on this?'

The change in Pepperstone's approach was laughable but she wasn't about to pull him up on it. 'You want to drive?'

'Let's go,' he said, dangling his car keys in front of her.

There was still an awkward silence between her and Pepperstone as they travelled to Wells. Within a few minutes, she'd been forced to switch on the radio to drown out the sound of his nasal breathing, and it was a relief when they finally arrived at the police station.

'DC Neil Maddox,' said Pepperstone, introducing her to the undercover officer who'd found the mother and son escaping from the camp.

Louise could see how Maddox would have fitted in. He was wearing rugged jeans and a short-sleeved flannel shirt, his long chestnut hair tied in a bun matching the colour of his beard. 'Hi, Neil. Louise Blackwell.'

'I know. I heard some people mention you in the camp.'

'Sorry if this has blown your cover.'

The DC shrugged. 'That remains to be seen.'

'Can you tell me what happened?'

'It was just pure luck really. My main interest at the camp was Teresa Willow, who I believe you've met. She's been leaving on daily visits and I've been trying to track her as best I can. She was staying at a hotel over in Frome last night. I monitored a dinner she had, and waited for her to return to her hotel room, which she left an hour after switching the lights off. I happened to be on the way back at the time Fi and her son were leaving.'

'Fiona and Max O'Sullivan?' said Louise, looking at the report sheet. 'What can you tell me about them?'

'Nothing beyond what Fi told me last night. I'd seen her once or twice around camp but hadn't come across the boy. She told me she felt in danger, and in particular she feared for her son. She mentioned Hugo Latchford as something of a catalyst. And I believe she put in an emergency call a week or so ago.'

Fiona O'Sullivan was a slight woman in her early forties. Her pale skin was almost translucent, sprinkled with freckles. Louise played the recording of her emergency call, as the woman fidgeted in her seat. They were alone in one of the interview rooms, Pepperstone and Maddox watching through the two-way mirror. 'That was you?' she asked.

'It was. I think I saw you in the woods with your colleague.'

Fiona explained about her life in the camp, how she and her husband had given up everything to live there, and how her son had adapted to life in the commune. 'If I'm being honest, I think I've always been a bit in denial, if that makes sense? It's hard to describe. On the whole, everyone is so lovely, but you have your given role and there is definitely a sense that you are duty-bound.'

'Were you ever hurt? You or Max?'

'No, nothing like that. Things have been a bit weird since Pete left. They've kept me in the caravan, which was nice at first, but it left me a bit isolated. I started to feel that I was losing Max. Do you understand what I mean?'

Louise nodded.

'Then there was that stuff with that boy in Banwell Caves. I knew it was linked to the Verdant Circle. There were whispers around camp about the boy's parents being part of the group somewhere else. I started thinking about how and why the boy had found himself in that position. Then there was this new man in camp.'

'New man?'

'He's called Silas. Look, if I tell you something, can I get into trouble?'

'As long as you haven't hurt someone, you'll be fine.'

'No, I haven't hurt anyone.'

'Go on then, Fiona. We're here to help you.'

Fiona's body language was a mixture of relief and extreme tiredness, and Louise feared she didn't have much energy left in her for more questioning. 'I went into Silas's caravan. I saw him have an argument with Teresa.'

'Is that Teresa Willow?'

'Yes, that's right,' said Fi, seemingly confused that Louise knew the lawyer's name. 'The argument was very strong, bordering on violent. I couldn't really hear what they were arguing about but they both stormed off and Silas left his caravan door open.'

'It's OK, Fiona, you're not going to get into trouble for snooping in someone's caravan.'

'I found some things. Some drugs, some money. But worse, I found this type of book. It had a leatherbound cover, but inside were a number of handwritten pages each protected by a plastic covering. I don't know what most of it meant. I couldn't really make out the handwriting, I wasn't sure if it was even English, but there were pictures and maps.'

'Pictures?' asked Louise, adrenaline hitting her system.

'Weird stuff. People dancing with masks on. But what really grabbed my attention, and made me sick to my stomach, were the images of children. For me it was too much of a coincidence, but there were drawings of a child being trapped in a cave, just like that poor Hugo boy.'

Louise looked at the two-way mirror, wondering if Pepperstone or Maddox knew anything about a book.

'Did you say anything to anyone?'

'No, but then they told me that they wanted Max to be part of a special celebration and that he would be staying away from camp. At the druid's altar, in Frome.'

'Did they say when this would be?'

'Over the solstice weekend.'

Louise recalled the flyer Georgina had given her at the Kalimera. The solstice was on Saturday. 'Just Max?'

'I don't think so. They said there would be a group of them, but by this point I didn't believe a word any of them said.'

'Do you know any of the names of the other children?'

'Max would know which other children had been selected, but I can tell you the names of all the children in camp. Although . . .'

'Although?' said Louise, softly.

'Most of them have changed their names.'

'I understand. It would still be a help.' She showed Fi photographs of some of the members of the Verdant Circle, confirming Teresa Willow's ID.

'And this man?' said Louise, more hopeful than expectant as she put another photo on the table for Fiona to look at.

Fiona's skin whitened. 'That's him. That's Silas.'

'This man, you're sure? He was at the camp and went by the name Silas?'

'Yes, definitely. Why, isn't that his real name?'

'Thank you, Fiona. You've been very helpful. I will make sure you get some help today. Somewhere for you and Max to stay.' Louise turned the photo she'd shown to Fiona towards Pepperstone and Maddox behind the two-way mirror.

The photograph they had on file for Jeremy Latchford.

# Chapter Thirty-Five

After the interview, Louise excused herself and made a call to Robertson. That Fiona had felt under threat and identified someone looking like Jeremy Latchford as that threat was hopefully enough to get a warrant to search the camp in Priddy. Added to that was the potential that other children were in danger, and the upcoming solstice celebrations. She felt a search warrant had to be inevitable.

'What has Pepperstone said?' asked Robertson.

'I haven't asked him, and I don't care. Jeremy Latchford is on a wanted notice and needs to be interviewed about the remains of his son. He's a viable murder suspect, Iain.'

'I understand. I'll get to work on it, but you need to speak to Pepperstone. Let's coordinate any search. Who knows, he probably has the resources to help. And he did come to you about the mother and child.'

Robertson was right, but she didn't like it. It wasn't that she completely distrusted Pepperstone, and he'd come to her immediately about Fiona and Max, but he had his own agenda and she didn't want that getting in the way. All she cared about was finding the person responsible for killing Hugo Latchford, and preventing them from doing the same again, and she didn't want to risk anything derailing that. But she also knew her hands were tied.

'I'm waiting to speak to the child, Max, first,' said Louise. 'I need to hear what he has to say.'

'OK, keep me updated,' said Robertson, ending the call.

Louise spoke to Maddox and Pepperstone as they waited for the child liaison officer to arrive at the station for Max's interview. 'You never noticed Jeremy Latchford was on site?' she asked the UCO.

'I'd only been there a couple of days. Never saw him, and there was certainly no indication he was in camp,' said Maddox, defiantly.

'What about this book?'

'News to me.'

'I told you there was some weird shit going on,' added Pepperstone.

'Once I've spoken to Max, we're going to have to search the camp. You OK with that, Gerrard? We can do it as a joint operation if you want to speak to Teresa Willow and anyone else.'

Pepperstone rubbed his nose and sucked in a breath. Louise thought he was about to offer some patronising insight, but instead he said, 'They would have already started preparations the second they realised the mother and child had escaped. It isn't going to help us, storming in there, but I understand why you need to. Happy to help with staff, but I need to be there.'

Louise nodded. 'Robertson is sorting the paperwork.'

The door of the CID opened. 'Ready for you,' said a uniformed officer.

Max O'Sullivan was sitting in the interview room with his mother and a police liaison officer Louise had previously worked with. He

209

was a healthy-looking boy, with a mop of brown hair that he kept brushing away from his eyes. Louise tried to ignore the fact that he was around the same age as Emily, and they could easily have been at school together if circumstances had been different.

Louise introduced herself, trying to keep everything as light as possible. Guidelines on interviewing children were strict, and it was the liaison officer's job to make sure Max was protected throughout the process.

'You need another drink?' said Louise, looking at the carton of juice in front of the boy.

'I'm OK, thanks.'

'I imagine this is all a bit weird for you, isn't it?'

Max shrugged. 'I guess.'

'Well, I won't keep you long. I just need to ask you a few questions if that's OK?'

'Sure.'

Louise started slowly, getting a feel for how Max liked his life in the camp. He came across as being well adjusted. His answers were confident, and he sounded as though he'd relished his time as part of the commune.

'Your mum says you've been doing really well at the school at the camp, is that right?'

'I think so.'

'She said you'd been selected to go on a special trip?'

Max glanced at his mum, who appeared to be on the verge of tears. 'Yes, for the solstice.'

'There were a few of you selected, is that right?'

'It was a prize for helping out in class and camp,' said Max, frowning in confusion as his mother grabbed his hand.

'Do you remember who else was going with you?' asked Louise.

'Yes.'

Louise handed him a pen and a piece of paper. 'Would you be able to write their names down for me?'

Max nodded and began writing.

The warrant had yet to be granted by the time Louise arrived at Priddy with Pepperstone. Robertson had spoken to a judge, who was assessing all the details and hoped to have an answer for them within the hour. Max had written down five names on his piece of paper, and with the solstice looming over them, Louise's first priority was finding those five children.

They parked out of sight, with eyes on the main route into camp. The view was tranquil, the road lush with trees, barely a sound reaching them. Pepperstone had a camera with a long-distance lens and was doing his best to photograph everyone coming and going.

'If Latchford was there, he'll be long gone by now,' he said, checking the results of a photo he'd taken of an ancient-looking Ford Focus estate.

'You always this positive?' said Louise, winding down the window and pulling the visor down to shield her eyes from the sun.

'There is a reason they change their names.'

'I plan to question everyone, including Teresa Willow. Fiona knew her, and she knew Latchford was in the camp. This could be an opportunity for you.'

Pepperstone placed the camera on his lap. 'Thanks for telling me how to do my job.'

'God, Gerrard, what is your problem? I'm trying to help. We can both get what we want from this.'

'Yeah, maybe,' said the DI, turning his attention back to his camera.

◆ ◆ ◆

It was another hour before the warrant was granted. Tracey had been heading things up back at headquarters and had put a team on standby ready to search the camp. Louise and Pepperstone waited for them to arrive before driving up the road.

'No one is to leave without our permission,' she told the officers positioned at the main entrance, though she knew it would be impossible to manage all the potential exit routes without sending up helicopters and bringing in more recruits, which wasn't feasible at present.

Miles caught up with her and Pepperstone as they were approaching the brick building at the heart of the camp, as fellow officers began interviewing members of the group, taking names and details and setting up further questioning.

It was Teresa Willow who was first to leave the building. 'What the hell is going on here? I told you before, this is private property,' she said, walking over to Louise and Pepperstone flanked by four men Louise had never seen before.

'Not all of this area is private property, Teresa, as you well know,' said Pepperstone.

'You've gone too far now,' said Teresa.

'We have a warrant to search the whole camp,' said Louise, handing her an iPad with the digital warrant on it.

Teresa read the document, undeterred. 'What is it you think you're looking for?'

'Jeremy Latchford. We have reason to believe he's in the camp. I would also like to see these five children immediately,' said Louise, showing her Max's list.

'Don't be ridiculous. Jeremy Latchford isn't here. As for these children, we don't keep an attendance sheet.'

'You sure you want to take that line, Teresa? We have a firm, irrefutable sighting of Jeremy Latchford. And not just that, but a sighting of you and him together,' said Pepperstone. 'Now might be the time for you to consider talking to me. As for the children, you know what your duty of care is. I need to see them now.'

The flicker of indecision in Teresa's face was unmissable. Her eyes darted around at Louise, at her guards, and the uniformed police showing photographs of Latchford to the rest of the camp. 'To be honest, I don't know what Jeremy Latchford looks like,' she said.

'That's convenient. Here,' said Louise, showing her the photo they had on file.

Teresa took a long look. 'This looks like someone we had in camp, but his name wasn't Jeremy.'

'What was his name, Teresa?' asked Louise, who'd realised the lawyer was going to use Jeremy's alias to get herself out of trouble.

'Silas.'

'And where is he now?'

'He left first thing this morning.'

It hadn't come as much of a surprise, but it was still a disappointment. Teresa refused to talk any further about Latchford's whereabouts until she had legal representation, but understanding the seriousness of the situation she had located four of the five children on Max's list. The only unaccounted-for child was Jayden Parsons. Jayden lived on site with his parents, Ian and Linda, and Teresa had taken Louise to the room where they lived, which was currently empty.

'Their belongings are still here,' said Teresa.

Louise looked around at the barren room. The only belongings she could see were a kettle and some packs of cereal. In the wardrobe, she found some items of clothing, but it wasn't much for a family of three. 'When did you last see them?'

'Not sure.'

'You need to do better than that, Teresa.'

'I saw the three of them in camp yesterday. They could be out walking. Lots of people aren't in camp at present.'

'Do they have transport?'

'No. They use our minibus when they want to leave camp.'

'And that is still here?'

Teresa nodded.

'I need all documentation on the family immediately. Do you understand?'

Teresa grimaced, her top lip twitching as if she was about to argue, before Louise instructed one of the uniformed officers to accompany her to the static caravan that acted as her office. 'I need it now,' she added, as Teresa stormed off followed by the officer.

Understandably, Fiona O'Sullivan hadn't wanted to return just yet, so Louise had to ask one of the camp members where the woman had lived with her son, and was led to the top of the camp, up a steep hill to the woodland, to the static caravans she'd seen on the walk with Miles and Molly.

The curtains were drawn, the interior dank and gloomy. Fiona had been carrying a small holdall with her, but not much had been left behind. Louise searched through the cupboards, wardrobe, and drawers, and instructed a colleague to pack up all the belongings in the caravan for later.

'And where did Silas live?' she asked the same camp member, who showed her to another caravan, a hundred yards further into the wood.

The caravan was almost identical to Fiona's but nothing suggested anyone had recently stayed there. Louise had managed to get details from Fiona about where the book, money, and drugs had been located, and found the cubbyhole, which was unsurprisingly empty.

As she was leaving, she caught sight of a woman walking down the pathway. 'Excuse me,' said Louise, jogging after the woman, who turned with a resigned look in her eye. 'DI Blackwell. Who are you?'

'Denise Ledbetter. I'm a friend of Fi's. Is it true what they're saying?'

'What are they saying?'

'That Fi left camp, and that she's been spreading some terrible rumours about us all?'

Louise studied the woman, who brushed a strand of blonde hair from her brow. She'd claimed to be a friend of Fiona's but hadn't even asked how she and her son were doing. 'What are these rumours you think she's been spreading?'

'I don't know exactly, but there must be a reason why you're all here.'

'How well do you know Fi?' asked Louise.

'Has she mentioned me?' asked Denise, a crease of panic spreading across her forehead.

'Not that I can remember, but we'll be speaking to her again later. I will find out what exactly has been going on here, and someone will be held accountable,' said Louise, thinking about Fiona's claim that her food and drink had been doped.

'I haven't done anything.'

'That's good to know, Denise. But you do know doing nothing when you were in a position to help can also get you in trouble. Best to tell us all you know now.'

'But I don't know anything.'

'You know this man?' said Louise, showing her a picture of Jeremy Latchford.

Denise nodded. 'Silas.'

'What do you know about Silas?'

'Not much. He's only been here a few weeks. He's been heading up the planning for the solstice celebrations.'

'Were you involved in this planning in any way?'

'Not really. He did ask me to keep an eye on Fi and Max.'

'What did that entail exactly?'

Denise shielded her eyes from the sun, pivoting so her face was out of the shade. 'I made sure she was eating, kept an eye on her.'

'And was she eating?'

'I brought her dinners.'

'Where did you get them from?'

'What is this? From the kitchen, where else?'

'So you brought them directly from the kitchen.'

Denise scrunched up her face, as if she thought she'd been caught in a trap. 'Well, no, Silas did, but . . .'

'Did you ever think that Fi and Max might have been in danger?' said Louise, keen to keep the conversation going for as long as possible.

'No, of course not,' said Denise, a little too quickly for Louise's liking.

'Why do you think she called the police on one occasion, and then fled the camp?'

Denise took a step back. 'She was paranoid. She was caught taking drugs and I really think it was getting to her.'

This didn't sound like the reaction of a friend to Louise. 'What was she paranoid about?'

'Lots of things. She hasn't been herself since Pete left.'

'But anything specific? She told me she was worried about Max's safety.'

Denise took another step backwards, and Louise wondered for a second if she was going to make a run for it.

'Best to tell us now what you know, Denise. The truth is going to come out.'

Denise shrugged. 'The thing with Hugo Latchford's remains freaked her out. His parents used to be part of our group. Fi started getting some strange ideas in her head about the same thing happening to Max.'

'What do you mean, "the same thing"?'

Denise shrugged again before pulling her arms in close to herself. 'I don't know. Whatever happened to him.'

'You think someone put Hugo in that cave to die?'

'How the hell would I know?' said Denise, trying to be defiant but failing.

'You think someone wanted to do that to Max?'

Denise shook her head, but didn't say anything.

'You know that Silas is actually Jeremy Latchford, don't you?'

'No,' said Denise, appearing genuinely surprised.

'Who was he working with, aside from yourself?'

'No one. I mean, he wasn't working with me.'

With Denise struggling, Louise pressed her advantage. 'It wasn't just Max who Silas was interested in, was it?'

'What do you mean?'

'The other children he was going to take to the druid's altar?'

'Well, yes, there were others in Max's class.'

'One of them is missing at the moment. You should help yourself out, Denise, while you still have a chance.'

Panicked, Denise began hopping on the spot. 'I don't know anything about this. Silas spent all his time with Willow.'

'Teresa Willow?'

'Sorry, yes. Who is missing?'

'Jayden Parsons. And his mum and dad.'

Denise had gone pale, as if she was about to faint. 'I'm sure they'll turn up. Probably out for a trek. They love walking together – and camp is pretty deserted today.'

Louise knew Denise was either lying or withholding something. 'Who else is involved?' Denise shook her head but Louise was sure she had more to say. 'This is your only chance. Best take it.'

'Listen, I know nothing about it. But I did see Silas leave camp this morning. He didn't know I was there. I woke up early and went for a walk. I saw Silas and followed him to the outskirts. There was a man in a car. A flash car. That's all I know.'

'Can you give me any more details. Colour, make, number plate?'

'I don't know anything about cars. It was maroon, some kind of sports car I guess.'

'And the man?'

'Sorry, I only saw the back of him. Can I go now?' The desperation was evident in Denise's voice.

'What aren't you telling me, Denise? Help me now, and I will make sure you're not held responsible for all of this.'

'I . . . I didn't think anything of it at the time. He wasn't forced into the car. He just got in and sat in the back with Silas.'

'Who did?' asked Louise, already knowing the answer.

Denise stared back, shame-faced and dumbstruck.

Louise struggled to contain her anger. The solstice was only days away, and it seemed a child was now missing. History was repeating itself. 'Who got in the car with Silas?'

Denise bit her lower lip. 'Jayden. Jayden Parsons,' she said, as a commotion broke out in the distance.

'Take her in,' said Louise to one of the uniformed team, rushing to the disturbance where a man and a woman, presumably members of the commune, were arguing with two uniformed officers. The adults were dishevelled, and as Louise approached, she could see their clothes were torn and blood was pouring from an injury on the man's leg. 'What's going on?' she said, catching her breath.

The woman turned to her, her face haunted and blank. 'They've taken my boy,' she said. 'They've taken my little Jayden.'

The search started within the hour. After settling Mr and Mrs Parsons as much as possible, Louise questioned the pair, who revealed that Silas/Latchford had taken Jayden earlier that morning. He'd arrived in their room carrying a gun and ushered the family into the woods, where he'd tied the parents to a tree and absconded with Jayden. The parents had subsequently escaped and returned to camp.

Search teams were in place, the hills being scoured by the search and rescue dog team, two helicopters, and numerous drones monitoring from the sky. Once again, Louise was taken back to the Madison Pemberton disappearance. Madison had been trapped within a cave system, and had managed to escape and return of her own volition. That seemed unlikely in this case. Denise Ledbetter had seen Latchford leave earlier that morning in a maroon sports car and was sticking to her story that Jayden had been with them.

They continued the search into the evening, though much of the work was now being conducted off-site. Although it was possible that Jayden was somewhere in the hills, the more likely scenario was that Latchford had taken him, so equal resources were going into tracking the car, Louise's team liaising with forces nationwide – though without a number plate it was proving an almost impossible task.

Louise reluctantly left headquarters at 1.30 a.m., when the search in Priddy was put on hold.

It was so frustrating to know that Jeremy Latchford had been at the camp, and had probably been there when she'd last visited. It felt like an oversight, a mistake on her part, and all she could think about as she made her way home was Jayden Parsons. She couldn't stop wondering where he was now, and what Latchford had in store for him.

Despite the late hour, Louise needed to decompress. She took a detour along the seafront in Weston. She parked up near the old Tropicana building, and sat looking at the lights dancing off the water, and the distant silhouette of Steep Holm, the small offshore island where her detective work in Weston had effectively taken off. Melancholy thoughts rushed through her mind. She tried to replay everything that had happened so far in her head, but all her mind conjured up was images of Jayden Parsons alone and scared, trapped somewhere in the darkness.

Almost too tired to drive, she restarted the engine and drove along the deserted seafront. She'd only reached Marine Lake when her phone rang – Miles's name appearing on the screen.

'I thought you'd be asleep,' she said, weaving the car up the Kewstoke Road.

'I'm still at headquarters. Sorry to bother you so late but we just had a call from Watford nick.'

'Watford?'

'Yes. An ambulance was called to one of the hotels in the town centre. Suspected suicide.'

Louise pulled over. Her pulse raised as she formulated a guess about what Miles was going to say next. 'You're going to have to tell me, Miles. It's too late for my brain to focus.'

'They've sent me photographs. I can say with ninety-nine per cent certainty that the deceased was Jeremy Latchford.'

Louise was forced to catch her breath. She hadn't expected this development, and her mind was trying to work out what Latchford's death meant. 'And Jayden?' she asked, fearing the worst.

'No sign of him, I'm afraid.'

# Chapter Thirty-Six

Louise rubbed her eyes and yawned. There was simply no way she could drive to Watford that night. Miles had informed her that the body was with the pathologist but no autopsy had taken place. Her phone pinged and she opened the message with the photographs of Jeremy Latchford taken from the scene. His last actions had been running a bath in a hotel, and dragging a razor vertically down his wrists.

Like any violent suicide, the room had been considered a potential crime scene and the CSIs were still on site going through everything. If it wasn't a suicide, then it was a meticulously staged murder, but she wasn't going to find out any more before the morning. Miles was working with the officers from Watford, and a search was ongoing throughout the town for any sighting of Jayden.

At home, everyone was asleep. Louise headed straight upstairs, undressed, and collapsed next to Thomas who was gently snoring. She felt guilty going to sleep, and so much was going through her mind that she doubted she would be able to drop off, but the next thing she knew the alarm on her phone was ringing, forcing her eyes to open.

'What time is it?'

'Six,' said Louise, getting out of bed, feeling more tired than when she'd climbed in.

'Six? I need some more beauty sleep. What time did you get back? I didn't hear you.'

'Not sure. Late.'

'And you're up again now because?'

'Going to Watford, of course.'

'Of course.'

Louise bent over and kissed Thomas on the top of his head. 'I'll tell you about it later. Get some more sleep if you can, but you'll have to take the kids in today.'

'That's fine. The Surrey project is all signed off, so I'll be able to take them during the mornings. Go get them, DI Blackwell. I hope you have a productive day.'

◆ ◆ ◆

She picked up Miles at Avonmouth services. As they drove to Watford, she checked in with headquarters. The search had resumed in Priddy, but the news about Latchford had thrown everyone. Louise felt torn, wanting to get to the bottom of what exactly had happened to Latchford, but worried that she should be back at headquarters doing more to locate Jayden.

They arrived at Watford before 9 a.m. The police station was on the same road as the hotel where Jeremy Latchford's body was found. The investigator in charge, DS Bradley Wittenberg, walked them both along Clarendon Road to the hotel. 'Some place for your last moments,' he said, walking them up the stairs to the chain hotel.

The room was sealed and had yet to be cleaned, but the CSIs had documented everything. 'The blood splatter is consistent with

223

the incisions on the deceased's wrists,' said Wittenberg. 'No signs of struggle or duress from what we could see.'

Louise looked at the photographs from the scene, matching the images of Jeremy Latchford to the blood-drenched bathroom.

'Guilty conscience,' said Miles, peering intently at the dried blood on the tiled walls.

Louise was thinking along the same lines, but there was more than a little doubt in her mind. Why had Latchford gone to all the trouble of avoiding the police all this time, including leaving the camp with Jayden, only to take his life the same day? Maybe Miles was right, and guilt had got the better of him. But if that was the case, why hadn't he given an indication of where Jayden was before killing himself?

Louise wasn't sure she really wanted to know the answer to that question.

But then there was an alternative explanation. According to Denise, Latchford hadn't been alone with Jayden in the car. It was feasible that the Verdant Circle had grown weary of the heat Latchford had brought on them and had decided to get rid of him. That was a much harder theory to accept, but for now it gave her hope that Jayden could still be alive.

They spent the morning in Watford working with DS Wittenberg and his colleagues, in between calls back to headquarters. Jeremy Latchford's suspicious death was effectively Watford CID's case, but Wittenberg was generous with his time and offered them a small office to work from. Louise and Miles tracked his death from the moment the hotel staff had forced entry after water had leaked from the room's bathroom.

Staff had been questioned, and others in Wittenberg's term were analysing the CCTV images, searching for any glimpse of Jayden. Louise had gone through the most pertinent footage, including shots of Latchford arriving alone at the hotel, and the last image of him alive as he'd entered the hotel's lift.

She was convinced there would be more to it than this, but it seemed unlikely that anything would happen that day. In the debrief with Wittenberg's team, the three of them were formulating a plan for the next steps when there was a knock on the door.

Wittenberg looked up. 'What is it, Grace?' he asked a woman in her twenties with pale skin and auburn hair who was entering the room.

'Think we might have a hit on Jeremy Latchford's car. We have footage of him arriving yesterday at the Palace car park.'

'DC Thornley,' said Wittenberg, as the three of them followed the DC back to her desk, where she played a video of Jeremy Latchford arriving in the multi-storey car park in a black Mitsubishi Outlander.

'It's definitely him,' said Miles.

Louise was unsurprised but dismayed as she watched the footage of Latchford arriving alone.

'The car is still there?' asked Wittenberg.

'Floor four,' said the DC.

Wittenberg sighed. 'Probably be quicker if we walk.'

By the time they took the short walk up Clarendon Road and crossed the main road to the large shopping centre car park, a specialist team were arriving and had cordoned off the area next to the Outlander. They made a visual search, before one of the team used a slim jim to open the door.

Wittenberg pulled on gloves, immediately alighting on an envelope on the passenger seat. Getting DC Thornley to video him opening the envelope, he pulled out the letter inside and placed it in an evidence bag. Through the clear bag, he began to read before handing it to Louise. 'Looks like we have our suicide note,' he said.

Jeremy Latchford's suicide note was short and to the point:

*I can no longer live with the guilt of killing my little boy.*

*May the world forgive me.*

# Chapter Thirty-Seven

Louise was back in the incident room by early afternoon with Miles, Robertson and DI Pepperstone, with photographs of Jeremy Latchford's suspected suicide and the note on the crime board, as a snapshot of Jayden Parsons, smiling and unconcerned, loomed over them.

'Watford CID are yet to confirm the handwriting belongs to Jeremy Latchford, but the note was found in his car. Everything points to the fact that he took his own life,' said Louise.

'And this all but wraps your cold case up?' said Pepperstone, sniffing.

Louise frowned, unsure if he was being serious. Her role these last few weeks had been to find out what had happened to Hugo Latchford, and a written confession from the boy's father seemed to be the closest they would get to solving that particular case. Of course, she wanted to know more – why and how Jeremy Latchford had killed his son, and how long Hugo had been imprisoned before he died. But it was likely that Latchford had taken those answers to the grave. All that paled into insignificance with Jayden Parsons missing, however.

'Do you think the Verdant Circle are aware of Latchford's death?' she asked, again playing to the DI's vanity.

'They're aware. There's more attention on them than ever, which was what we were trying to avoid from the beginning.' Pepperstone got to his feet. 'Look, you have someone for the Hugo Latchford killing, and Fiona O'Sullivan and her child are now safe. I will help as much as I can with the missing child, but everything going forward to do with the Verdant Circle will be handled by my division. Do I make myself clear?'

Louise smiled. 'Whatever you say, DI Pepperstone,' she said, before Pepperstone shook his head and stormed off.

Louise decided the best course of action with Pepperstone was to ignore him. Things with the Verdant Circle had been ambiguous before, but now they had a missing child to contend with. The last sighting of Jayden had been in the maroon sports car, and locating that, and in particular the driver, was of great importance. Without more information on the type of car and the number plate, there was little use trying to gather CCTV images from the various sources at her disposal. Instead, she began trawling through the interviews from the camp held during the search, looking for any other mentions of an expensive-looking car being nearby on the day of Latchford's disappearance.

An hour later, she closed her laptop, fearing she was going round in circles. For now, there was only one obvious place for her to go – and that was to see Valerie Latchford. She didn't know how the woman would react to her ex-husband's death, or his apparent confession. But with Jayden missing, Louise needed to see her reaction in the flesh.

Leaving Miles to work through things at headquarters, she drove to Taunton, parking outside the last-known address they had for Valerie. Peering through the window of the terrace, she saw the same mess as last time, with the addition of Valerie Latchford slumped across one of the sofas. It was good to know she was here, but Louise wished she could see a hint of life through the grime-smeared glass.

She knocked on the door, relieved as she returned to the window to see Valerie pushing herself up from the sofa. A few seconds later the front door opened, a dazed-looking Valerie sticking her head out of the doorway. 'Oh, it's you,' she said.

'Good to see you too, Valerie. May I come in?' asked Louise.

'I guess, but you'll have to excuse the mess.'

Louise followed Valerie to the living room, which seemed to be doubling up as Valerie's bedroom. In the corner of the room was a duvet and pillow, each covered in stains. The air was stagnant with the smells of nicotine, stale lager, and body odour. 'I have some news for you,' Louise said, moving a pile of sodden clothes from the sofa so she could sit down. 'We've discovered the body of your ex-husband, Jeremy. We believe he may have taken his own life.'

Valerie squinted her eyes and recovered a plastic bottle from the armchair she was sitting on. She unscrewed the cap and took a long swig of the orange-brown liquid Louise presumed was some kind of scrumpy cider. 'He's dead?'

'Yes,' said Louise, not sure if she should be offering condolences considering what Valerie had gone through with him.

'That's the best news I have heard in years,' said Valerie, her hand shaking as she took another drink.

Louise sighed. 'He left a note,' she said, showing Valerie a photo of the note they'd found in the car.

'*My little boy*,' said Valerie, wiping her eyes. 'He wasn't his fucking little boy. How dare he do this now. After all these years, he finally admits it and takes the coward's way out to avoid serving justice.'

'I know it's of little comfort, but once we close this investigation, we can give Hugo a proper burial.'

Valerie looked at the bottle and put it down. 'That would be nice.'

'I'll do everything I can to make that happen as soon as possible. In the meantime, Valerie, I need your help. There is a boy missing from camp, Jayden Parsons.' She showed Valerie a picture of the missing boy. 'We believe Jeremy took him.'

Valerie stared at her, her mouth hanging open.

'Prior to Jayden's disappearance, there was another boy who had been in danger at the camp. Fortunately, his mother got him to safety. When we interviewed her, she told us about a book she'd found in Jeremy's possession. It was a very old manuscript which she claimed contained images of human sacrifice. Did you ever see such a book when you were with Jeremy?'

'Is that why he did it? Because of some stupid book. He killed my son because of that?'

'It's something we'll be looking into. Our concern is that even though Jeremy is gone, the book might be linked to why Jayden is missing. Can you think of anyone who could have that book now?'

'I don't know anything about a book. As I told you before, there were things about that group I didn't have access to.'

'But Jeremy did? Why was that?'

'I'm not sure.'

'Do you think it's possible that Jeremy already knew about the group before you joined?'

'What do you mean?'

'Is it possible that he intended all along for you to join?'

Valerie glared at the cider bottle, as if daring it not to be the answer to all her problems. 'Maybe. Sometimes I did wonder that. At times it was as if he knew Hugo wasn't his from the beginning.

230

I was so out of it most of the time that I didn't really understand what was happening.'

'Was there anyone he was particularly close to in the group?'

Valerie shook her head. 'I can't remember their names, there were so many of them. But I was always surprised at how respected he was, as if he was an integral part of everything when I always thought I was an outsider. Why are you asking me this now? He's dead, isn't he?'

'He is, but Jayden isn't,' said Louise, softly. 'What happened to Hugo was terrible. I have a son myself and I can't imagine what you've gone through all these years, Valerie. But there is a missing boy out there and I need to find him. Please help me.'

Valerie shook, her eyes focused on the cider.

Louise stood to leave. It seemed she wouldn't be getting anything of use from Valerie today, however much she pleaded. Telling her not to drink would only fall on deaf ears, so she placed her card in the woman's trembling hands and told her to call if it all became too much. She was about to leave when Valerie stopped her. 'If they came for him, then they'll come for me,' she said. 'I told you that before.'

'We don't know if anyone came after Jeremy. From what we can see, he took his own life.'

'I know you don't believe that. He messed up and they sacrificed him. They'll kill me just as easily.'

'Why would they come after you? You haven't been part of that group for years.'

'I need protection. I'm begging you,' said Valerie.

'What is it you're not telling me?'

'What?'

'Valerie, ever since we've met there has been something you're withholding from me. If you want my help, you need to help me.'

Valerie reached for the cider, but Louise put out a hand to stop her. 'No. Tell me.'

'There is a lot you don't know about the Verdant Circle, and Jeremy's involvement. Not that I have all the answers for you, but there was some weird stuff going on even before we joined them.'

'What sort of stuff?'

'Strangers. Sometimes they would be wearing strange costumes. Sometimes, there was . . .'

'You're not making any sense, Valerie.'

Tears ran down Valerie's face, but she seemed oblivious to them. She stared at Louise as if she were replaying some horrendous memory in her mind. 'Sometimes there were children.'

Louise's pulse spiked. 'What are you talking about? Where was this?'

'I stayed upstairs. I was never part of it, I swear.'

'What do you mean, "upstairs"?'

Valerie was borderline incoherent. Her face was flushed as she rambled, but Louise let her continue, hoping she could make sense of what the woman was saying – hoping there might be a clue, however small, that would lead her to finding Jayden. 'I only went there once when Jeremy made me. It was the drugs, I promise. I couldn't help myself. He gave me what I wanted and I did what I was told. But I didn't want to go down there. It was dark, and the smell. But he made me. I lied to you before, when I said Jeremy wasn't Hugo's father. Hugo *was* Jeremy's child. Beneath the house was where Hugo was made.'

'What are you talking about, Valerie?' asked Louise, wanting to shake the answer from the woman.

Wide-eyed, Valerie's face was smeared with make-up and tears, like she was wearing a type of war paint. 'He raped me. That's how Hugo was made. I don't know if that's why he hated his own son so much, but I don't think that really mattered, do you? They all knew what he had done, because they all did things like that all the time.' Valerie grabbed her stomach. 'I feel sick,' she said, vomiting on to the stained carpet.

Louise went to Valerie. She was trying to process what she'd been told, but needed answers. 'Where did this happen to you, Valerie? I need to know. It could be where they have Jayden.'

'The house,' said Valerie, wiping vomit from her mouth. 'Beneath our old house.'

# Chapter Thirty-Eight

Within the hour, Louise had a full team at the Latchford house, ripping up the carpets from the ground floor, searching for access to the supposed basement beneath the house. It rankled that she and Miles hadn't uncovered the hidden basement last time they were here, but there was definitely no obvious sign that it existed, and it was another hour before they had a result. Miles had taken a team to the first floor, and had eventually found a door behind one of the freshly painted walls that turned out to be a recently built partition wall. The door opened to reveal a metallic spiral staircase leading down beneath the house.

'I knew there was a reason for the fresh paint,' said Louise, recalling their last visit. She handed Miles a torch and sent him down first. She followed close behind, fighting feelings of the claustrophobia that she'd developed after the shipping container investigation.

The staircase seemed to be never-ending, and she was relieved when Miles hit solid ground. He shone his torch around the low-ceilinged basement, which appeared to be empty.

Wary that there could be forensic evidence in the area, they walked the perimeter, Miles deep on his haunches as they searched for a secondary exit. 'Here,' he said, pulling open a hatch in the south-east corner.

Louise was on her knees at this point. She shone her torch through the opening, which was an entrance to a tunnel barely wide enough to fit a human inside. 'This would go beneath the garden?'

'I think so,' said Miles. 'Do you want me to go through?'

Louise weighed up the possibilities of Jayden being within the tunnel. The partition wall had been in place before Jayden had gone missing, so it didn't seem feasible that the boy was somewhere here. 'We have no idea how stable it is. Let's get specialist teams in,' she said, retreating back to the house, relieved when her hand touched the metal staircase, and she reached the house proper and was able to step out into the fresh air.

The same specialist team who had retrieved Hugo Latchford's remains from Banwell Caves arrived thirty minutes later. Louise refused to be cowed by the darkness and confines of the cellar, and led the team to the tunnel.

'Any idea where this leads?' asked the leader of the team, Sergeant Giles Matheson.

'There's something called the druid's altar, but that must be at least eight hundred yards from the house, if not more. Also, I've been there and didn't see any visible signs of an opening that would lead to this tunnel.'

'I'll need to check that out first, and see if there's anything on record for this tunnel. It could be a long afternoon,' said Giles.

'Understood,' said Louise, retreating once more to the safety of the staircase.

Giles could find no record for the tunnel, and instructed everyone not in the specialist team to wait upstairs as they investigated further. Although it seemed unlikely that Jayden might be somewhere in the tunnel, a distant part of Louise still hoped that Giles would radio from beneath the ground to say the boy was safe and sound within.

Tracey called as Miles and a member of specialist teams set up a video link. 'I think I have a match on the car that picked up Jeremy Latchford and Jayden from the camp. I made a search of the closest cameras to the site and we picked a car travelling east at 6.27 a.m. A maroon-coloured Audi R8,' said Tracey.

'What makes you think this is him?'

'The number plate. Belongs to Rupert Gosling.'

'Gosling? Do we know where the car is now?'

'We're on it,' said Tracey.

Things were escalating all at once. It could be a coincidence that the husband of the head of the Verdant Circle was driving close to the camp in Priddy the day Jayden went missing. But it seemed unlikely.

What it did suggest was some form of conspiracy, and it also put further into doubt Jeremy Latchford's suicide. Was it possible that Latchford had been killed for what he knew? And if so, did Rupert Gosling have Jayden in captivity? Ending the call, Louise turned to the screen Miles had set up.

'They've entered the tunnel,' he said, pointing to the grainy image on the screen, which wasn't showing much beyond the slow progress of one of the specialist team as he made his way through the dark space. Louise shivered involuntarily. It wasn't a job she envied, and she wasn't looking forward to making the journey herself should the route be cleared.

'More space in front of me,' said the specialist officer through his headset. 'Everything seems secure. There are turrets in place, looks like they've put a lot of work into this,' he added, breathlessly.

Louise watched with Miles as the officer crawled further into the tunnel before getting to his feet. Shining his torch around the interior, he said, 'Looks to be approximately thirty yards or so deep. Natural cave formation.'

The images from his body cam were indistinct but Louise could make out the rock structure as he walked the perimeter of the cave. She thought about Jayden and where he might be, the thought leading her to dwell on her own children. It seemed so long since she'd seen Jack and Emily.

'I think I have something. Sweet Jesus,' said the officer, turning his torch to a hidden section of the cave where, curled up in a heap next to manacles chained to the rock wall, was a small bundle of bones – the scene reminiscent of the discovery of Hugo Latchford several weeks earlier.

# Chapter Thirty-Nine

Any fear that the remains belonged to Jayden Parsons was immediately ruled out – the bundle of bones had been in that position for years. But the question remained – whose were they?

The CSIs were called in, and they waited for the specialist team officers to return before the head CSI, Janice Sutton, and her colleague were led through the tunnel, where they would begin photographing and filming the area ahead of the difficult task of collecting the remains and bringing them back.

'Do you think it's Ben Carter?' asked Miles, when they managed to get a quiet second.

'It would be my guess, but we aren't going to know for days . . . if we ever know at all.'

'There must be a connection.'

Louise wasn't sure if it was a question or not. The obvious connection was the Latchfords, but with Jeremy dead, and his father long since gone, the only person left was Valerie – and she was in protection, and had been running scared of the Verdant Circle ever since Hugo had disappeared. 'That's for us to prove, Miles. But for now, all I care about is Jayden. Where are we on locating Rupert Gosling?'

Miles shook his head, his tiredness showing. Like her, he'd been working full-out, and if her current state was anything to go by, he must be exhausted. 'Take thirty minutes in the car,' she said. 'Get some food if you haven't had anything. It could be a long night.'

Louise wanted to take her own advice, but she couldn't rest. The investigation was moving too slowly, and with tomorrow being the solstice she needed answers now. Even with the feed showing Janice Sutton and the CSIs reaching the cave, she felt like she was wasting her time. She called Tracey for an update, and even made contact with Pepperstone on the off-chance he had anything for her.

'That complicates things,' said Pepperstone, when she told him about the discovery beneath the Latchford house.

Louise was still unsure about the offhand way Pepperstone seemed to deal with everything. She'd just told him that a second set of remains had been discovered, and it sounded like it had barely registered. 'Certainly gives more credence to the possibility that the Verdant Circle were involved in these deaths,' she said. 'And there's more. We have CCTV image of Rupert Gosling's car driving away from the camp on the morning of Jeremy Latchford's death.'

'He's supposed to be in Germany. Do you have facial identification?'

'Not at the moment. We're trying to track the route the car took from the first sighting. Listen, Gerrard, I want to be upfront with you. I'd like to see Ella Gosling again. This time without prior warning. Maybe you could join me. If we can link the Verdant Circle to these deaths, and we can get a hold of where Jayden might be, then surely that will help bring the organisation down. Sounds like a win-win to me.'

Louise waited, moving the phone away from her ear at the sound of Pepperstone's breathing. She was going to see Ella Gosling with or without his permission, but it made sense to get her fellow DI on side.

'Sounds like it's all coming to a head. I appreciate the call. When are you thinking of leaving?'

'Now.'

'I'll do the same. I'll meet you near her house. But for now, Louise, I would keep this very quiet.'

'Understood,' she said, hanging up.

Louise checked in on Miles before leaving. He looked a little crestfallen when she told him she was going to see Ella Gosling without him, but she reinforced the necessity of finding out where Rupert Gosling's car had gone after leaving the camp. If they could get video evidence of Gosling being with Jeremy Latchford and Jayden, then it could help prove a link between the deaths and the Verdant Circle.

It was another long journey. Louise thought of the floating parts of the investigation as she drove, searching for that final piece that would link everything together. Two children had died, most likely murdered by someone linked to the Verdant Circle, and she couldn't let Jayden be the next.

Pepperstone texted and they agreed to meet a few streets down from the Gosling house. He was waiting for her, standing outside his car, his shirt covered in sweat. 'I have confirmation that Rupert Gosling is back in the UK,' he said.

'He could be at the house?'

Pepperstone shook his head. 'We've got it under surveillance. He hasn't returned there since he left. At present, Ella Gosling is alone.'

Louise hid her surprise and annoyance, marvelling at the budget Pepperstone must have in place to keep the Gosling residence under permanent surveillance. 'You've met her before?'

'Numerous times. She's not my number one fan.'

That, Louise could imagine. 'I'll lead then.'

'She'll know what's going on. She's a savvy operator. She'll have a contingency plan in place. But I think you're right, if there was ever a time to lean on her, it would be now.'

They walked together to the front gates, Louise pressing the video doorbell and informing Ella that she was there with DI Pepperstone. It could all go wrong at this point. Ella was within her rights to deny them access and they had no real grounds for arrest, but after a pause the gates opened.

'Come through,' said Ella, after they had made the short walk down the driveway to the front of the house. She was dressed in an elegant summer dress as if she was due at a wedding or a party. Louise followed her through to the dark-walled library where she had sat before. This time Ella didn't have a lawyer or an assistant with her, and didn't offer any refreshments. 'This is about Jeremy Latchford, I presume?' she said, inviting them to sit.

'You've already heard?'

'Terrible business. I didn't know him very well, but from what I understand he was a very troubled man.'

Louise noticed Ella was focusing all her attention on her, as if denying Pepperstone's presence. 'You may have also heard that a young boy, Jayden Parsons, has gone missing from the camp in Priddy?'

Ella appeared confused. 'No, this is news to me.'

'Your husband was close friends with Jeremy Latchford, I believe?'

Ella frowned, taken aback. 'Not that I'm aware of.'

'Jeremy Latchford and Jayden Parsons were picked up from camp yesterday in a car belonging to your husband: an Audi R8.'

'My husband has lots of cars.'

Louise showed Ella the photograph of the same car on the outskirts of Priddy. 'The number plates are a match.'

'I don't understand. You think Rupert has something to do with Jeremy's death and this missing boy?'

The question was matter-of-fact, as if Ella wasn't surprised by the possibility. 'Do you think Rupert is capable of such things?' asked Louise.

'Listen, I think I should call my lawyer.'

'You're free to do that, Ella,' said Louise, before she was interrupted by Pepperstone.

'It's all coming apart, Ella. I think you know that,' he said. 'Rupert and all the others are going down. The option for you is simple: you help us and we can help you. If you don't want to, then be prepared to fall with the rest of them.'

It wasn't the approach Louise would have taken, but it seemed to have the desired effect. The colour drained from Ella's face. She was scratching her neck, looking from Pepperstone to Louise, as if deciding who she could trust. 'What is it you want to know?' she said, finally.

Pepperstone was the first to speak. It was clear to Louise that they both still had completely different agendas. Pepperstone's questions concerned the financial irregularities of the Verdant Circle, while all Louise cared about was finding Jayden.

In the end, Louise persuaded Ella to show them to Rupert's office, which took up the whole of the third floor of the house.

'I don't imagine you're going to find anything of use here,' said Ella.

Pepperstone looked at the laptop on Gosling's desk, but without a warrant it was all but useless.

'You know how this all came about, don't you, Ella?' asked Louise.

'What do you mean?'

'Why Jeremy Latchford fled the camp in Priddy . . . Why he took his own life.'

Ella grimaced, but was too sharp to incriminate herself. 'Enlighten me.'

Louise told her about Fiona O'Sullivan and Max, and the second set of remains they'd found beneath the Latchford house. 'You see, it's much more than a corruption case now, and I won't rest until I've got to the bottom of everything. You need to tell me exactly what you know, now.'

Ella collapsed on to one of the office chairs as Pepperstone flicked through the files, requesting permission every time he opened something. 'It has nothing to do with me,' said Ella, her body slumped as if all her energy had dissipated.

'You knew this was going on, though?' said Louise.

'Of course not. There have always been rumours. This isn't what Mummy wanted for the group but . . .'

'But others wanted something different.'

'There were rumours.'

'Rumours isn't enough, Ella. You need to tell me what you know now, or I'll arrest you and search this place top to bottom,' said Louise, ignoring the sharp look from Pepperstone.

Ella began biting her fingernails. 'The Verdant Circle existed long before my parents made it official. Mummy wanted to do some good with it. She truly believed in collective organisation, as did I, but there were darker roots to the group. I thought all that was gone, but every now and then I would get a hint of it. Why Hugo Latchford went missing all those years ago, and other things . . .'

'Such as?'

'I need to speak to my lawyer,' said Ella, some of her earlier energy returning.

'You're free to do that, but do remember there is a little boy who's missing. We don't know what has happened to him, or where he is, but delaying everything with lawyers could jeopardise finding him. Do you think you could live with that?'

Ella went to speak, but her mouth hung open.

'Fiona O'Sullivan told me about a book she'd seen in Jeremy Latchford's possession. It told of human sacrifice, amongst other things. She was convinced Jeremy was going to replace Hugo Latchford's remains with her son. It's the solstice tomorrow, Ella. I think someone plans to sacrifice Jayden. Please help me find him.'

Ella had gone so pale, Louise thought she might faint. Pepperstone had stopped fiddling through Rupert Gosling's files and was watching intently. Eventually, Ella got to her feet. 'Through here,' she said, opening the doors to a walk-in wardrobe and pulling a sliding door apart to reveal a large wall safe. 'Rupert doesn't think I know the code but I do,' she said, her finger hovering over the keypad.

'Please,' said Louise.

'Before I do, I want you both to know that I have never looked inside before. Do you understand me? I know the code because he uses it for everything. But I've never looked inside.'

Louise nodded. 'I understand. Please open the safe.'

Ella entered a six-digit code and the safe opened. Louise eased Ella aside and looked inside. 'We need to call backup,' she said to Pepperstone.

# Chapter Forty

Louise had requested backup because the first thing she had found in the safe was a handgun. 'Is it loaded?' she asked, putting on gloves and taking the gun from the safe.

Ella stood with her arms folded. 'I've never seen that in my life.'

'Take a seat, Ella,' said Louise, and she waited until Ella had left the wardrobe before handing the gun to Pepperstone, who put it in an evidence bag. Slowly, she retrieved the rest of the safe's contents – documents, passports, and four bundles of currency; two of sterling, one of dollars, and one of euros – until she came across a leather zipped folder at the back of the safe. 'What's this?' Louise asked Ella.

'I've agreed to help. I told you I know nothing, except that Rupert keeps his secrets in there.'

With her gloves still on, Louise unzipped the leather file. Inside she found four USB drives, and a second leather folder. *These keep getting smaller*, she thought, as she opened the second folder and retrieved an old leather-bound folio. The book was called *The Verdant Circle*, and contained fifty or so pages of stained parchment covered in handwritten ink.

Louise lay the book on the bed so Pepperstone could see it. She moved through the pages one by one. The text was small and densely packed, each page probably containing over a thousand words. Images appeared nearer the end of the book, reminiscent of what Fiona had described, of a boy being sacrificed by a group of dancing adults wearing animal masks.

'Fiona said the pages she'd discovered were loose within the covers,' said Louise.

'A copy, or this is the original?'

Louise peered closer at what appeared to be a set of maps, marking out a number of underground cave systems. 'What does that say? The *sacred sites?*' she said, squinting.

'The twelve sacred sites. What the hell is this shit?' said Pepperstone.

Louise tried to read through the passages but the cursive was all but unreadable. 'Here,' she said, finding an entry for the druid's altar in Frome, and then Banwell Caves. 'We'll need to get an expert to examine it, but Banwell Caves is where Hugo Latchford was found, and the druid's altar, here, is next to where Ben Carter went missing.'

'That's great. For now, I'm very interested to see what we have on these thumb drives,' said Pepperstone.

Louise pointed to the book. 'What does this mean, Ella?'

'I've never seen it before.'

'Save it. You're cooperating and it's being duly noted, but I know you've seen this book before. Your parents formed the Verdant Circle.'

'I told you, that's not quite the case. It existed long before they were involved.'

'They would have seen this book, and I refuse to believe you haven't.'

It was evident Ella was losing her fight. She sat on the bed, hugging herself. 'I've seen it, but it's a relic. I've never read it, it's impenetrable. It's not the basis of what my parents wanted to do, or what I wanted to continue.'

'But other people think differently . . . your husband included?'

Ella shrugged.

'Have you ever heard of these twelve sacred sites before?'

Ella rocked herself side to side, hugging her body. 'They're myths. Supposedly there were twelve sacred sites set across the country, long before my parents were ever involved. This goes back to pagan times. Twelve sacred sites and twelve guardians for Gaia. Twelve sacrifices. My parents never took any of that seriously, and neither do I.'

'But they're real places, Ella, you can see that? We've found two sets of remains. What does it mean? It's solstice tomorrow, is Jayden in danger?'

'I don't know,' said Ella.

Backup arrived, and Louise arrested Ella for possession of an illegal firearm. She spoke to the local DS who had come to the scene, and asked for his help in carrying out a search on the property. 'Is there anywhere we can view these?' she asked, pointing to the thumb drives in the evidence bags.

'I'll call my tech team now. Got some machines back at the station you can use.'

Within the hour, they were at Madeley police station, working with one of the IT specialists who had prepared a clean laptop, currently unconnected to the internet, so they could try the thumb drives without risk of contaminating the whole system.

Pepperstone's eyes all but popped out of his head as the specialist bypassed the rudimentary protection on the drive to open the files. It made little sense to Louise, watching the specialists click on links to hundreds of spreadsheets and bank statements. 'This is what you've been looking for all this time?' she asked.

'It's certainly not going to hinder us,' said Pepperstone, something approaching a smile appearing on his face for the first time that Louise could remember.

Similar documents appeared on the next two drives, but it was only when they reached the fourth drive that Louise found what she'd been looking for, though seconds into the playback, part of her wished she'd never found the file. 'That's Hugo Latchford,' she said, as a grainy image of a campfire played on the screen. Hugo was sitting in the middle of a circle of people, all of whom were wearing animal masks. Louise searched for a clue as to the location, the petrified boy shaking as the group began chanting and the video was abruptly cut off.

A second video appeared. This time the footage was filmed inside. The area was dimly lit, the only illumination coming from the fiery torches held by the masked people. It was hard to see for sure, but it looked to Louise as if this was Hugo's final resting place. She watched transfixed, knowing these images would never leave her mind, as the boy crawled through a small crack in the cave and lay on the floor, before his image faded from sight as rocks were piled up against the opening and the video stopped.

The three of them stared at the blank screen in silence. It was impossible to say if any of the masked people had been Jeremy Latchford, but it was clear that more than one person was responsible for Hugo Latchford's death, which meant that more than one person had to be involved in Jayden Parsons' disappearance.

Louise didn't reach headquarters until late, the incident room still full of officers. With the revelation in the books about the twelve sacred sites, and the solstice tomorrow, no one was planning on leaving.

She'd called Thomas as she drove back, explaining the situation. Not for the first time in recent weeks, she was pleased that she'd married an ex-copper. Thomas didn't need any explanations, and understood her absences even if they were far from ideal. How Emily and Jack would deal with them was a different matter, but Louise couldn't focus on that now.

She'd agreed with Pepperstone that he would take the first three flash drives, and she the last with the images of Hugo Latchford on them, and that they would pool their results. She wanted her IT expert, Simon Coulson, to go through the flash drive in detail that evening, as there were numerous files she hadn't had time to analyse.

She was also carrying the Verdant Circle book, and had instructed a team to be ready to work through it. There was a bustling incident room waiting for her when she eventually returned.

Images of Ella and Rupert Gosling had been added to the crime board, but Louise was focused on the smiling image of Jayden Parsons staring back at her.

Miles stopped her before she'd time to get her bearings. 'We've made some progress on finding Rupert Gosling's car,' he said, thrusting a laptop into her arms.

Louise pulled the laptop away to see a clear image of Rupert Gosling driving Jeremy Latchford along the M5 in the Audi R8. She squinted, catching a blurred image of a third person in the background. She thought that it had to be Jayden. She wondered what the men had said to him, whether the boy had been restrained.

'We've tracked the car to the outskirts of Watford. The last image we have is in Garston.'

Louise glanced at the image. 'That's definitely Jayden,' she said, trying to read the blank face of the young boy in the back seat.

'Gosling has an office there,' said Miles.

'Yet Latchford drove to the shopping centre in a different car?'

'We have images of him in the car park as well.' Miles pressed some buttons on the laptop, and Louise watched Latchford leaving the car park and taking the elevator to the ground floor of the shopping centre. The images followed Latchford as he made his journey to the hotel, cutting out now and then, until the camera in the hotel lobby picked him up.

'Doesn't look like much coercion going on there,' said Louise.

'Maybe his guilty conscience got the better of him finally?'

'Maybe,' said Louise, 'but that doesn't explain where Jayden is.'

Simon Coulson arrived in the incident room and took the thumb drive from her. He had worked with Louise on a number of investigations, and she trusted him as much as anyone in the station.

'I can scan the book you have as well,' he said. 'See what matches we can get online?'

'OK, I'll come with you. You too, Miles. You're going to need to see this.'

Coulson led them through to his department, where he gave the Verdant Circle book to his colleagues to work on before loading the flash drive on to a designated computer.

The next couple of hours were probably the worst Louise had ever experienced as a police officer. Usually, specialist teams would trawl through such material, after significant training with lots of support, but there wasn't time for that. There were more videos of Hugo Latchford, and other children held in captivity. At one point, Miles had to rush to the toilets to be sick, and returned a few minutes later ghostly white and covered in sweat. Of all the things Louise ever encountered in her duties, the abuse of children was always the hardest to understand. There was no sexual abuse in the videos themselves, but the torment and psychopathic cruelty were evident on the dazed faces of the victims. The perpetrators were masked in every frame, using the cover of their costumes, and their supposed beliefs as an excuse for their monstrous crimes.

'We need to find every single person in this video,' said Louise, not recognising the growl in her voice as the most recent video mercifully ended.

'We've found matches of the book in one of our online files,' said one of Coulson's colleagues, Grace Levy, who looked as shaken as Louise felt. 'Here,' she said, handing Louise a printout with typed-out words instead of the illegible scrawl on the manuscript. 'It was already in our database in various forms. There are snippets from various sources, some going back hundreds of years, some less than a century. This is one I think you will find most relevant.'

Louise read through the text of the twelve sacred sites she had discovered in Ella Gosling's house. As the title suggested, and Ella had alluded to, it was a list of twelve locations, UK-wide, believed to be sacred to members of the Verdant Circle. Only, there was a caveat to the sacredness of these places. Louise read through the manuscript. There seemed no logical reason for the locations of the twelve sites, beyond the fact that they ranged the length and breadth of the UK.

'Where do they come up with these monstrous ideas?' said Louise.

'There are links in the document. I'll send you the online version so you can read in more detail. The beliefs stem from ancient pagan rituals. The belief was that human sacrifices were needed to appease Gaia, to ensure good harvests, that sort of thing. For this to work they believed a human sacrifice had to be innocent and alive, and entombed in the land.'

'Which appears to be what happened to Hugo Latchford, and Ben Carter,' said Miles, the colour yet to return to his face.

'Yes,' said Grace. 'Only, the theory was that for the sites to be protected, the sacrifices had to be in place before the summer solstice. Here, look,' she said, pointing to a passage she'd typed out:

*If a soul be unearthed, ere the solstice night's zenith, another must take its stead beneath the moon's gaze by the stroke of solstice's midnight.*

# Chapter Forty-One

Louise caught a couple of hours' sleep at the station. She had no option. Everything pointed to something happening today. She missed Thomas and the children, but how could she go home when they hadn't found Jayden? She was awake again before 6 a.m. and changed into a fresh set of clothes she kept at the station for situations such as this. She sent a text to Thomas, explaining what was happening, and told him to kiss Emily and Jack for her while trying to ignore the guilt eating away at her.

Taken literally, the book they'd found at Ella Gosling's house suggested a replacement had to be in place for the remains of Hugo Latchford before midnight today. However, subsequent translating of the text suggested that a like for like replacement wasn't necessarily needed, therefore it didn't necessarily need to happen in Banwell. It seemed the so-called sacred sites were highly generalised, and covered regions more than specific places, which made the job of finding a potential location even harder than it already was.

Louise had already positioned a team at Banwell Caves to watch the site, even though it seemed highly improbable that Rupert Gosling would risk taking Jayden there, and other units had been sent to other possible locations in the region.

CID was full before 8.30 a.m., and not long after they had a minor success. 'We've found Rupert Gosling's car,' said Miles.

'Please tell me it's nearby,' said Louise.

'Outskirts of Shepton Mallet. The car was left at a supermarket. Monitoring cameras clocked it as being over its four-hour limit.'

'That's close to where the Jenkinses live,' said Louise. 'See if you can make contact with them. I'm going to take a look at Gosling's vehicle.'

A local patrol car was already at the supermarket by the time Louise arrived. Rupert Gosling's car was on the ground floor and was locked. Louise walked around the car, which was worth more than her yearly wage, and shone her torch into the immaculate interior. As she was deciding what to do next, Miles messaged to say they had CCTV images of Rupert Gosling arriving last night in the car at 8.30 p.m. Louise flicked through the images, wondering why Gosling was in the area and where he had gone next. She told Miles to scour the local area for CCTV images of Gosling before instructing the officers to break into the car.

Louise hadn't expected much, but was still disappointed there was nothing to be found that would aid them in finding Jayden. After making a preliminary search of the interior, including the boot, she told the officers to get the car towed to headquarters for further analysis.

She had to keep dismissing images of Jayden in captivity from her head, convincing herself there was still time to find him, but it was the solstice and time seemed to be going quicker than normal.

She called Miles before leaving. 'Did you get hold of the Jenkinses?'

'No, I've left them messages,' Miles said on the other end of the line. 'And I've sent a patrol team over there but they're out. However, I just cross-checked with social services and they only have one child staying with them at present. One of the children they were looking after has successfully been adopted, and another has been returned to the system and is currently awaiting another foster placement.'

'Who are they looking after now?'

'Simon Wilson, aged nine.'

'OK, I'm coming back. Make sure that patrol car stays there and alerts us when the Jenkinses return,' she said.

Louise wanted to be everywhere at once, but she was experienced enough to know how to delegate. Everyone was working towards the same goal, and she had to trust the other members of the team. Still, something pivotal felt just out of reach. If she could just concentrate hard enough, she could manoeuvre all the various pieces into a whole. She knew something was definitely about to happen to Jayden, she just needed to know where and when it was to take place.

Back at headquarters, the tension was palpable. Although they only had the word of the Verdant Circle book that something was going to happen today, they had a missing boy to find, and that had the whole station focused.

'Can I have a word, Louise?' said Robertson, tapping her on the shoulder.

Louise jumped, realising she had been so fixated on the crime board, and thoughts of Jayden Parsons, that everything else had faded to the periphery. She followed her boss out of the room to his office. 'I know now isn't the time, but I thought you should know we have an official date for your interview panel. Ten days away,' he said.

'You can't wait to get out of here, can you?'

Robertson smiled. 'Why don't you take a break. Five minutes. I'll leave you my room so you can get used to it.'

'I don't think I'd ever get used to sitting on that side of the desk.'

'No one said you could sit in my seat,' said Robertson with a grin as he left the office.

Louise took a breath, savouring the silence for the briefest of seconds before calling Pepperstone.

'We're still working through the flash drives. Some useful stuff for us, nothing that would help you as of yet. We've come across a number of encrypted files that could be of interest. Our team is working on them presently. I'll notify you if we find anything of use,' said Pepperstone, sounding the most helpful he'd been since they'd met.

'OK, thanks.'

'How are things progressing? Any luck finding the boy?'

Louise told him about the discovery of Gosling's car at the supermarket. 'If that bloody book is anything to go by, we're running out of time.'

'We're working full-out here as well. I'll make sure everyone's focus is on finding the boy,' said Pepperstone.

'Appreciate that, Gerrard,' said Louise, hanging up just as there was a knock on Robertson's door.

'The Jenkinses are home,' said Miles.

It felt like the hottest day of the year as they got into the car and it was relief to be able to switch on the air conditioning. As they drove back to Shepton Mallet, she could sense Miles drifting in and out of wakefulness in the passenger seat, as if he was fighting to stay awake. Louise understood how he felt, and buzzed down her window for some fresh air as she sped along the back streets towards the Jenkins house, passing the fields where Hugo Latchford had gone missing twelve years ago.

'Vehicle's there,' said Miles as they reached the house, pointing to a rusty, brown camper van which had seen better days.

Louise peered in through the smeared windows of the van, which seemed to be used as a dumping ground for various sweet wrappers and crisp packets. Leslie Jenkins was already at the front door by the time they walked up path, his face a mask of consternation. 'Why are you two back, and why are you looking in my van?'

'Sorry to bother you, Mr Jenkins. May we come in?' said Louise.

Mr Jenkins sighed, then opened the door. 'What the hell is it?' he said, as he let them in and led them into the living room. 'My wife is trying to sleep. She has a headache, and knowing you are here will make things worse. You dragged up a lot of bad memories the last time you visited.'

'I am sorry about that. There have been some developments since we last spoke,' said Louise, explaining about Jeremy Latchford's death and what had happened to Jayden Parsons, stopping short of the remains that had been found in Frome.

'I am sorry to hear about that, but what has it got to do with me?'

Louise looked around the room, wondering if Mrs Jenkins really was sleeping. 'We believe a person of interest in the investigation is active in this area.'

'You said Mr Latchford took his own life. In Watford?'

'Yes, that was why we were surprised to find a car belonging to the last person seen with Mr Latchford in the local supermarket less than a mile from your house.'

'I really don't understand.'

'Do you know this man?' said Louise, showing him a photo of Rupert Gosling on her phone.

Mr Jenkins took out a pair of spectacles and squinted at the image. She studied his response, his look of surprise appearing genuine. 'Never seen him before in my life. Who is he?'

'His name is Rupert Gosling.'

'Sorry, I have no idea who he is. If you think he might be in the house, please feel free to take a look.'

Louise didn't think Gosling was anywhere nearby, but she couldn't risk ignoring the invitation. She gestured to Miles to make a search of the house.

'My wife is sleeping in the second bedroom on the right.'

Miles nodded and walked away.

'The house is very quiet at the moment,' said Louise.

'Isn't it just.'

'Why is that?'

Mr Jenkins went to answer, his mouth opening to speak when he changed tack. 'What is this?' he said, part perplexed, part angry.

'I believe you're looking after a foster child at the moment. Simon Wilson?'

'How would you know, and why do you . . . Oh, I see. You think Simon is in danger, is that it?'

'No, it's not that—'

'Yes, it is,' said Mr Jenkins, interrupting. 'Well, may I suggest you check your facts before you come to my house flinging around accusations. Simon is back with his biological mother. We have been away today to do the handover. Surely that came up on whatever system you work on?'

Miles returned before Louise had time to answer, shaking his head, which infuriated Mr Jenkins more. 'You need to leave now, both of you,' he said. 'I don't know what you think is going on here, but we're not involved in any way.'

'Did you look in on the wife?' asked Louise, once they were back in the car.

'Door was ajar so I snuck a quick look in there. She was asleep.'

'We'll keep the patrol car here for now. Get confirmation Simon Wilson returned to his biological mother today,' said Louise, as she headed back to headquarters once more.

They stopped at a petrol station for coffee on the way back, the caffeine rush doing little for Louise other than to put her more on edge. She felt they were being reactive at the moment, and it wasn't the way she liked to work.

'What time is it?' she said, placing her paper cup in the bin of the petrol station's forecourt.

'One thirty.'

Louise watched the other patrons filling their cars. She didn't need any reminding that this was the longest day of the year. At that precise moment, it felt like it would never end. 'Miles, get me another one for the journey,' she said, as her phone began to ring.

Miles nodded and ambled back to the kiosk as Louise looked at her phone. 'Hope you've got some good news for me, Gerrard,' she said, answering the call from Pepperstone.

'Where are you, Louise? Do you have access to a computer screen?'

'On location. What do you have? Can you send it by phone?'

'Needs to be secure. We've managed to access the hidden files. There's an old recording you need to see. Looks like an old Super 8 film that has been digitised. Same sorts of people in the same stupid outfits, only this time there are some missed moments.'

'What do you mean, "missed moments"?'

'It looks like whoever was recording played a little trick . . . a little later in the footage, the same people are caught on camera without their masks on.'

259

# Chapter Forty-Two

Louise rarely got carried away with the promise of new evidence. She'd been disappointed too many times in the past. But she couldn't deny the skip in her heart as she ran to the petrol station's shop and told Miles to forget the coffee.

She tried not to speed as they headed back to headquarters. Pepperstone was sending over the files securely, and she needed access to a police-issued computer to prevent jeopardising the evidence trail.

She'd primed Simon Coulson, who was waiting in the incident room. 'Files are coming through now,' he said.

Louise watched the system go through its checks before the files were ready to access, her heart hammering in her chest as she pressed play on one of the video files.

As Pepperstone had suggested, the quality of the footage suggested it had been taken a long time ago, as did the decor of the room on the screen. 'You recognise it?' she said to Miles.

'It's the Latchford house,' he said, as four masked figures appeared on screen. Five including the camera person.

Louise's initial thoughts were that the masks were the same as in the other files recovered from Ella Gosling's house, each person wearing the face of an animal. A fox, a badger, a boar and a raven. It was the largest of the figures, the one with the boar's head, that drew the camera person's interest, just before the feed phased out to be replaced with a new location.

'That's where we found the remains,' she said, as the figures came back into focus.

Once more the camera person focused on the boar-headed figure who was speaking, though the footage had no sound.

'The area is well lit,' said Miles.

Louise nodded as the boar moved to the side to reveal the semi-clad figure of a boy in chains. 'If I was to guess, I would say that's Ben Carter,' said Louise, as mercifully the image faded out, this time replaced with a much clearer scene, the camera steadier than before as if it had been placed on a tripod.

It was the living room area of the Latchford house. Where now it was whitewashed, everything in the footage was tinged with browns and beige, including a sofa and two armchairs where five people were sitting, drinking and smoking.

Louise leant closer to the screen, only now realising she was holding her breath. 'That's Lee Latchford,' she said, pointing to a burly man sitting alone on an armchair, smoking a cigar.

'Like father like son,' said Miles. 'Do you recognise the others?'

Louise shook her head, before leaning closer to the screen, her focus on a petite woman sitting opposite Latchford projecting almost undisguised lust. 'Jesus,' she said, noting the mole beneath the woman's right eye. 'I think we met her the other day.'

'Marion Parker, that old woman?' said Miles, as Louise drove them towards Castle Batch park in Worle.

'I'm sure it's her,' said Louise.

'I suppose it makes sense in a way. She was a neighbour of both the Latchfords and the Carters.'

Louise rushed around the late-afternoon traffic as safely as she could, all the time recalling the meeting with Marion Parker, trying to remember if there was something she had missed. Louise was convinced it was her on the video. Fifty years younger, maybe, but definitely her. She checked the time on the car's dashboard. It was coming up to 7.20 p.m. 'That footage was from fifty years ago. She said she'd needed to get away from everything that had happened. Let's hope she's remorseful and can help us,' she said, parking up outside the house.

There was no answer, so Louise tried her next-door neighbour, a woman of similar age to Mrs Parker answering. 'If you're looking for Marion, she's gone,' said the woman.

'DI Blackwell,' said Louise, showing the woman her ID. 'Where has she gone?'

'I thought it was odd, but I didn't want to say anything. A car picked her up a couple of hours ago. Two men. I came out to say something, to ask Marion where she was going, but they'd already gone.'

# Chapter Forty-Three

Marion Parker may have been hiding out these last few decades, but it appeared she was intrinsic to whatever sick games those involved were playing. 'What's your name, madam?'

'Jean. Jean Watkins,' said the woman, who seemed to be having the time of her life.

'Have you ever seen the men before? Is this usual behaviour for Marion?'

'Not at all. That was why I tried to find out who they were. I only saw one of the men, who came to the door. Lovely looking guy, tall, grey hair. Marion greeted him as if he was family. To be honest, I was a little jealous.'

'Was this him, Jean?' asked Louise, showing the woman a photo of Rupert Gosling on her phone.

'Yes, that was him.'

'And this boy?' said Louise, showing the woman a picture of Jayden.

The woman shook her head. 'No, sorry.'

'Could he have been in the car?'

'Maybe. I only saw the car from the window.'

'I don't suppose you know what type of car they were driving, do you?' said Miles.

'Have you not seen the sign on my window, young man?' said Jean, dismissively, pointing to a sticker for the neighbourhood watch. 'I wrote it down, hold on.'

Louise and Miles stood in silence as they waited for the woman to return. 'Here you go,' said Jean, handing Miles a piece of paper with a car description and a number plate written down.

'You're sure it was an S-type Jaguar?' said Miles.

'Yes, the big cat on the front gave it away,' said Jean, tutting as she shook her head. 'And it was maroon. Could hardly miss the bloody thing.'

The car belonged to a leasing company in Shropshire, five miles from where the Goslings lived. Louise called Robertson as Miles took on driving detail. She explained everything that had happened with the new footage and Marion Parker.

'What exactly is it you think is going to happen?' asked Robertson, his tone unreadable.

'If I'm being brutally honest, I think they intend to sacrifice Jayden Parsons tonight. I just don't know where.'

'What do you need?'

'I need more staff, Iain. Over at the fields by the Latchford house in Frome, in the woods by Priddy. Miles and I are heading to Banwell Caves as we speak, and I could do with some people over there as well.'

'Leave it with me,' said Robertson, after a long pause.

A light was on in the small house near Banwell Caves where this had all started almost a month ago. Miles checked in on the undercover car situated down the road from the house before they made the short walk to the property.

Malcolm Landry answered the door. He was in his dressing gown, and Louise smelled alcohol on his breath. 'Hello, Detective, fancy seeing you here again.'

'Mr Landry. I need your help,' said Louise. 'May we come in?'

Puzzled, Landry let them in the house. 'Excuse my attire. Decided to have an early bath today, as it were. My wife, Samantha,' he said as they entered the dining area. Mrs Landry, dressed in jeans and a light-coloured blouse, was holding a glass of red wine. She offered them a curt smile.

Louise gave them an edited version of recent events. 'I'd like you to show me the cave again, please, Mr Landry.' The cave was private property and technically they needed permission before entering.

'What, now? You don't think the boy is there, do you?'

'If you don't mind.'

They waited in awkward silence as Mr Landry went upstairs to get changed. Mrs Landry clearly didn't want them to be there, and didn't offer them any refreshments as they stood in the kitchen area.

'Come on then,' said Mr Landry, returning. 'Though I can assure you no one has accessed the cave since you were last here.'

The light was starting to fade as they walked to the cave, but the day's heat hung in the air as if it was still midday. They passed through the Druid's Temple, the tower looming in the distance. Louise wondered what relevance the place had to the Verdant Circle, and wished now they'd conducted more research into Landry and his wife.

'Come on then,' said Landry, torch in hand as they crossed the threshold. Miles lowered his head, despite not quite being at risk of hitting the top of the stone entrance, as they moved into the bone cave.

'Haven't been back since you took those remains away. It's had a horrible impact on us if truth be told. Hard to accept we've been living here all this time with that boy's body only metres away,' said Mr Landry, as he walked to the centre of the cave, the collections of animal bones almost a mockery of what had happened there.

Louise realised she hadn't considered how the Landrys would have fared after Hugo Latchford's remains were taken away. Violent crime always had a lingering effect, its tentacles spreading far beyond those directly involved.

Both she and Miles had brought torches with them, and together they searched the small area. Louise shone her torch through the small opening where Hugo's remains had been found, her pulse spiking as if she somehow expected to see Marion Parker and Rupert Gosling there, ready to sacrifice Jayden.

'What were you hoping to find?' asked Mr Landry, once they were back outside. In the fading light, he looked pale and old, and Louise chided herself for not considering how the discovery would have affected him.

'I'm not really sure. Have you ever heard of the Verdant Circle?'

'I've heard of them. Nutcases, the lot. You think they're responsible?'

Louise told him what she could about the book they'd found, and the twelve sacred sites.

'The solstice. That figures. I'll keep watch here if you like. But I can't see it happening again.'

It may have been the longest day of the year, but the light was disappearing fast. 'Let's say for argument's sake you needed to make another sacrifice tonight, but doing it here was impossible for various reasons. Where would you go instead?' said Louise, to both Miles and Mr Landry.

'It would have to be somewhere where the body wouldn't be discovered. Nearest cave structure?' said Miles.

'You'd need to speak to the two men who were here before,' said Landry.

Miles checked his notebook, using the light from his phone. 'Steven Webster and Patrick Morton?'

'Patrick lives not far from here. I know him and Steven are always out in weird and wonderful places. I'm sure they could give you some ideas.'

◆　◆　◆

Louise had never felt an investigation was more out of her control. Exhaustion kept hitting her in waves, only the forced adrenaline of knowing that the solstice was about to end keeping her awake, as Miles drove them to Patrick Morton's address in Uphill.

Unlike Mr Landry, the surgeon was not dressed for bed. He recognised Miles and Louise immediately, and invited them into his house, which was full of people. 'We're having a little summer party,' said Patrick.

'Can we speak somewhere quiet?' said Louise, as her phone went off.

'Through here,' said Patrick, leading them into his study.

'Explain the situation,' Louise said to Miles, as she walked to the corner of the room and answered her phone. 'Tracey?'

'We've had a sighting of the S-type Jag. It was caught by the traffic lights next to the Grand Pier, and then further on the road. Last sighting it was taking the old toll road to Kewstoke. He likes his maroon cars, doesn't he?'

It was the same road that led to her parents' house, where Thomas had planned to take the children that evening. 'Send everyone we can out there searching for that damn car,' said Louise, hanging up.

'I've explained the situation to Mr Morton,' said Miles, as Louise walked over.

'I'm afraid it's a tough ask. There are so many complexes around here that I wouldn't know where to begin,' said Patrick.

'They would be looking at somewhere all but inaccessible. A place where they could leave a body without discovery.'

'That could narrow down the search. Lots of these places are mapped but there are always uncharted places, and if they know a specific spot, they could always make it inaccessible, or difficult to locate. All it would take would be the blocking of a small opening. Not that easy to do, but from what your colleague told me it sounds like they're used to that sort of thing.'

'What about the Kewstoke area? Anything specific we could look at there?' asked Louise.

'There are some coastal caves by Sand Point. Not easily accessible, and tide dependent. I guess there could be somewhere within that structure if you know what you're looking for,' said Patrick.

'We just had a sighting of the car heading to that area,' Louise said to Miles. 'Sorry to ruin your party but would you be willing to come with us, Mr Morton? We could do with all the help we can get.'

Patrick nodded. 'Let me tell my wife.'

A few minutes later, Patrick left the house and carried a large bag towards the car where Miles and Louise were waiting. 'Some things that might help us,' he said, placing the bag in the back seat.

Louise ran through the case file as Miles put on the integrated police lights and headed towards Weston. She'd already called Tracey to instruct teams towards Sand Point, where they were headed now.

Although most of it was ingrained in her memory, Louise read through everything she had on the Verdant Circle. As Weston's promenade flashed by in her periphery, she decided to call DI Pepperstone, Miles slowing rather than accelerating through the red light next to the Grand Pier where the S-type Jag had been caught.

'Good to see you're working as late as I am, DI Blackwell.' For once, Louise wasn't annoyed by Pepperstone's breathing on the other end of the phone. He'd been more amiable since the discovery of the flash drives, which had been a major breakthrough for him in his investigation. She told him about Marion Parker being picked up by Rupert Gosling in the maroon Jag.

'Where exactly is it that you're headed?' he asked, a clicking keyboard audible.

'Kewstoke, towards Sand Point on the peninsula.'

Pepperstone struck a few more keys. 'OK, that rings a bell. Leave it with me, and I'll get back to you soon,' he said, hanging up.

Miles glanced at her before turning his attention back to the weaving road, the car only inches away from the side of the road and the sheer cliff drops. 'He's going to get back to us,' said Louise, her voice full of incredulity as Miles took a sharp left towards Sand Point.

A few minutes later, flashing blue lights pierced the darkening sky as they approached the car park at Sand Point. Louise left the car and spoke to the local officers who'd arrived before her. She glanced around the all but desolate car park. 'We're looking for a maroon S-type Jaguar,' she said.

'Yes, ma'am,' said the officer. 'No sign here I'm afraid. We have a car searching the area, and two of my colleagues have gone up into the hills.'

Louise checked her phone, pleased to see a message from Thomas stating everyone was safe and in the house. 'Where would we need to start looking for these coastal caves?' she asked Patrick Morton.

'The other side of that,' said Patrick, pointing to the hillside. 'The tide is out so we can access it by foot, but it would be time-consuming. Furthermore, by the time we reach there the tide would be on the way back in.'

'If someone is in the caves now, could they get back safely enough?'

'At this time, yes. In an hour or so's time, however . . . much more tricky. Obviously, this is dependent on where exactly they're trying to reach and how they're trying to get there. There could be other access points I don't know about. They could have climbed down from the cliffs.'

'We're working on the presumption that they have a seventy-five-year-old woman with them, and a ten-year-old boy.'

'Then maybe not the climb. Sorry, I'm not being much use.'

Louise was wondering how fanciful it was to hope for a maroon S-type Jaguar to arrive in the car park, when a radio call came in for the uniformed officer.

'There's a group of teenagers on the hillside. They've set up a campfire. Looks like there could be some underage drinking but they claim they haven't seen anything out of the ordinary.'

Louise tried to shake the feeling they were on a fool's errand out of her mind. She had to think logically, free of emotion. The truth was there was no S-type Jaguar in the car park. The last sighting they had for the car was heading out on to the old toll road, but unfortunately that road also worked as a back route to Worle and then the M5 and A370. Until the car was spotted again, they had no idea where it was headed.

'I'm happy to go searching,' said Patrick. 'I can call some of my friends. It would take some time but we can do our best.'

Louise checked her watch, dismayed to see it was 10.25 p.m. It may have been the longest day of the year, but it was nightfall now. 'Thank you, Patrick. I'll let you know when we make a decision.'

She walked over to the other side of the car park, gazing out to the mud plains that would soon be covered in water. Remaining focused, she reminded herself of what she'd seen on the horrendous footage on the thumb drives. Hugo Latchford at Banwell Caves, and an unknown boy, most likely Ben Carter, in the dungeon-like cave under the Latchford house. And there was the sight of Marion Parker and Lee Latchford with the others, unmasked and celebrating.

It was up to her to stop the same thing happening to Jayden.

'The officers are bringing the teenagers down for questioning,' said Miles, joining her.

Louise felt more powerless than she'd ever felt. A solution seemed at once just out of reach and a million miles away. Time was ticking as they stood there in the empty car park waiting for something that might never materialise.

Her phone rang, startling them both from their stupor. Louise glanced at the name Pepperstone, the energy draining from her as she answered. 'Tell me you have something good, Gerrard.'

'I have something. That's all I can say. I ran a search on the coordinates you gave me with the files we've recovered. Might be nothing, but the VC have a number of properties in the area. Mainly small dwellings, but one large development on the outskirts of Kewstoke. Wick St Lawrence? Just pinged you the address.'

Louise wasted no time. She asked Patrick if he could stay and assist with the other officers, before taking the car keys from Miles. 'Get in. We have a new address, I'm driving,' she said, speeding out of the car park a split second after Miles got into the car.

The address in Wick St Lawrence was only a few minutes inland. The property owned by the Verdant Circle was a former farmhouse close to a small inland channel that led to Woodspring Bay. Miles searched the address as Louise raced through the narrow back roads. 'According to the Land Registry, the place was purchased seven years ago by Gosling Management.'

The sky had fully darkened, peppered by a sprinkling of stars. Louise slowed the car down as they approached the address, parking up next to a large metal container in the centre of the front yard, where a sign stated the area was being developed into a number of luxury holiday homes.

'Call for backup,' said Louise, as she saw the maroon-coloured S-type Jag parked among the other vehicles.

# Chapter Forty-Four

*This time there was no camera. This time he was the Fox.*

*Things were different this time. He'd messed up, and that was why they were here instead of the cave. But it would still work; the Raven had promised them. But things had to be different.*

*As soon as he put on the mask, he stopped feeling conspicuous about being naked. The Raven had insisted on it. They had to be closer to mother Gaia, and couldn't bring the trappings of their materialistic lives to such an important ceremony.*

*The smell of the Fox's mask was more majestic than the mask he'd worn before. He could smell the animal deep in his sinuses, was becoming the Fox with every passing second.*

*The Raven read from the book, and one by one they lit their torches and began the chanting. They had to get it right this time, and they had to do it by midnight.*

*'It is time,' said the Raven, walking to the secondary area where everything was already in place.*

*He felt a stab of envy as he watched her go, the giant mask dwarfing her old and wearied body, but it had to be her.*

*He turned back to the others, their chanting increasing in tempo and harmony until they were one voice, and waited for the day to end.*

◆　◆　◆

Louise checked the plates of the S-type, which matched the car that had picked up Marion Parker. The car was unlocked and she did not hesitate before checking inside.

'It's 11.12 p.m.,' said Miles.

'Send the plates of the other cars to Tracey,' said Louise, checking the doors of a locked Land Rover before moving to the other three cars, which were also locked. She pinched her nose. Despite the adrenaline-inducing situation, she felt otherworldly with exhaustion. 'Come on,' she added, moving through the building site. The night was balmy, sweat sticking to her blouse despite the late hour. 'Did you hear that?'

They both stopped, the uneasy sound of choral singing coming to her, the words and melody jarring, mournful, rather than joyous.

'Where are we on backup?' said Louise, checking her watch before inching forwards.

'A few minutes away.'

Without any time to waste, she urged Miles onwards. The area was a labyrinth of different building plots, each unfinished as if the development had been halted mid-project. Building materials were strewn across the ground. Louise narrowly avoided some discarded bricks which had been left under a tarpaulin. 'Smell that?' she said, lowering her voice.

'Fire,' said Miles, as they moved towards the source of the singing and the burning smell.

Louise kept checking her watch, which seemed to be ticking down to midnight quicker than was possible. 'Over there,' she said, pointing to a development surrounded by a wire fence where smoke was rising from deep within the excavation.

They should have waited for backup. For a brief second Louise remembered the Walton farm in Bridgwater, where she'd once been forced to confront the serial killer Max Walton, and had shot him dead.

There were no firearms tonight. All they had to protect themselves were police-issued expandable batons and pepper spray – and most important of all, their wits.

'Through here,' said Miles, holding open a gap in the fence so she could slip through before he squeezed his huge bulk into the opening.

The sound of the singing, now more like a monotonous chant in words Louise didn't recognise, was coming from deep within the foundations. She checked behind her, wondering where the flashing blue lights were, before stepping towards the edge of the excavation. Dropping to her knees, she peered over the edge, with no idea what she would see.

Miles followed suit, lying close to her, his breath rapid as they gazed at the sight below.

It was at once ludicrous and harrowing. Maybe if Louise hadn't known the history, hadn't seen the footage of the other two sacrifices, she would have laughed off the sight of four grown adults – two male, two female – holding torches of fire, naked except for the grotesque and bloody animal masks covering their heads and shoulders.

'Fox, Badger, Boar, Hare,' said Miles, under his breath. 'Where's the Raven?'

'Where's Jayden?' asked Louise, her voice equally as low. She had no idea if these were the same masks she'd seen in the footage, and it seemed unlikely they were the same people. The footage they'd recovered was fifty years old, which she imagined would have put most of those present at the time in their seventies, closer to Marion Parker's age. In the dim firelight glow, it was hard to make out the shapes completely but the bodies she could see dancing to the maudlin rhythm of the chanting appeared much younger.

'It's 11.45. We need to approach them before backup arrives,' said Louise, wondering to herself what exactly that would entail.

'There,' said Miles, pointing to a spot twenty metres away, where the tip of a ladder jutted from the exterior walls of the excavation area. 'I'll go first. See if I can get down there before they come out of their trance.'

'OK, ready,' said Louise, following as Miles crawled along the dry ground and swung himself over the edge.

The dancers may have been enraptured in their ceremony, but not enough to miss the sight of Miles's huge figure bearing down the ladder. The chanting stopped immediately, the four of them standing stock-still, the Fox, Badger, Boar and Hare all staring at one another. Their masked faces added to the absurdity of the situation as Miles landed at the bottom of the pit, moving to one side so Louise could join him.

She estimated that the excavated area was twelve metres deep and over thirty metres wide. The ground was uneven, with pipes and wires snaking across the ground. 'Police. You are all under arrest on the suspicion of child abduction,' she said, thinking the technicalities of the arrest could wait for later. Louise switched on her torch. 'I'd like you all to safely extinguish those fires and remove your masks.'

None of the four moved, each staring through the dead eyes of their masks, which looked horrifically realistic in the glow of the fires. 'Now,' said Louise, raising her voice as she withdrew her extendable baton.

Miles took a step forward, following her actions. 'Now,' he repeated, his body tensed for action.

The four masked humans looked at each other, before the Fox removed his mask, revealing himself to be Rupert Gosling. 'You must be DI Blackwell,' he said.

'Mr Gosling. Who else do we have here?'

The two women – the Hare and the Badger – also removed their masks, revealing the lawyer Teresa Willow and a younger woman Louise recognised as Denise from the camp.

She checked her phone. It was 11.49. There was no sign of any potential sacrifice. 'You, now,' she said to the man in the Boar mask. The man looked about him, standing tall. Up close, his body was withered, his skin and atrophied muscle dangling from his frame.

'It's OK,' said Rupert Gosling, as the Boar took off his mask, revealing the face of an elderly man closer in age to Marion Parker.

Louise took a step closer. The man squinted at her, a snide smile appearing on his face. Louise squinted back, concentrating on his features, realising where she'd seen him before. 'Lee Latchford?' she said.

'Very good, DI Blackwell,' said Gosling.

Louise didn't understand how and why Hugo Latchford's grandfather, who had supposedly died ten years ago, was with them, but it wasn't her pressing concern at the moment. 'Where are Marion Parker and Jayden?' she asked.

Latchford glanced at Rupert Gosling, who looked at his watch. 'Better late than never,' Gosling said, dropping his fiery torch, and from nowhere bursting into a sprint towards the far side of the pit.

It was only as she watched him run that Louise realised the snaking cables on the ground were connected to a cylinder in the far corner of the excavated area. 'Stop him,' she shouted to Miles, who was on that side.

Gosling was quick, but Miles was quicker. In three giant strides he was on top of Gosling, bringing him down to the ground with a rugby tackle that winded the man.

As Miles cuffed Gosling, Louise sensed the other three were weighing up their chances. She waved her baton in the air, her other hand poised by the pepper spray on her belt.

Lee Latchford smiled, and Louise thought she'd never seen anything more sinister in her life. 'It's on a timer anyway. You're too late,' he said as backup arrived, two uniformed officers entering the pit and cuffing Denise, Teresa and the still-smiling Lee Latchford.

Louise bent down to the wires on the ground. 'We need to get everyone out of here,' she shouted, tracking the wires from the cylindrical object she presumed was the detonator to the far side of the pit.

As the officers pulled the suspects out, Louise followed the wires to an opening in the pit floor.

'It's a tunnel,' said Miles, sticking his head through the opening.

'I'll go through, you wait here,' said Louise, climbing through the opening before he could argue. 'I mean it, Miles. Do not follow, you could bring this whole thing down.' The dry ground ripped her knees but she crawled towards a faint light at the other end of the tunnel, where there was a small drop into a second excavated site.

Louise stepped through the opening, her eyes alighting on another masked figure. This time it was the Raven.

# Chapter Forty-Five

'DI Blackwell. I was so hoping it would be that handsome friend of yours instead. How lovely it would have been to spend eternity with him.'

'Mrs Parker, is that you?' asked Louise.

'But the three of us should be enough,' said Mrs Parker, ignoring her.

Louise turned to her right. In the corner, bound and gagged, was the figure of Jayden Parsons. 'It's OK, Jayden, I'm here to help you. What's going on, Marion?' she asked, as Mrs Parker took off her mask.

'I thought you would come. I could see you were smart, and the others messed everything up.' Mrs Parker placed the grotesque Raven mask next to her. 'We needed to do something before the solstice ended. You understand that, don't you? This is the foundation of a new building, a new era. If it wasn't for you, we could have just offered up the boy. But I was sure you would find us.'

Glancing at Jayden, Louise moved closer to the woman, who was slumped by the wall. The area was damp, the air rich with ammonia. As she got nearer, she noticed Mrs Parker was holding something in her hand. 'What are you doing, Marion?'

'I'm going to bring it all down. I'm sure they'll dig us out and take us to our graves. I can only hope Gaia will accept our larger sacrifice as compensation. Not that we'll rest,' said Mrs Parker, her face contorting in rage. 'We'll have another body guarding the land by next solstice. You mark my words.'

'You don't need to do this,' said Louise, inching forwards.

'Oh, but I do.'

The air in the room was thin, and Louise saw the exhaustion on Mrs Parker's face. 'Who are you doing it for?'

'Don't you understand? I'm doing it for all of you,' she said, as Louise threw the dirt she'd been holding in her hand directly into the old woman's eyes. She didn't hesitate, rushing forwards as Parker coughed and splattered, tearing the object from her hand, which appeared to be some type of rudimentary detonation device.

With Parker still rubbing her eyes, Louise retreated to the other end of the room and took the gag from Jayden's mouth. 'Are you OK?'

'My legs,' said the boy, glancing down at his zip-tied ankles.

Louise retrieved a penknife from her belt. 'Hold still,' she said, snipping the binds. 'Let's go.'

Jayden began crawling to the exit. Louise urging him onwards, as she checked her watch. 11.57 p.m. 'Through there,' she called, trying to control the mounting panic. If Lee Latchford had been telling the truth, then the tunnel could come down at any second.

She stopped by the entrance to the tunnel. Marion Parker was sitting with her back to the wall, a serene look on her face as she put the Raven's mask back on. 'You need to come,' said Louise, offering her one chance before scrambling after Jayden, who was halfway down the tunnel.

She tried to think only about moving forwards, but images of Emily, Jack, Thomas and her parents came to her mind as she battled through the dirt. She felt like she'd let them down, that they would always blame her for stepping into the tunnel when she knew what could happen.

It urged her onwards, her hands pulling at the dirt as she approached the end of the tunnel to see two huge hands waiting by the entrance.

Miles dragged her out, and together they sprinted to the edge of the pit, where other officers helped them out just as an explosion ripped through the ground.

# Epilogue

The grey August weather contrasted starkly with the heatwave of early summer. Louise was wearing waterproofs as she made her way through the dense undergrowth of the New Forest. Next to her, in cuffs, was Rupert Gosling, who was leading them to one of the twelve so-called sacred sites of the Verdant Circle.

'Miraculous how quickly people's resolve fails them,' Louise said to Miles, who was walking next to her.

The explosion in Wick St Lawrence had entombed Marion Parker. By the time her remains were recovered, most of the existing senior members of the Verdant Circle were under arrest. To Louise's surprise, the group had stuck to the same central line. Despite the evidence presented in the found footage, all members of the group had maintained that their actions were a direct consequence of their beliefs, and stuck to Marion Parker's mantra that they had been doing it all for the good of humanity.

Of course, it didn't explain the litany of abuse, and Louise was sure there was more to the group than mere outdated pagan beliefs. For years, children had been abducted and sacrificed for the cause. Marion Parker and Lee Latchford, the latter having faked his death ten years previously, had been the ones to take the hardline approach fifty years ago, taking to heart the passages they'd found in the ancient Verdant Circle books that had been passed down from generation to generation.

When Hugo Latchford's body had been found, the plan was to sacrifice Max O'Sullivan, but when Fiona had successfully escaped the commune, attention had turned to Jayden Parsons.

They stopped at a row of stones. 'He's in there,' said Rupert Gosling, pointing to a small rock formation in the ground. 'About four hundred yards in.'

◆　◆　◆

Miles poured them coffee from Thermos flasks as the specialist teams set up. The steam from the liquid billowed into the air, and Louise caught Gosling's envious look as she took a drink. It took all her willpower not to throw the cup in his face.

The body at the Latchford house had subsequently been identified as Ben Carter, and with Lee Latchford identified on the footage, the man had been charged with the young boy's murder alongside joint charges for the death of his grandson, Hugo Latchford, and the abduction of Jayden Parsons. But Latchford senior was unrepentant and uncooperative, and was awaiting trial in a Cat A prison.

Rupert Gosling had found it much easier to talk. And that was why they were here today – searching for the remains of Aaron Speed, who had disappeared forty years ago when he was eight. It wouldn't keep Gosling out of prison, which he would probably never leave, but there were some advantages to cooperating for him, such as little day trips like this, and the leverage of holding information on the other nine bodies he claimed were buried throughout the land.

It was Louise's hope that they could extract the information from him sooner rather than later, but the gleam in Gosling's eye suggested that wouldn't be the case. Out of everyone she had talked to, he seemed the least interested in the legacy of the Verdant Circle. It had made her think that there was more to his involvement in the group. From the numerous interviews she'd conducted with him, she was sure he had derived pleasure from his actions beyond upholding the legacy of the group. It was likely the same was true of Lee Latchford and Marion Parker, but with Gosling it had been possible to play to his vanity and that was why he'd finally cracked.

◆　◆　◆

It was another day before the remains were found, and two weeks on they still had no positive identification, beyond Gosling's word, that the bundle of bones found in the cave were the remains of Aaron Speed.

'Look at you,' said Tracey, as Louise entered CID. It was the day of her final panel interview for the role of DCI, which had been delayed over the summer period, and she was feeling conspicuous in a full business suit.

'Have to make the effort,' said Louise, walking towards her office where Miles was waiting.

'Warm-up coffee,' he said, placing a cup on her desk.

'It won't be long before you're up for promotion if you keep going the way you are,' said Louise, noting that the young officer was also wearing his best suit for the imminent arrival of Avon and Somerset's top brass.

Miles smiled, then frowned. 'DI Pepperstone would like you to call him,' he said. 'I was going to wait until you'd finished the panel but I thought it might be important.'

'Thanks, Miles,' said Louise, waiting until he'd shut the door before calling Pepperstone.

Her relationship with her colleague from London had improved dramatically since the first day they'd met, and Pepperstone greeted her call with a warm 'Hello, Louise, thanks for getting back to me. I hear you're up in front of the panel today.'

'Sure am.'

'Well, best of luck with it. Thought I'd send you a bit of good news before I do.'

'I'm all ears, Gerrard, as always.'

'I've just sent you a file. I wanted to be on the phone when you opened it.'

Louise tapped on her screen, having to go through the procedure of logging in before she could see any of her messages. 'Don't keep me in suspense, Gerrard,' she said, as she searched through her messages.

'We had a breakthrough on the final set of encrypted messages on the drive,' said Pepperstone, as Louise clicked on the message.

'This is the list?' said Louise, breathless.

'Sure is. Exact location and names of the twelve missing children, Hugo Latchford, Ben Carter and Aaron Speed included.'

'That's amazing, Gerrard, thank you. I guess Rupert Gosling no longer has anything to bargain with.'

'Couldn't happen to a nicer fella. Let me know how it goes. It'll be difficult calling you DCI but I'll get used to it.'

'Thanks, Gerrard, I will.'

That weekend, Louise joined her family on a day out to Bath. It was the last weekend before the schools started again, and it was lovely to see Emily with her grandparents, Jack smiling away in his pushchair as his grandfather wheeled him through the ancient streets.

Louise held hands with Thomas. Things had been better of late. They'd managed to get into a routine of sorts, and with the Verdant Circle investigation winding down, Louise had been getting home at a decent time most days.

'It came through,' she said, walking slower so they were out of earshot of the rest of the family.

'The promotion?' said Thomas, the delight evident in his broad smile.

'How does DCI Blackwell sound?'

'It sounds fantastic,' said Thomas, hugging her. 'When did you find out? Why haven't you told me?'

'Friday. I don't know why I haven't said anything. I'm still undecided.'

'Oh, really? What's holding you back?'

Her parents had stopped outside a coffee shop and were looking back at them.

'Go in, we'll be there in a minute,' said Louise, before turning her attention back to Thomas. 'When I was scrambling through that tunnel, I kept having thoughts about Jack and Emily, about you and my parents. If I'd left it any later, I might not be here today.'

'Don't say that, Lou.'

'No, listen. You know better than most what the risks are. I'm not sure I want to take them any more.'

'Doesn't that make the DCI role even more attractive?'

'Maybe. Maybe it's just time to call it a day.'

She'd been feeling this way ever since Miles had grabbed her from the pit in Wick St Lawrence. She kept thinking about Marion Parker entombing herself in the ground, and how close she'd come to ending up next to her.

'You know you have my support. We can make do while you find something else to do. Anything in mind?'

'Lady of leisure?'

Thomas laughed. 'You wouldn't last a day.'

'You might be right. Come on, let's eat some cake and think about it.'

# ABOUT THE AUTHOR

*Photo © 2019 Lisa Visser*

Following his law degree, where he developed an interest in criminal law, Matt Brolly completed his Masters in Creative Writing at Glasgow University. He is the *Wall Street Journal* and Amazon bestselling author of the DI Blackwell novels, the DCI Lambert crime novels, the Lynch and Rose thrillers *The Controller* and *The Railroad*, and the standalone thrillers *Zero*, *The Running Girls* and *The Alliance*. Matt lives in London with his wife and their two children. You can find out more about him at www.mattbrolly.com or by following him on X, formerly Twitter: @MattBrollyUK.

# Follow the Author on Amazon

If you enjoyed this book, follow Matt Brolly on Amazon to be notified when the author releases a new book!

To do this, please follow these instructions:

### Desktop:

1) Search for the author's name on Amazon or in the Amazon App.
2) Click on the author's name to arrive on their Amazon page.
3) Click the 'Follow' button.

### Mobile and Tablet:

1) Search for the author's name on Amazon or in the Amazon App.
2) Click on one of the author's books.
3) Click on the author's name to arrive on their Amazon page.
4) Click the 'Follow' button.

### Kindle eReader and Kindle App:

If you enjoyed this book on a Kindle eReader or in the Kindle App, you will find the author 'Follow' button after the last page.

Printed in Great Britain
by Amazon